D1755565

Hooded Crow

DJ Gilmour

Douglas J Gilmour has asserted his rights under the Copyright, Designs and Patent Act 1988 to be identified as the author of this work.

All rights reserved. No part of this publication may be reproduced, stored in a retrieval system or transmitted, in any form or by any means without the authors prior permission in writing.

This is a work of fiction. Names, characters, and incidents either are products of the author's imagination or are used fictitiously. Any resemblance to actual events or locales or persons, living or dead, is entirely coincidental.

Copyright © Douglas J Gilmour 2023

Front Cover: Penny Garner, all rights reserved.

With thanks to the Coalville Writers Group for stress testing various parts of Hooded Crow. Additional thanks to Richard Ashdown and David Gilmour as beta readers for excellent feedback, thought and encouragement.

There is not enough space to adequately thank Lesley Jones of perfecttheword.co.uk for her editing skills. Every part of the manuscript had been scrutinised, from the use of a single word through to the whole story arc for cohesion and clarity. A transformative and educational process.

Douglas Gilmour grew up in Balloch, Helensburgh and the Isle of Lewis before a stint at Glasgow University. He then went south to seek fame and fortune. After various adventures in the Berkshire Badlands, he settled in Leicestershire where people still have the time to talk to strangers. He is lucky enough to be married with two sons and has a dog that can walk him back from the pub.

All proceeds will go to www.alzheimers.org.uk/

First Edition 2023

Hide and Seek

Chapter One

Thunder growling down the streets of Islington reminded Ken of heaven's postponed vengeance. A breeze hinted at the cooler air outside but even with all the sash windows as wide as Ken could manage, the Victorian walls held on to the summer heat far longer than seemed possible. He sat by one of the open frames hoping to escape the suffocating warmth. Below, the roads were empty apart from sporadic travellers. A few carried umbrellas, but most seemed to be unprepared for the storm that had sat above London for hours now. Piano music drifted from the floor above.

The old man played Bach's *Goldberg Variations* to help drown out the sound of his wife fighting for every breath. Ken could still hear her though. He had lost most faculties as his body had aged, but he could still hear the bats hunting and the woman breathing on her deathbed from where he sat by the window. The couple had moved into that apartment upstairs in the Sixties, all full of hope and excitement. They had shown him washed out Polaroids of them redecorating and their son taking his first steps. Now the son worked in Vietnam. There was a long pause in the music; she used to turn the pages for him and now he would have to try and do it himself. Ken could picture his hands, so sure on the piano keys, stabbing almost uselessly at the sheets as they slithered off the rest.

Ken sighed and pulled down the window. The sash stuck about halfway down, and Ken panted as he tried to pull it fully closed. He looked around for his cane to beat the frame. Not that it would help; he was simply frustrated. But he had already broken two panes of glass and the insurance man had been quite clear that they wouldn't pay for a third.

'Bugger it. The thieves would have to fly in.' Ken put his head outside into the sought-for cooler air. Reassured by the lack of flying monkeys he walked across the hardwood floor of the flat and pulled the door behind him. He looked at the stairs as an old adversary. They curled around a central space but there were too many of them for Ken to attempt in one go. He had put a chair on the landing once, beside the small table with a hydrangea that gamely added colour to the scene. But somebody had stolen the furniture last winter – for firewood, Ken suspected. Times were hard. They had left the flower bowl. He sat on the floor halfway up, aware that the sound of his heart beating now drowned out the piano.

Ken let himself into the flat above with a key given to him a while ago so he could feed Felix while the couple were regularly in hospital. The scent of the flat filled his nostrils. Not the bitterness of the young and unwashed, just the smell of things that had grown stale. Ken went to the living room first. Stacks of magazines and periodicals tall enough to obscure the line of sight across the room barred his way. Since those on the tables had achieved a dangerous height, new collections had sprung up on the floor. Behind all of this, the old man sat playing. 'Variation Eight' transformed him into a sinuous creature lithely moving above the keys. It came to a joyous end and his shoulders slumped as he stared at the pages, willing them to turn by themselves. Ken reached across and deftly turned the sheet over.

'Thank you, Sarah,' said the man smiling. He looked at Ken. 'I'm sorry, Mr Austin.'

'No need. You carry on. A cup of tea?' asked Ken.

The man nodded and turned to the piano again. 'That would be very nice. Would you see if Sarah wants one?'

Ken walked through to the kitchen. Dishes had gathered like dirty seagulls above a trawler. He filled the kettle but it refused to start. Ken checked the plug and the switch on the wall. This kettle's boiling days were over. Sighing, Ken poured the water into a pan and lit the gas on an equally decrepit stove. Lighting a match near it seemed the most dangerous thing he had done in years. He looked at the uneven flame barely escaping the burner cap and grimaced. This would take a while.

Ken went into their bedroom with a little trepidation. He had seen death many times before, caused it often enough. Though it held no fear for him he still didn't like it. She lay on the covers, her eyes closed. The rise and fall of her chest, Ken thought for a moment, synchronised with her husband's playing of 'Variation 13'. The sound was the same as the one he had heard from downstairs. Every breath was fought for, consuming what scrap of energy she had. A nebuliser sat by her bed. Ken checked that it still worked and that the steroid capsule still had some liquid in it. It was a more expensive machine than the couple would have been able to afford themselves, and fed oxygen into the mask as well as the medicine. Ken had wanted to help and still wasn't sure he had. The action had at least kept the sense of powerlessness away for a brief while. He brushed the hair from her eyes and smiled as he saw the echo of the beautiful woman in the faded Polaroids.

Water hitting the hot pan supports hissed in the kitchen and Ken left her side to return to the stove. He found a cup and a saucer that looked serviceable, then reached for the tin of shortbread he had bought last week, untouched it seemed since his previous visit. Ken left the tea and a finger of shortbread on a coaster on the piano and then returned to the kitchen to hunt for a second clean cup. He picked a round biscuit with a thistle motif.

Sitting among the towers of papers, Ken became aware he was being watched. The two yellow eyes of Felix were fixed on him from under the sideboard. They reminded him of ancient, more deadly terrors. Ken was fairly sure that the cat could see past this frail old body to his true nature. As a result, any visit by Ken to the apartment tended to descend into a game of hide and seek as Ken attempted to verify if the cat was still in the flat and alive. He rubbed the back of his left hand where the scars from his last encounter were slowly healing. Not that he bore the animal any ill will. Felix had a good grasp of who was on whose side.

Ken wolfed down the shortbread, washed it down with tea and closed his eyes. He felt quite worn out by all the exertion. Although the biscuit helped, nothing seemed to aid him in really recovering any of his former strength. This world seemed to be a plane bereft of magic in any form. The old man finished 'Variation 15', but Ken didn't have the energy to get up and assist him as he tried to control the treacherous stack of pages. Ken sat, keeping his eyes shut, willing the player to be able to turn the page himself. Above the rustle he could hear Sarah's breathing like some terrible slow grandfather clock counting down the minutes to death. The music started again and after a moment Ken worked out it was 'Variation 24'. Two more minutes of rest then.

Chapter Two

Ken took the umbrella rather than his cane and, leaving his flat behind, made his way through the wet streets of London. The streetlights were coming on individually, as they seemed to do these days. The air was cool after the storms but not enough to make him shiver. He picked his way carefully through the busy roads. A red bus ploughed through a deep puddle resulting in a flurry of curses and phones amongst the pedestrians who had been caught in its wake. A cheer went up as the people pointed above one lad's head and he bowed to the crowd in acknowledgement.

'There will be a chorus of disapproval,' the lad said, and the group laughed in a not entirely pleasant manner. Their masks lit by their bright phone screens, they looked other worldly. Ken looked on, mystified, though he had learned long ago that people didn't take kindly to him asking questions, bearing in mind his appearance and accent. He was old enough that most often no one saw him anyway. He could still look. At the traffic lights a woman was tilting her large green umbrella – her own portable, flattering lighting effect. Across the road, waiting at the same crossing, five identically dressed and umbrella-ed young women bobbed about like they were taking part in a girl-band photo shoot. Even when it was raining in London it was always time for a show.

At last he came to A1 Kitchens. The sign said 'For all your Bespoke Kitchen and Bathroom Needs', but Ken had never seen anyone in the shop, never mind buying anything. At the side of the display room window, an easily overlooked red door instilled a sense of excitement. The presence of a bouncer hinted that there was something more interesting than innovative corner units. He must have been three times the size of Ken and usually found a chance to make sure Ken acknowledged it. Today, though, he limited himself to a laugh and a pat on the head.

'You go on up. She's waiting for you. That should speed you up.' He laughed again, a deep chuckle that Ken felt as much as heard.

When he eventually reached the top, the staircase took Ken to a landing. What had once been the hall of someone's home was now just a series of rooms, all closed, with girls' names on them, some custom made and glittery, others just written in pen on a torn piece of A4. The hall smelt like all neglected public spaces, slightly damp, inadequately cleaned, unloved. Ken shuffled past them to the door at the bottom of a further set of stairs up. A small plaque depicting a unicorn holding up the word 'Candy' told him he had arrived. He had bought that for her. He knocked on the door.

'Come in.'

Ken nudged open the door. The room was a mass of pink cushions and toys piled up in one corner of a double bed, itself pushed up hard against the wall. The curtains were closed but Ken knew there was an iron balcony out there to enjoy on summer afternoons. Tonight, the whole space was brightly lit with a couple of lamps rigged up where the central light would normally have been, and two more spotlights on stands opposite each other that made it difficult to see properly.

Ken squinted. 'Hello Candy. Can you turn some of the lights off?'

Candy moved from the bed to the isolated pair of kitchen units at the far end of the bedsit.

'Hi, Ken. I'm going through a JJ Abrams phase.' She laughed though Ken didn't get the reference. 'Do you want a cup of tea?'

'Yes, please.' Ken took his usual seat behind the door, facing the bed and the galley. Candy was wearing a big T-shirt and long socks. As she reached for the tea, the lilac shirt rode up her thigh. Ken looked away before she spotted him and smoothed the brim of his hat. She faced the other way, long dark hair spilling down her back.

'I have some clean cups somewhere. Oh yes.' She had to stretch up once more to a shelf almost out of reach. With Candy's back turned, Ken could look at her all he wanted. The T-shirt slid up again revealing the bottom of her cheeks and the possibility of no knickers. Ken's fedora shook so much he dropped it on the floor, and he scrambled to pick it up again as the kettle boiled. After a minute she passed him a cup of tea and he pulled out a long tube of dark chocolate digestives.

'Oh, lovely, Ken – I think these are my favourites.'

'You say that whatever biscuits I get – I don't know which ones really are your favourite,' he pointed out.

Candy blushed slightly, looping her hair behind her ears. 'What can I say? I'll do anything for a biscuit.' She raised one eyebrow suggestively at Ken and sat back on the bed, folding her legs under her, facing him. No knickers right enough.

Ken had to put the tea down and took a moment, breaking his digestive into pieces, his eyes downcast. Had she noticed him looking? He glanced back up at her eyes, bright, trusting.

'Tell me, what have you been up to? How are your neighbours?'

Ken recounted what he had been doing, trying to get the prescription sorted for the man in the flat above, the latest on the cat. She talked about her acting career and how she was still hoping to break out of the chorus line and onto the centre stage. All the while Ken tried to keep his gaze fixed on Candy's as she shifted around the bed and ran her free hand over her hip, past the bruise on her thigh and down to her foot.

'Your knees look sore,' Ken said.

'Oh yes.' She looked at the scabs on her knees as if seeing them for the first time. 'I was cleaning yesterday and wasn't really paying attention.'

'Carpet burn?'

'Yes.' Candy smiled. 'I was scrubbing hard. You'd be surprised how much effort it took to get this place clean.' She put down her cup and stretched. No bra either, Ken noticed. If it had been fifty years ago he could have made this woman a princess … and the joy they would have had. Instead, he could barely raise a smile, and she had to clean to keep the roof above her.

'They should look after you better here.'

'They do look after me well here, Ken. It's safe. They're only ever a shout away. Safer than being on the streets.'

'Where is home? Not London, I think?'

Candy slid another biscuit off the top of the packet and bit into it, her full lips catching all the crumbs. She tilted her head to one side, her glossy hair spooling off her shoulder. 'Burnley,' she said. 'Home was Burnley, Lancashire.' Her voice sounded quite different as she spoke, with more rounded vowels.

'Do you ever go back there?'

Candy looked sad; Ken didn't remember ever seeing her look sad before.

'No, Ken. There's nobody there for me now.' She looked past him to one of the many mirrors that made the tiny room look bigger than it was. When she spoke again the Lancashire accent was gone. 'Look at the time, Ken. I need to get changed for tonight's show. Will you stay while I get ready?'

Ken had stayed many times while she washed in the sink of the bedsit and picked out her clothes for the evening with as little care as if he had faded into the mirror behind him. It was for the same reason that she could chat to him freely; he was no longer a threat, no longer a man in this woman's eyes. Nothing would happen. He looked down into his lap. Nothing could happen.

'No. I will go.' He pulled out five twenty-pound notes and left them under one of the lamps.

Candy looked disappointed. 'Are you sure you wouldn't like to stay?' she asked, but she was looking over his shoulder again. Ken glanced round to the reflection but only saw himself and Candy in the room; there were no demons in this world. He stood up, collecting his hat and umbrella, moving quickly from the scene of his humiliation.

'Look after yourself, Candy.' He opened the door and tried to walk purposefully down the corridor. The door to one of the other rooms was open. A man and a young woman were hunched over a bank of televisions; cables snaked across the floor through grey conduits connecting a dozen black boxes. Each computer glowed from within in a shifting pattern of colours. The two looked up like children caught with their hands in the cookie jar. The woman, who had short and surprisingly white hair, took Ken in with her brilliant blue eyes and pushed the door hard enough for it to close.

Ken continued walking without slowing, his anger with himself delivering the energy.

The bouncer at the bottom of the stairs was still looking at his phone, the purple-blue light bleaching his dark face. 'Not hanging around today then, Ken?' he chuckled with a mocking air. Or was that just in Ken's head? 'It's not too late, you know. You could go back and surprise her?' He held the screen up in his massive pink palm and Ken saw Candy, top off now, dancing in front of the washbasin singing along with some music. Ken hurriedly glanced away. The phone shook as the bouncer laughed.

Rage washed through Ken, a strength of emotion he had not felt for decades.

'It's just not the same without you. You should go back in. It's more fun with you pretending not to look!' The bouncer had to shout the last bit as Ken strode away as best he could.

By the time he reached City Road his heart was pounding. The light was fading and the LED lamps, much vaunted as a green improvement when installed, made it clear that the energy saving was largely based on being less effective. The rain was heavier and the streets had cleared of pretty women or indeed anything pretty at all. Now that the shutters were down the graffiti was omnipresent and the wind whipped rubbish that had built up on the street corners. Ken fought for breath for a moment, trying to make sense of what he had seen. Some sort of CCTV system to protect the girls? Candy had said that she only had to shout for help. But the idea that the bouncer had been watching his discomfort for his entertainment … Ken would inform the management on his next visit about their guardian's bad behaviour.

Feeling a little mollified, Ken continued his walk home, hoping to get back before curfew. The clouds had come down to cover the tops of the towers now. Distant flashes from the citadels distributed by the mist created a silent lightning storm above the glistening streets below. A group of youths stood at the corner huddled against the weather, faces bright from their cigarettes in the poor light. Ken couldn't tell if they were AntiFa, the UK League or Neo-Soviets. They all just seemed like angry young men to Ken.

'Bloody chink,' said one as Ken hurried past. 'Get back to Hong Kong.'

UK League then. But no one else picked up the cry and Ken kept his eyes down, making it clear he wasn't worth the effort. He let out a little sigh of relief when he got to Middlesex Street and his home run. He paused, making sure the UKL hadn't followed him for want of something better to do. His only pursuers were rubbish zephyrs that ran the squall line of heavier rain down the road and collapsed at the crossroads.

Ken entered via the shared front door and rested his head against the woodwork before gathering himself for the first flight up to his flat. When he got there he glanced briefly at the stairs up to the apartment above. Not tonight.

Chapter Three

Ken had a sleepless night dreaming of women arguing on the Underground. The argument about pandemic control seemed real enough, but then they all got their phones out and showed him pictures of Candy. He woke up with their laughter still in his ears. The orange LED on the clock said it was 5:05. He got up and stood by the window. It was dark outside; the street lights were off as part of the new green measures or the curfew, depending on who you believed. Above him, he could hear the woman continuing to fight for her life. Ken understood that; he too was dying. He looked at his own body in the window's reflection. The pyjamas he had purchased last year hung off him as if they had been bought by a cost-conscious mother expecting him to grow into them. The arm he held out to steady himself was not just lacking the muscle he had once enjoyed, but the bone beneath had thinned to the point of fear.

Haunted by the images on the mobile, early the next morning Ken took himself to a café in the Bishopsgate Centre. He had seen a leaflet about a phone course there – all part of an 'inclusion' programme. Ken didn't really want to be included but he liked Bishopsgate; there was something about the scale of the place that seemed safer than the chrome-and-glass giants that surrounded it. He showed his Vaccard at the door and the mechanism flashed green, letting him in. The same leaflets were scattered over all the tables. 'Don't be left behind!' said the flyer.

A woman in her sixties sat down opposite him. She looked concerned behind her mask. 'This new world can seem very daunting,' she said, clearly trying to look reassuring.

'It's not that new,' Ken replied. 'I have been here quite a while now.'

She smiled thinly. 'Yes, but keeping up with technology. That seems to be harder every day.'

Ken nodded. 'That's why I'm here. I understand there are classes?' He hesitated – he wasn't sure if he had ever said that word before. 'I need to know more.'

'We can help with that. This class today is about choosing a phone. But in a couple of weeks we have a software developer coming in to tell us about what you can do with them, and then a few weeks after that she's coming back to talk about what her company is doing in terms of augmented reality.' Her smile indicated that she really didn't want him to ask if she understood what she had just said.

'I was okay as far as the "choosing a phone" bit. When does that start?' he asked.

'The class starts at ten thirty, so you have time for a cup of coffee and a cake.'

'Excellent.' Ken picked up his small satchel and looked carefully at all the cakes before buying a pot of tea and a pack of Viennese whirls. The room filled up slowly. Given the age of the attendees it would have been difficult for them to do it any other way. Ken watched them settle in; he felt so much younger than they looked as long as he couldn't see his own reflection in a mirror.

'So, let's see your current phone. It'll give me a better idea where to start.'

Ken looked round and saw that he wasn't alone in having no phone at all.

'Okay, you four should move together onto one table and we can talk to you separately.'

Ken made a show of standing up and being ready to move towards the ones who looked like they couldn't. The four sat looking around at the rest of the class but not each other while the lady in charge talked in what sounded like English but didn't relate to anything that Ken had learned so far. He had picked out 'mobile broadband' 'chorus' and 'augmented reality', but only because he had heard the piano player's son use those words in a similar futile discussion with his father.

Eventually, the organiser came over with some phones that Ken was pretty sure she had kept aside for her special group.

'I think these would be good for you. You can see this one has large buttons so it makes it easier for you to dial people. And it has actual buttons, which makes it much easier to tell what you have done.'

The ancient man beside Ken wheezed into life. 'Actual buttons as opposed to what? Pretend buttons?' he asked with a bitter smile.

'Well, yes, you get real buttons and virtual buttons. This phone, for example, is just a screen with haptic feedback so it feels like you're pressing a button when it's really just a flat bit of glass. This phone has quite a nice projector that creates the illusion of a keyboard ...' she flipped out a little stand from the phone so that it stood by itself '... when you say the command word – "*Jian*".' She repeated the same sound. '*Jian*. Ah, there we are.'

Ken jumped back slightly as a computer keyboard appeared in front of the phone. 'And then what's also neat is, if your eyes are struggling with the size of the screen, you say "*Huǒyàn*".' She laughed. 'I never get this right. I think you need to be under thirty really to drive these things properly.' On the fourth attempt another light leapt into life at the back of the phone. This instruction created what looked like a full-scale television, though mostly projected over the man who was still coming to grips with the concept of a virtual button.

'Can you still use it as a phone?' asked Ken, holding his empty hand up to his head.

'Oh yes. You just repeat the commands and the projectors turn off. But it's too complicated and you would be better off with these. With this one, for example, you can put a picture of your son or daughter on the front so you don't have to remember their number. Just press the picture and you can talk to them.'

'Oh, that sounds more like it,' said the lady beside Ken.

'I can't see,' complained the wheezing man. 'What's the point of having a class if the first thing you're going to do is blind people?'

'*Huǒyàn*,' said Ken. The TV disappeared. He felt a little twinge of excitement. '*Jian*.' The phone was back to being just a phone again.

'That's very good. Have a look at this one though. It's probably more age appropriate.' She passed Ken a device that had an improbably happy-looking older woman on the front. 'And if you slide your finger across it ...' A younger black man now emerged. He also looked happy but there was a touch of concern there too.

'That's not my son,' said the old woman, quite definitely.

'That's just an example. You can put any picture you like in there.'

'I still can't see. This could be permanent damage, you know.'

'I wouldn't want to cut up a picture of my son to stick on there. I only have the one photo. Before he went to sea.'

'I hope you have insurance.'

Ken put down an age-appropriate phone he was holding but as he did so the screen changed again. 'This daughter seems to live somewhere very warm,' he pointed out.

The course runner looked at the phone with resigned embarrassment. 'Bloody kids. They help set these things up for free but you know one of them is going to do something like this. But that phone is really good – it has a panic button on the back and a fall detector.'

'Well, a panic detector might be quite useful. Especially if you're unexpectedly blinded.'

'I want this one,' said Ken, picking up the one with projectors. When he stroked it the sense of charge, of life, seemed to vibrate into his fingers, or was that just the haptic feedback?

'That Xiaomi is really complex to use and expensive. You might find it better to start with one of these and then work your way towards something like that.'

'Oh, I think I'm sure I'll start with this one,' said Ken.

'So you can go round blinding people? Typical of your kind. We let you come here when your city sank and how do you repay us? By shining laser beams in our eyes. I have a good mind to call the police.'

Ken pushed over the one with the pictures for phone numbers. 'Here, use this one to phone them. Or you could call her?' As he looked the picture changed again. 'And her, er, friend.'

Ken walked out from the class and into a phone shop where he met the same resistance to buying the Xiaomi. In the end he only succeeded in obtaining one by picking the most expensive data option they did.

'This is the Executive Slice package. You'll be able to get, like, all the bandwidth you want when everyone else can't even load Facebook. Not that anybody does anymore.'

Both assistants in the shop laughed at their own joke but Ken didn't join in. After they had set it up, he finally had the phone in his hand and it felt alive, the same way the one in class had. It was like hearing singing in the distance, and it reminded Ken of the magic he used to wield, the sense of power tingling through his skin. How could he gain access? How could he release it?

'Is there an instruction manual?' he asked.

'What, like one of those old Haynes manuals?'

'Yes.'

'No. Nobody does manuals anymore, buddy. You go online.'

'For which I need a phone.'

'Yeah ... but, like, you have one now.'

'So the way I find out how to get online is to get online.'

'Yeah.'

Ken looked for a smirk from either of the assistants but there was nothing, only blank stares at his incomprehension of the obvious solution they were offering.

He pointed at them each in turn to make sure there was no doubt in their minds who he was referring to. 'You two are too stupid to be allowed to be in this place on your own.' They both looked hurt. Ken thought about saying more but there was no point. He gathered all the packaging and put it in the bag they had charged him for. 'Have I missed anything?'

They shook their heads. 'Like an apology?' asked one of them.

'Do I need anything else to make this work?' Clearly too frightened to speak in case the horrible old man savaged them again they could only repeat their headshakes. Ken pulled the door open, but as he stood in the doorway trying to create a gap between his hat and mask he heard the two shopkeepers bleat like wounded sheep behind him.

Ken held the phone like a torch on the way home. The squawks of scooter horns rose to a deafening level when the riders saw him embarking on a pedestrian crossing and realised that he would qualify for the extra twenty seconds for the over eighties. Normally he would try and shuffle across a bit faster, but now it didn't seem to matter that they were piling up six deep waiting for this old man to cross.

'Hurry up and die!' shouted one of the riders wearing an open-face helmet.

'Too late!' another yelled. 'This one's a zombie.'

Ken stopped to look at him but they were all identical. How could he pick any one out? The artificial intelligence in the pedestrian crossing, aware that he had slowed, gave him an extra ten seconds to get to safety. The frustration of the traffic felt like a wave towering above Ken now, but nobody moved. The enforcement cameras would snap them the instant they drove onto the black and white banding. Ken understood that the new CCTV caught everything, including an old man struggling to cross. If a pack of frustrated scooter drivers did mow him down at least his death would be recorded for posterity and, potentially, for prosecution.

'Yeah, but have you seen his granddaughter!' someone shouted. Ken's left foot landed on the pavement and the road snapped back to its usual black. The scooters whined away, taking the laughter of their riders with them, free at last from their fifty-second prison.

When he reached home Ken had to sit on the telephone table for a good ten minutes to recover enough to make the final stretch into the kitchen. He took the charging pad out and plugged it in, then placed the Xiaomi on top. The phone lit up with an orange logo Ken didn't recognise and a picture of a battery slowly filling with green light. Now, he thought, time for a cup of tea and then to unravel the power the phone held.

Chapter Four

The weeks waiting for the next class had been a time of frustration for Ken. At each point he thought he understood how the menu system worked, something else would appear that would throw him. Even just turning the phone sideways seemed to hide everything he was used to. He took to stuffing the phone under cushions, but it was still there in his mind, taunting him with that sense of vibrant energy hidden within – a puzzle that had to be solved. He realised he had been so absorbed that he hadn't visited Candy since that night summer had ended.

Ken was sitting in the Bishopsgate café waiting for the talk to begin. He was surprised to see that it was even fuller than it had been two weeks ago, but his inability to distinguish people made it hard to judge if this was the same group as the first class or new enthusiasts.

The organiser stood up at the front. 'Thank you all for coming. I know most of you have put a lot of work into mastering your phone since these classes started. But today we are going to try to give you an idea of what they are really capable of doing now and perhaps a little bit into the future.' She looked around the room and waved at the back. 'Hello, Ellie, Ellie Chassagne. I hope I've pronounced that right?'

'Close enough,' said the woman walking forward to take over the slightly raised platform. 'Can everybody see the monitor?' She was young but the severe white bob, which was probably surprising to her peer group, fitted right in here. 'Okay, this screen is bound to my handy so what I can see on this, you should be able to see on there.' She pointed to the full-size display. 'So let's turn everything on and see what we can see.'

She lifted the phone, some folding one Ken had seen since buying his and discovered there was a world of connectivity options out there.

'The handy is showing you in the room now as you are. What I want to show you is that it can also add information on top of that view. *Detail hinzufügen.*' She paused. 'My phone is still in German. I can do everything else in English but somehow I just can't make the switch when it comes to voice control on phones.' Ellie shrugged her shoulders. The screen now showed the café's address superimposed; emergency exits were highlighted with a green outline and as she moved the phone around Ken could see a dotted green line now drawn on the floor. She followed another blue line until a toilet sign came into view. 'The red line you can see is the route you came in. This is often not the fastest way out of a building but it can be really useful if you've dropped something.' Her fingers slid around her phone.

'This is a video I made in the street before I came in. I tried to make it as relevant as possible. So what I'm doing here is adding detail. This augmented-reality system allows you to access information in the most appropriate way. Everything you look at will have these tags that give you more data about the things you are interested in. You can see here the tram stops and the times of the next tram, the walking time to the nearest public toilet and which direction it is, the sequence of lights so you know how long it's going to be until the next pedestrian crossing appears and where it will be. But you can do more.'

A slightly tinny version of Ellie's voice came from somewhere repeating '*Detail hinzufügen*' every few seconds. The screen became a mass of highlights and information, the road in front a cord of coloured paths to take.

'So this one, this line here.' Ellie pointed at the coloured ribbon on the road in the video. 'This goes to the nearest Café Nero. This one, the nearest Tesco and the offers they have today linked to your preferences. The phone knows what I usually buy and can tell me which shop I should go to for the cheapest basket of goods. This is my way back to the office, and if I turn the other way …' She paused, waiting for the film she had made on her way to Bishopsgate to catch up with her commentary. 'Yes. You can see my path here and how long I have to make sure I'm not late. Looking up I can see the air quality around me, how long it will be until the sun sets. Weather forecast hangs off that. The company that owns that plane, where it took off from, where it will land and its last known mechanical problems. A list of all the people on the street and the current alerts from the governments Communicable Disease Management Service.' By now there was almost no real world left on the screen at all. 'If you look at each building, you can now see if the fire regulations are …'

'My phone doesn't work,' said a voice that broke the spell Ellie had woven. Ken recognised the man from the first class who had threatened to call the police. He had chosen to sit next to Ken again and Ken wondered why.

'How is that?' Ellie asked.

'Well, I can bring up the exit path on the phone but when I look at the floor it's not there.'

'That's not the way it works. This is augmented reality. The path only exists on the handy, not in real life.'

'Well, that's no use to anyone,' he exclaimed.

Ken reached across to touch his arm. 'I don't understand how you make living this hard and yet have managed to live this long,' he said quietly.

'I know you! You're the chink that goes around blinding people and tries to push porn,' he said, the volume of his speech rising slightly.

The organiser appeared from nowhere. 'Mr Ashworth, this is a safe space and you need to keep your voice down or I will have you removed – again.'

'It's not right,' muttered Mr Ashworth before settling into what Ken supposed was meant to look like a silent, innocent pose focused on Ellie and her demonstration.

'This is something a lot of folk struggle with,' continued Ellie after a pause. 'The phone knows where you are, what direction you're facing, and then maps a digital world on top of the real one. But it doesn't change the real world – only what you see through the screen.' She looked out at the sea of glazed eyes before her.

'So next thing for you to try today. Who has signed up to Chorus? It can be very useful to know who people are, for them to know who you are. And it's a very neat way of personalising the world around you.' She switched the monitor back to what her phone could see. 'Chorus,' she said in a strong German accent and smiled.

'It's the same word in both languages. Okay, so now you can see what information you are already broadcasting.' She panned the room and stopped at Ken. 'Ken Austin, oh, *scheiße*.'

At the same time Ken remembered stumbling down the corridor after leaving Candy – this woman's bright blue eyes and the short white hair disappearing behind a deliberately kicked door.

Ellie killed the display and looked up at the bewildered as a whole. 'Thank you very much for your attention. I hope you found this useful. I think I'm booked for another session where I can go through things in a little more detail and also give you an idea what my company does. I am Ellie Chassagne and the company is Starflame. Thank you.' She stepped lightly down from the platform, but several people managed to block her from leaving while waving their phones at her. By the time she had disentangled herself, Ken had positioned himself by the exit.

'Ms Chassagne, can I buy you a coffee?'

'I'm not sure I have the availability.'

'You were due to speak here till three. That gives you twenty minutes before you should be anywhere else. And I would like to know why you swore when you saw me.' Ken knew he didn't have a winning smile anymore so didn't try. Ellie glanced at the door. For a moment Ken thought she was going to just pick him up and put him to one side like a child.

'Okay, Mr Austin. But there's a pub close by and you can buy me a gin.'

Ken sat in a corner getting his breath back while Ellie bought the drinks. She returned with a whisky, a gin, and two packets of cheese and onion. She had clearly been thinking about what to say before she returned to the table. 'So, Ken. What I think happened is that your handy has worked out who you are from your online presence.'

'I didn't know I had an online presence.'

Ellie winced. 'I had a feeling you were going to say that.'

'And this is somehow connected with your company and Candy.'

'Judith? Yes. Okay. So my company, Starflame Graphics, does software development for the kinds of things I was showing them today. We have a really neat product – you saw the thing with the air quality? We have a real-time prediction algorithm where we can lift your health records and give you a personalised warning about the toxins you're breathing in and forecast whether you're going to have an attack or not. Whether you should get on the next train based on the air quality in that carriage, level of infection and so on. It's super cool. Anyway. It also isn't ready – software development is always so tricky. Not that anyone understands why.' She focused on Ken, still not smiling. 'Or cares. So we need money to fund the company and the project while we work on delivery.' Ellie took a long drink from the gin glass. 'So ...' She drew out the word.

'So?' Ken responded.

'We help broadcast stuff from the rooms next door, you know in Spitalfields. Mostly it's fake porn.'

'People pretending to make love?'

'No, they're doing it all right. It's just that we overlay body doubles of media celebrities. Sometimes the whole thing is computer generated. Do you remember when the deep fakes of Boris and Kate came out? Not that that was us. But that kind of thing.'

Ken knocked back the whisky. 'Is that what you do to me?' he asked.

Ellie laughed and put her hand on his knee for a moment. Her strong fingers easily fell through the cloth to a thigh that was barely there. 'No. You were a minor hit all on your own. It was just you watching Judith while she got ready for a party, or whatever. She would get undressed and the fun was watching your reaction.'

'Fun?'

'Hey, I'm not judging anyone in this. I was just paying the bills.'

'By broadcasting my reaction to Candy.'

Ellie didn't respond, but her face flashed through some options. 'So your phone has recognised who you are and tagged you with a link to the website that we put together for Candy's ...' Ellie struggled to find a word. 'Employer, in your Chorus handle.' Ellie snapped a picture of Ken and then showed it to him. There was his name floating above him and an image of Candy. 'So if I, if anyone, clicks on your handle they see this.'

A short loop of Candy dancing in front of the mirror in bra and pants loaded on screen. Ken could see himself in the seat by the door, his leg trembling. He felt himself deflate; only his hands stopped his face from reaching the table.

Ellie was still watching the clip. 'She knows how to use her body, that girl. Even her ponytail has an artistry of its own. Not that anyone notices.'

'It was all pretend.'

'She had a soft spot for you. You could tell.'

'Why not tell me?'

'That was the charm of the set-up. You were either a brilliant actor or had no idea what was going on. And if you were that good at acting you wouldn't be appearing in that kind of video.'

'What should I do now?' Ken was speaking to his feet.

'Stand up and fight. Pick up your handy and do something about it.'

Ken looked up, head still in his hands.

'It's up to you,' Ellie continued. Her blue eyes looked deeply into his. 'You have an air of a fighter about you. Were you a fighter?'

'Before you were born,' said Ken, who felt unsure if he could stand, never mind fight.

'Pick it up then. I'll show you how. And then I have to go.'

Ken was fascinated by the way Ellie used her phone in a combination of words and gestures – it was as if it was an unconscious extension of her thought processes. As he copied her, the phone came alive in his hands; it reminded him of the flame he used to form with magic, to shape it, bend it to his will.

'Oh, that's it. So take the link away. Excellent. Now you can change what it says there.'

He thought of changing it to say 'Hail Kenato Orin, the Prince of Hell, the Lord of Elementals, King of the Kobolds, Seraph Friend, Freer of Dwarves, master of debate. All hail Kenato Orin, whose harnessing of magic has brought joy and hope to all the peoples of the world.' It was a very different hell from the one they had in this world. In that world spiritual essences like Ken took on real bodies of flesh and blood. You could eat and drink, make love and die. It's what made the place so attractive. Every day could be your last. There was a heaven too, not some abstract concept that you hoped to attain after some arbitrary penance, but a real city full of angels. Insufferably smug angels that had unjustly banished him from their city and then driven him out of that world entirely. Leaving him here, broken old and forgotten. But was that really true? All he had to prove he had been the Prince of Hell was a tin of shortbread that had turned out to be from Edinburgh. Maybe he had just escaped from some institution in the Sixties and never been caught.

Ken jumped a little, faced with Ellie's single eyebrow raised.

'Ken, you've been staring at the handy for a couple of minutes now. You okay?'

'I just can't be sure what's real anymore,' he said quietly.

'Maybe skip the text for now.'

'Right.'

'I really need to go, but I think you've got enough to get started. Most people are frightened to press buttons because they don't know what it will do. Press them all, see what happens, that's how you learn.' She stood up, finishing her gin in one move. She looked embarrassed. 'Bye, Ken.'

'Bye, Ellie.' He sat for a moment wondering if he should look up Candy's website. He used to go to sex shops when he was still capable but that had been years ago. He had gone to see Candy because he missed female company, the simple joy of looking at a beautiful woman. The thrill of what could happen but never would. Watching Candy on a website would only shift him one step further away. He would become a ghost, no longer able to interact in any way. He ordered another whisky and soda and returned to the same table, pulling out his phone again. He felt it pulse in his hand in the same way he used to feel with his flaming sword. It felt good. Mastering this the way that Ellie did, an unconscious extension of her being, that was what he should be doing.

Night had long since fallen when Ken left the pub. The phone warned him the battery was down to minimal and he must have drunk half a bottle of whisky. But it was okay. Fuelled by the water of life he made it all the way home and up the stairs to his flat in one go. He tore his clothes off and collapsed on his bed, his heart racing fit to burst. But in his hand he still held his sword – no, the phone; he squinted at the screen. Based on his biometric information it was offering to call for medical assistance. Ken laughed deeper than he had done in years and fell asleep dreaming of burning castles.

Chapter Five

Ken was woken by somebody snoring. He was going to complain until he realised he was the source. He looked out over his naked body following the line of abandoned clothes to the open front door and the occasional neighbour shuffling by to go to work. One raised a smile and said 'Morning,' but most looked shocked and some hid their eyes.

I could have died on the stairs last night and they would still pass me rather than be late for their precious jobs! Ken rolled off the bed, crawled to the door and pushed it shut. He sat with his back against the wood. He felt awful; his head pounded.

'If I'm in pain I must still be alive,' he said to himself and chuckled. He had met plenty of people who applied that measure to themselves and some who applied it to others. He thought about Naomi and the Queen of Heaven, something else he hadn't done in an age.

He looked at his empty right hand and laughed. 'The phone!' It had slid off the duvet, perhaps bounced off by his snoring. Ken plugged it in and felt that tingle in his arm again. He reached into it as he would have reached into a fire in the world he had come from. His head resisted, rusty from decades of lack of use or possibly the whisky. He tried to picture a question in his head rather than say it out loud or press buttons. The mobile showed him where he was and the shops around that sold fizzy drinks and paracetamol.

At the next technology class Ken was able to outperform the rest of the group, though he made a show out of pretending to press the keyboard. He was disappointed that Starflame had sent someone else to run the session and quickly grew bored with watching the others struggling to open settings and change the screen brightness. What he was really interested in was this 'Internet' that they all talked about. It became clear that although everyone knew of it, no one understood what it was, where it was or how it worked. Ken needed answers, but the only person he trusted was Ellie, and he didn't think he could go back to Spitalfields again, if only because the mobile had made him aware of the violence on the streets. On the way back from Bishopsgate it tried to route him away from the high-frequency muggings, stabbings and shootings that seemed to be rife around him. Had it always been like this and he hadn't noticed? He considered the young folk on the street corners looking for offence and making great efforts to find it.

Well, he thought, *maybe I can discover her online.* Ken was pleased with his use of the phrase. Safely sitting by the window in his apartment, he sent the consciousness of the phone off as he would have dispatched a minor elemental in a previous life. It was back within seconds saying that it had found her but could not reach her. 'Firewalls,' it said.

'Now that's something I understand.' Ken sent his own mind racing off after the phone to this wall that prevented him reaching what he needed. The transition made him feel ill. This was not like any of the planes of existence he was used to. There were no terms of reference. Several times he felt as if his mind was being torn apart and then gathering together again. Eventually, some of him collected in front of what his new-found familiar called the firewall, but he could no longer remember why he was there. Parts of him kept arriving, making him stronger, more focused. *Ellie,* he thought, and reached through the curtain, feeling the resistance grow and lessen as he tried to push, drawing on the power around him as he had done on so many worlds before.

'Hello?'

'Ellie.'

'Who is this?'

'Ken Austin. We met at the old folks' technology class a couple of weeks ago.'

'Ken?'

'I need your help to understand the internet.'

'If you can reach me here then I don't think you need my help.' Something slid, creating a window that Ken could look through. Ellie was there illuminated in blue.

'I can see you,' Ken said involuntarily.

'But I can't see you, nor where you're coming in from.' She was tapping her keyboard and looking below where Ken's window was. He tried to make himself visible. Ellie let out a little scream. 'Okay, that was very scary.'

Ken gave up on that and concentrated on the voice. 'I would like to see you. I need to understand more about the internet. I can buy you lunch?'

'I usually charge one thousand pounds a day,' said Ellie.

Ken thought for a moment. 'I just want to know what you know.'

'That's what I'm saying. Wait, what else do you …?'

The window slid closed and the impression of something beyond the wall disappeared. When he returned to his form, he found vomit in his lap and the stomach-churning smell of incontinence came from his trousers. This would need some practice. When he had finished cleaning himself up there was a message on his mobile. A contract from Starflame Graphics offering consultancy at eighteen hundred pounds a day.

By the third day of working with Ellie it was finally making sense to Ken – the banking, CCTV, payment devices, power generation, games, it was all there. The machines were all talking to each other without anyone really understanding what was going on. The average person in the street had no idea how the information got on their mobile or what was being taken off it. To Ken it seemed like humans had managed to build another reality, parallel to their own, and then almost ignore it completely.

'The only time they use it is when it impinges on the real world.'

'What else would they do?' Ellie asked.

'They could live there, do anything, the energy is incredible.' And it was; this internet had its own power from phone batteries to entire wind farms. Ken in turn drew off it in a way he hadn't been able to since the fires of hell so many years ago.

'I've been meaning to ask, Ken – what's your secret?'

Ken felt his smile freeze. 'That's a difficult question to answer. I have so many.'

Ellie laughed. 'No, I don't mean it literally – it's your looks, Ken. When we first met you looked ancient.' She laughed again. 'That sounds bad. But you look younger now than you did. Not young, but more alive somehow.' Ken thought of the twenty-four-ounce steak he'd had last night at the Malvinas.

'I've gone vegetarian,' he said. She didn't look convinced. 'I think it's just this. Having an interest. Meeting you.' She looked surprised. 'These meetings, your training. It's given me a reason to live. There's so much more I can do than I ever dreamed.'

'Well, you're certainly doing well on it.'

'Thank you.'

Coming back to the flat was depressing though. He became conscious of the stacks of his own newspapers he had to navigate around. The kitchen and bathroom, though nominally clean, were ingrained in forty years of grime. When he sat in his favourite chair the cloud of dust it exhaled blocked out the light from the dim bulb far above in the high Victorian ceiling. Now that he had worked out money was virtual, getting more wasn't a problem. He just had to be careful not to cross any of the tripwires the banks had attempted to put in place to stop people doing what he had in mind. Small, repetitive actions soothed the watchdogs into looking elsewhere. He rang A1 Kitchens, but no one picked up the call and they didn't have a website, but Ken found a long list of companies who would be very happy to refurbish his flat.

Ken returned to his home after all the work was done and was busy rearranging his new furniture when someone knocked at the door.

'Hello, Mr Austin.' It was the piano player from upstairs. 'I don't wish to disturb you. I …' A tear ran down his cheek like a marble down a stair. 'Oh dear. It's Sarah. What should I do?'

Ken rested his arm on a bony shoulder for a moment. 'I'll come up.'

'Thank you, Mr Austin. I think we might have to call for an ambulance but I'm not sure we have the money if it turns out not to be an emergency.'

Ken pulled the door to and heard the old man behind him as he climbed the stairs. The woman was in her bed as before, a more sallow colour, her face drawn in to make her almost unrecognisable. Her hand was cold, the breathing nearly inaudible, seemingly random. There was a bitter smell in the air. Her husband stood at the doorway as if seeking permission to come into his own bedroom.

'What should I do, Mr Austin?'

Ken reached into her soul. Her fight was over; she was ready to go, a faint spark left inside a husk. What good would an ambulance do?

'Put the kettle on please. Do you have any biscuits?' Ken asked. The man shuffled away, his slippers fitting into two worn brown grooves in the mustard carpet. Ken stretched his right hand to her chest. His palm popped like a badly lit gas ring. He tried again, tried to remember what it was like to bend fire and life to his will. Warmth from him spread out across her lungs. She breathed deeply and again. Ken's fingers flared and then faded. He still held her other hand when the old man returned with the tea and a packet of Rich Tea, slightly soft from being open too long, but Ken ate through the pack like a hamster eating sunflower seeds.

Sarah's eyes opened a crack and she took in the two men. 'Hello. I had such a lovely dream.' She smiled and she looked less dead, more like herself again. Now Ken felt a hand on his shoulder. He looked at the mess of pink and purple impactless bruises and veins wandering free under the pianist's skin.

'Thank you, Mr Austin. I hoped I was overreacting. Will she be all right, do you think?'

Ken had seen the damage done throughout her body. He had only helped, not cured. 'For a while.'

Ken walked back down the stairs considering the hand on his shoulder. Naomi used to look like that when she was trying to put the angels off their meals. She had come through into this world with him. Thinking about it, though he had provided the power, she had picked the way. She had chosen to come here and he had never asked why. They had escaped from the destruction of hell and arrived in the middle of an ancient stone ring – a fire elemental and a husk of a man falling out of the sky on a freezing cloudless night. They had argued on frosted grass; Naomi stomped off, her green footsteps steaming in the light of the full moon. Ken, exhausted by creating the portal, hadn't had the energy to follow her. But now perhaps he could. He walked slowly back down to his own flat not really paying attention to each step or the grain of the wooden rail under his hand. Maybe now with his strength returning they could get the old gang back together again.

Four hours later the phone lay in the corner of the room where he had thrown it. Nothing. No presence at all. He stood looking out of the window as if he might see her walking down the street. But he saw only the scooters weaving in and out of each other and potholes. He recovered the Xiaomi, checked to see if he had broken the screen, and called Ellie.

'Ken, been a while. How are you?'

'Alive. How do I find somebody that's not on the internet?'

'Not on the internet?'

'I'm pretty sure not.'

'Well, you can look through articles, news stories, pictures if you know what they look like.'

'I've looked through all the social media.'

'No, you need to go through archives, old newspapers, magazines. A lot of it is just images so the content doesn't show up in a search.'

'That sounds impossible.'

'If you think about it, there's usually a link, a thing that ties you to that person. Start from there.'

'Nothing springs to mind. We were very different people back then.'

'When did you last see her?' A good guess from Ellie there.

'1962, I believe.'

'Well, Ken, you know that was a very long time ago. She may not be with us anymore.'

'She will still be alive. There's nothing on this planet that could kill Naomi.' He pulled out a piece of shortbread and looked at the picture of Edinburgh Castle on the front of the tin. Naomi used to eat these while she was in heaven. He had never made the connection before. She must have been visiting here all the while she was building hell.

'Hello, Ken?'

'Thank you, Ellie, invaluable as usual.'

Chapter Six

The sleeper to Glasgow cost enough to make Ken hesitate in buying the ticket. But now he was on his way he was quite excited about his plans. He spread out the printed articles he had found. Rereading them made it feel like less a wild-goose chase. Naomi, it seemed, had been a major patron in Edinburgh for a while. Even though she changed her look every now and then, Ken had been able to pick her out in pictures of new art events grateful for her sponsorship. They seemed to be mostly dance troupes of various kinds. Property appeared to be her source of income and Ken had enjoyed building a picture of the buildings and housing associations she had invested in. But then it had all stopped in the mid-nineties. There were notices of sale, land all round Scotland being sold off under a variety of names. The trail had gone cold. Then, while aimlessly browsing through articles about housing north of the border, he had seen her in a piece in *The Scotsman* from 2010 about people living off the grid after the first collapse. There was an image of some of the folk in a place called Carbeth, mostly men with beards and woolly jumpers, but there she was at the back, not looking at the camera so perhaps not even aware her image had been caught at all. That was all Ken had needed. He laid the hard copy of the article down on the train table. This was where the line of enquiry stopped. It was where he would start.

Ken sat in the back of a taxi from Milngavie to Carbeth. The countryside was becoming wilder again the further they went from Glasgow. Green rolling hills hid the higher, browner peaks behind. The taxi driver spoke but Ken had no idea what the man was saying. They had several goes at talking to each other during the drive, but the conversations had all ended in the same mutual incomprehension.

Instead, Ken reflected on what he was going to say to Naomi. He had thought about it on the train from London to Glasgow and the smaller line from Glasgow to Milngavie. But despite all that thinking he had failed to come up with anything concrete other than 'Let's get the gang back together and destroy heaven.' Not the most compelling argument, but he was so excited at the idea of meeting Naomi again he was sure she would feel the same and that would be sufficient. The taxi pulled up, but the driver was peering out through the windscreen. He talked again as they crept up a narrow road.

'I'm sorry?' asked Ken.

'I said there used to be a pub here.' The driver spoke slowly now as he might have done to a difficult child. He continued to peer out, clearly not happy at what he was seeing. Rain was falling now and the windscreen wipers shuddered over the glass then shrieked back. 'I was looking forward to a pint and a charge before going back, but anyway, this is you.'

'This is me what?' Ken was confused now.

'Out!' the driver shouted. Ken picked up his suitcase and folder and bounced himself out of the back seat. He just had time to close the door before the car whined away, leaving him on the edge of the main highway with the darkening sky above. Ken abruptly felt very alone. He pulled out the print of *The Scotsman* article and headed along the single-track road. Taking a path to the right he looked at each house carefully to try and work out where the picture had been taken. He then took a left but realised that he was looping back on himself. The dwellings varied from small houses to glorified wooden sheds that looked desperately in need of care. He saw two people on his tour – one was spinning wool, the other was reading a book, but neither did more than raise an eyebrow as he passed. Clearly he was not from round here. When he saw a third man making detailed carved birds on his porch, Ken unconsciously stroked his chin. Shed dwelling seemed to demand a full, uncontrolled beard.

The rain picked up pace as Ken walked slowly further into the settlement. Each reference to the damp picture made it a little more fragile and he became reluctant to use it further. The water forced its way past his jacket's collar, and he felt its chill fingers spreading over his body. He stopped at the end of the road; he saw only open moorland beyond. This was hopeless. The folded paper refused to come apart one last time, and was now just a squishy white blob in his hand.

'Kenato Orin. I hoped you were dead,' said a voice loud enough to cut through the hissing downpour. Ken felt a tug at being called his old name. For a moment the rain didn't seem quite so cold. Ken looked round, trying to push his plastered hair out of his face, but only succeeded in mixing in the pulped print. A figure in a grey cagoule had followed him up the road to the moor's edge. The black hood had been pulled forward into a snorkel, making the head all but invisible. The figure raised a black arm, storm cuff hiding the hand within. 'How did you find me? If you used magic you may have killed us both.'

'A picture. There was an article about the way you all live here – off grid. In a newspaper. You were in the picture. No magic.'

'Okay, that's a start. You look worse than the day I left you. I was sure you would have recovered your strength by now.'

Ken tried to imagine what was left of his thin grey hair stuck to his scalp, the jacket and trousers clinging to his slight frame. Not the way he would have wanted to be seen, the mighty ogre long forgotten.

'I'm better than I have been. I have finally discovered a way to get my powers back. And I thought once I found you, we could, maybe …' Ken hesitated. 'You know …'

'Don't say "get the gang back together", Kenato Orin.'

'No, absolutely not. I—'

'Let's be clear, fifty years is not long enough for me to have calmed down after what you did. A hundred years wouldn't be enough.'

'I understand you might be angry.'

'That would be a first. I have gone over that day again and again. What could I have done differently that would have saved hell from being crushed? If we could have picked up the host movements sooner? Could we have disrupted their magic better? Had we had the full strength of the kobolds would we have prevailed? And then it came to me – there was a simple answer that could have prevented hell being laid waste.'

'You were always the best strategist we had.' Ken tried to smile but he was shivering uncontrollably. 'What was it?'

'It was "Don't shag the Queen of Heaven". That was all you had to do. Then Alfin would be alive. And Lorcan. And you wouldn't have to die on a cold and rainy day at the arse end of Scotland!' The arm came up again and Ken flinched. 'Hell was the best set-up we had ever had, that we were ever going to have, and you had to throw it away.'

'You were there in the halls of the Heavenly king – you saw I truly loved her.'

'We were in the middle of a battle I would've really liked to win. But no, you had to set up a royal therapy session and share it with everyone. You made Arden see Lorcan, the man she idolised, fucked one way by the High King and the other way by the High Queen. And then all of us watched Alva going cowgirl on you, which is not an image I felt the need to see then or now. I think I'll just kill you. You're so slight, the midges and rain will get rid of any evidence.'

'Please, Naomi!' Ken's teeth chattered together. The seams on his jacket had given way and water that seemed colder than ice washed over him now, determined to steal away any signs of life before Naomi could.

'What was it, Kenato, were you bored?' Naomi asked.

Ken hadn't thought of it in those terms. He hesitated to respond. 'A little, yes. Quite.' He tried to blink the rain out of his eyes and found it difficult to open them again, to look into the righteous anger of the Procurator of Hell. 'There is no excuse.' The only sound now was the driving downpour strong enough to break up the streams flowing down the gravel track from the moorland.

'Okay.'

Ken looked up and realised he was being left behind the shifting curtains of grey. He followed the shrouded figure back down the hill to a house he had walked past at least twice. It looked like it had been extended out in several directions, part seemingly an integral greenhouse that they stepped round to get to the front door. A decent-sized felted porch kept the worst of the weather off though it bounced up from the concrete path with force.

'Thank you,' said Ken as they entered the hallway.

'Don't thank me until I've decided not to kill you,' said the figure as it pulled off the cagoule and hung up the streaming jacket on a hook alongside other damp garments. Naomi stood before him looking much as she had when he had last seen her. The hair was wild and grey but the stance unbowed, and there was a quickness to her movements that belied any sense of age. 'Get your wet things off. I'll put the kettle on.'

They took a few steps down a corridor. Ken looked round the inside of the house, which widened out into a narrow room. A wide hall pretending to be a room. There was a table set up for a meal under an oil lamp – three wicker mats and sets of cutlery with three chairs pushed in around it, though none of it matched. Naomi came out from a small kitchen to Ken's right and disappeared into another room. 'Get your trousers off as well and I'll do what I can to dry them.' There was the sound of wooden drawers opening and closing. She came back and threw a pair of jeans, a shirt and a black cardigan at him. 'Here. These were …' She stopped and looked at Ken carefully. 'The less you know about me, the better. Okay, you get changed and I'll put your stuff above the stove. It should take off the worst of it.'

'You've picked up a Scottish accent.'

'After more than fifty years I would hope so.'

Ken dressed in clothes that made him feel child sized while Naomi hung up his soaked garments. She brought out a pot, two porcelain cups and a tin of shortbread. Ken recognised the brand.

'That's the same make you left me with in Avebury.'

'Yes, I used to go to Edinburgh quite a lot. Came for the Enlightenment, stayed for the biscuits.'

'How did you expend the energy?' asked Ken.

'You don't have to do the whole showboat "I'll rip a hole in reality" thing,' Naomi mimicked, pulling apart the space in front of her. 'You can sort of slide through. Especially if you know where you're going. And if I'm on my own, the path becomes easier somehow. Anyway, when you did your ...' She grunted with mimed force again. 'It was quite easy to nudge us somewhere close to a place I knew. Which is why we're both here on this world.' She bit on a biscuit, brushed the crumbs off her grey jumper and smiled to herself a little. 'While the rest are scattered across all the multiverse.'

Ken felt emptiness at the thought of all his demons, so powerful together, now strewn across so many worlds.

Naomi continued. 'I had expected to find that Candice had already tracked you down.'

'She was always a good time girl. And these are not good times. It was...you know, if we could get things going again she might find me. Or I might find her.' Ken smiled a broken smile and they sat in what he hoped was a comfortable silence.

'It is really good to see you, Naomi,' Ken said, and was surprised how moved he felt just being able to say it. A clock somewhere out of sight marked the passing of time and the rain hit the roof to remind them that it was still there, waiting. Ken was relieved she didn't feel the need to say she would destroy him again. Small victories.

'You said that if I used magic it would kill us both. Why?'

Naomi got up and went behind Ken to another room. Ken wondered how long it would take to get used to the layout of this randomly built place. He looked round the room at the china dogs each side of the fire and a picture of a younger Naomi, a broad man with a beard, and a girl in a cream Aran jumper about the same height as Naomi. Serious grey eyes peered out from under a black fringe. The picture had been taken in this room with the same china dogs. Naomi returned with something wrapped in a towel. She put it in the centre of the table leaving Ken to reluctantly tug away a corner. A skull, translucent white, more like marble than bone. The back of the skull was elongated, the rest all sharp edges – eyebrow ridges, cheekbones, teeth.

'An angel? But how did it get here? Have you been back?'

'No, well, I have been back, but I was summoned by some of my old followers.'

'I didn't know you could do that.'

'Nor did I,' Naomi said. 'It was a weird experience. With heaven in chaos, some of the crew we had left behind wanted some advice on what to do. They were a bit sad when I said I wasn't coming back.'

'Aren't you?'

'To what end, Ken? Take up the unrighteous war? Have tens of thousands more die to install myself as absolute ruler? They need to sort themselves out. That was the point of Eden. It gave people options – tried to spread the power out a bit. Get heroes to fight the good fight rather than rely on gods, along with breaking heaven's monopoly on reincarnation. Choice is good. Of course, then the angels just called Eden Hell and that made some of the choices bad. Anyway. No.'

'And you picked up the skull then?'

'I had a limited presence, a bit like being a spirit again, a ghost. I don't think I could threaten much more than blow a candle out. I came back with one of these sods hot on my heels. What didn't help was I'd messed myself here while being summoned. I can tell you fighting an angel while your knickers are full of your own shit is no laughing matter. Anyway, I beat him, obviously, burnt the place down and fled. It took me a while to figure out, but magic is definitely the way they find you and then they seem to be able to use technology in some way to narrow it down. This World Wide Web is the key to power in this world. That's why I'm living here. I don't think there's a mobile or an internet connection within three miles of here.' Naomi refilled both cups from the pot. Ken remembered the laptop and phone in his bag and thought they'd better stay unthought of. 'Since I moved here twenty-something years ago I haven't had a visit.'

'How many have you had before?'

'This little beauty was actually number six. I stopped using my powers to kill them and they stopped coming.' Naomi patted the skull. 'I sold the other five to collectors. I'm keeping her for a rainy day.' She laughed as she looked out the window. 'There's good money in alien artefacts here.'

'Alien?'

'Did you not notice out of the dozens of worlds we've visited this is the only one I can think of where there's only one intelligent species?'

'It hadn't occurred to me.' Ken was slightly bewildered. When had he stopped thinking, stopped caring?

'These guys, humans, killed any competition off just after they invented spears and canoes. Can you imagine the level of aggression required for that? Well, you don't have to, you've been here. And this has been a quiet period for them. I've never seen anything like it. Tell one half they're blue team and the other half they're red and that's enough for them to go slaughter for it.'

'Not all of them.' Ken thought of his piano-playing neighbour and his wife.

'No, not all.' Naomi reached out and picked at the cardigan Ken was wearing. He was sure Naomi was seeing the original wearer. 'But people will pay for concrete proof that there are, or were, something else, others.' She wrapped their common enemy up in the towel and took it away back down the wooden corridor out of sight. When she returned she seemed less tense.

'Kenato, I'm sort of glad you're here. I knew I didn't want to go back to that life.' Ken felt the question rise on his face. 'I had thought about it, only maybe not quite as much as you. But I'm done with the Queen of Heaven trying to kill me.' She paused for a long moment. 'And you. You've pushed me into not wanting to stay here either. Some very slow game of hide and seek. Hoping for people to come back and find me. Fearing that they will. I used to travel the worlds. It was what I was good at. It's how I found Alfin, on the run. I always was a sucker for someone down on their luck. It's too easy for the angels to come here and vice versa. Maybe all my shopping trips built a path between here and heaven? It doesn't matter. Time to move on. Discover somewhere new and start again rather than spend any more of my life here living with ghosts. Being a ghost.'

'I could come …' Ken wanted to follow her, to see the flame-wreathed Naomi in action again. 'We were a good team. You know, I can give you a sense of direction, purpose,' Ken ended hesitantly.

'And that's why you don't have friends, Kenato.'

'I have lots of friends,' he said defensively.

'Unless you've changed, you either pay them to be your friends or they're frightened you will kill them if they're not.'

Ken didn't feel he could win that argument. 'All I was saying was that we were better than the individual parts.'

'Yes. Yes, we were,' she said without conviction. 'Now, let's see how much your clothes have dried off.'

They were warm but damp as Ken pulled everything back on again. When he picked up his anorak, water was still dripping from it onto the rug at the door. 'That jacket was meant to be waterproof.'

'Only if you're south of Watford. We have proper rain up here. You can take this.' Naomi handed him a yellow oilskin with the words 'Hebridean Offshore Power' in black letters on the back. Ken pulled it on and it swamped him.

Naomi laughed. 'Sorry, Kenato. But when I think of what we were and here we are.'

'We could win, Naomi.' Ken could see the glory days again; with Naomi at his side, anything was possible.

'Aye, right. We have no army, no allies, we're hiding our magic in the shadows, fearful of the heavenly light falling on us, always wondering when an avenging angel will appear with their flaming sword and sense of smug righteousness.' Naomi passed him his suitcase and went to pat him where his shoulder should have been. Naomi looked round her own house like a stranger. 'Time for us both to go,' she said.

Ken found himself being pushed out of the front door and back into the patient rain. Pleased to see him, it intensified, ripples in the air coming up the road towards him. The oilskin, though, was impervious, and he took a couple of steps down the short path pulling the hood tightly around his face. An odd-looking grey crow sat opposite the door. It had black wings but the black head made it look like it too was wearing a cowl against the weather. The bird turned his head to look at them through the cascading spray.

'No food at the moment,' said Naomi in a raised voice.

Ken looked from the woman to the bird. 'You used to look like that. I thought you had made it up.'

'No.' Naomi shook her head for emphasis. 'It's a hooded crow. We're right on the edge of their territory here. South and east of here it is all carrion crows. North and west these fellows are the norm.' She looked around the outside of her hut, oblivious to the gushing water from the overflowing gutters. 'That's why I came back here – somewhere to hide, shortbread and hoodies. But it's not enough. Goodbye, Kenato Orin.' She went inside and closed the door.

Ken tried to protect his phone from the incessant downpour as he used it to order a taxi when he was back on the main highway. Once he had finally established where he was, they said it would be half an hour for a pickup, but it was closer to an hour and a half when the taxi whizzed up the road to gather up its bright yellow passenger. Ken would return to London alone. This was not what he had planned, what he had hoped for. No procurator to plot his victory with. Then, he thought, what was the point of going home? He turned away from the approaching taxi whose tyres hissed on the smooth wet tarmac. Having come this far he should try again, at least. But smoke from the burning house was climbing above the trees. A tongue of flame curled up into the sky, defying the storm, vanquishing it with fiery intensity. It towered above all the huts of Carbeth for a moment, red and gold and black. Ken wondered at the shapes in its writhing form. Now he could hear the distant sound of sirens. He pulled the taxi door open, and as he leaned forward the rain trapped in the oilskin poured out as if from an opened tap.

'Glasgow, Central Station.'

Chapter Seven

Ken had booked a table seat on the train back south. He needn't have worried; the mobile had already announced a raised threat level for the next fourteen days, so most people were staying at home. He spread out all the material he had planned to show Naomi, partly to allow it to dry off and partly because he was sure he was looking at pieces of a puzzle. If only he could see how they fitted together. He thought of the description Naomi had given of being summoned and how it mapped to his own experience exploring the internet. Could he use the same technique to visit heaven even though he didn't have the strength to do it himself? If he did so, to what purpose? He saw himself as a spirit drifting through the wreckage of hell taunting unseeing angels. He dozed fitfully through most of the journey back to London. His phone woke him up twenty minutes before arriving.

'Thank you, Naomi,' he muttered sleepily. Ken laughed at himself; he changed the name of the phone and added a picture of the odd Scottish bird as the phone's avatar. If he couldn't have Naomi herself then the Xiaomi would have to do its best to fill the gap. The train had been delayed in York so Ken didn't get back into London until after curfew. Even with his Vaccard it was hard to persuade a taxi to take him home. He was exhausted and irritated when he finally reached the haven of his flat and closed the gate behind him.

He was too distracted to crawl out of the giant oilskin. He sat for a while by the front door trying to work out if he was happy or sad about the events of the last couple of days. It had been good to see Naomi. It had reaffirmed in his mind that it had all been real – he really had been the Prince of Hell. He had fought heaven and lost. Just that was almost enough to compensate for her deciding not to be at his side. So, what should he do now?

In answer there was a horrible noise from the flat above. Ken put down his phone and concentrated on the ensuing hush. The sound of his neighbours playing the piano to briefly escape life and fighting for every breath to keep it had been his soundtrack for years. Now it had been taken away, the silence was deafening. He rolled over onto all fours and pulled himself up the door until he stood, his head resting against the woodwork. His body ached with tiredness. He should just go to bed. Then that wail again. Felix?

Ken climbed the stairs as quickly as he could, the oilskin rippling as he climbed. He let himself into the flat above with the key he still had. The light from the landing lit up a portion of the hall and the living room beyond. The stacks of papers had been knocked over creating black and white waves of paper washing out to the shoreline of the hall. Ken slipped into the shadow, leaving the light to obscure his entrance. The smell of blood filled the apartment so he didn't feel the need to say hello.

He found them both in the bedroom. The husband had been tied up, facing his wife; his fingers appeared broken but left in place as though he was trying to carry something on the back of his hands. Blood had pooled around the feet of the chair from an unseen wound. Tears were still wet on his bruised face as he stared with sightless eyes at the love of his life. She looked unharmed but, as Ken approached, he felt a breeze from the pipe to her mask. He squeezed the tube slightly and a dozen tiny cuts gaped open showing their betrayal.

Ken sat beside his neighbours piecing together what had happened. Someone had sliced the tube to limit the airflow but had turned up the oxygen flow to full. To what end? To keep her on the edge of consciousness as long as possible while continuing to cut the pipe as she watched? All the while her husband would have looked on, powerless to help. This was no robbery gone wrong. There was that cry again, very close. Felix pulled himself into view. His orange fur had been carved along the side allowing his intestines to escape. The act of entering the bedroom had wrapped his guts round his hind legs. He stopped crawling, looking at Ken with a palpable sense of disappointment.

'Naomi, light on,' he said, and the phone shone out brightly like a car headlight. Four eyes blinked back at him. Above the shivering cat crouched an angel, sword in hand. He held up his arm to block the torchlight.

'Call upon the Procurator of Hell if you want – she won't be able to save you,' the angel said confidently. 'But if you tell me where Naomi is your death will be swifter than for these three demon worshippers.'

Ken sat stunned as he took in the details of the angel in front of him – the almond eyes, the elongated ears, the badge on his leather armour that should mean something, but it had been oh, so long. Deep scratches ran down one superbly defined cheekbone; well done Felix.

'Now ...' The angel paused, sword drooping. 'Fuck me, Kenato Orin!'

At the sound of his old name he felt that tug again, stronger this time, still an echo of what it had been, but closer.

'I need to tell the High Queen.'

'Queen's Rangers,' said Ken clicking his fingers. 'I knew it would come to me.'

The intruder looked quizzical for a moment then turned and ran towards the front door. Ken's phone blazed. Ken sprang up with an energy he had never felt in this world; it was an ogre's talons that pulled the angel off the landing and back into the hall.

'Don't kill me!' pleaded the angel. 'I'll ...' And there he stopped, for what could an angel offer the Prince of Hell?

Ken did not hesitate; his hand burst into flames as he pulled the angel in for a fiery kiss. The Ranger screamed in the face of death but there wasn't much more than the smell of burning leather. The fire flickered and then burned out. An angelic foot to Ken's stomach freed its owner and with another kick off the wall, he leapt into the cruel room.

Ken caught him again, using the wrecked lives in front of him to supply the anger he needed. 'What have you become that you could do this?' he demanded. Rage swept through him and his hand sparked into flames again. The air itself seemed to burn. The angel exploded over Ken as the pair were thrown back against the brickwork, another blast smashed into them both and Ken felt himself falling.

'Welcome back to the land of the living.' The voice was calm and reassuring. He opened one eye and looked out into a white world. A doctor stood beside the bed in a Hazmat suit.

'Are you sure?' asked Ken.

'I am amazed you're alive at all,' said the medic, 'Mr Austin. How old are you?' Ken knew the answer to this one. His paperwork stated that he was eighty-nine and he said so. 'Well, you have kept yourself in good condition. For a man of your age to survive such trauma is remarkable.'

'I drink a lot of milk,' he said before drifting off.

He struggled on the edge of consciousness for the next couple of days – a wakeful drifting punctuated not quite by sleep; it was more like being switched off.

'It's been ten days now. What can you remember?' Ken hadn't been aware of the policemen coming in and tried not to look too alarmed. He could recall nothing after the blast and said so.

'Can you explain what happened?' one of the officers said.

'There was an intruder upstairs. I heard the cat and went up to have a look.'

'We found the cat,' the policeman confirmed. 'We think he used up all nine lives that day.'

'What about the intruder?' Ken asked.

'He saved your life,' said the policeman. 'Albeit not intentionally. The fire brigade said the oxygen bottle blew initially. Your burglar caught most of the blast, saving you from the worst of it.'

'Initially?' asked Ken.

'Yes. The old stove in the kitchen went off second and took out that corner of the house. The first responders discovered you in the street. You were covered in so much of the other guy they assumed you were a goner. Just as well they decided not to ship you straight to the mortuary.' They both laughed. It didn't seem that funny to Ken. He found their lack of concern worrying.

'What about the couple upstairs? Did you find them? I think they were already dead when I arrived.'

'That's what we want to determine,' said the first policeman. 'Let's start again from the top. Don't miss anything out, however unimportant you might believe it to be.'

Ken told them as much as he could, but once he had confirmed that it was some mad guy who thought he was an angel and not terrorism they seemed to lose interest. The torture he had witnessed kept them engaged but none of it made it as far as their notebooks.

'That's a new one on me,' said the first cop as they stood up to leave.

'Just as you thought stuff couldn't get any weirder,' said the other. 'Right, we better be going.'

'What happens if I need you for anything?' Ken asked. The cop looked confused for a moment.

'That's not really our problem. Look, I'll send you our Chorus tag.' The policeman looked around the room.

'My old phone was destroyed in the blast and I haven't had the concentration to set up the replacement yet.'

'Hang on.' The detective pulled out a card. 'Always carry a couple of these for emergencies.' He left it by Ken's bed and the pair left.

The medical staff were back in and started packing everything up.

The nurse smiled at him. 'Your results have come back negative for any of the current notifiable infections so it's back to the outside world for you.'

Ken pulled his blankets up to his chest and held them tight. He felt mixed emotions over the prospect of leaving the safety of the hospital. It was difficult for him to judge but he felt stronger than he had before; his arms had some hint of muscle now. His body had somehow grown in the fire and destruction. He had been dreaming of Candice. Her tail had slid up his back as she whispered in his ear. He had woken with an erection; he really couldn't remember the last time that had happened.

The doctor looked from her pad to Ken again. 'And the blackouts have stopped?' she asked.

'Yes,' Ken lied automatically. 'None since a couple of days ago.'

'It would be good to get this bed back. I'm afraid with the new rules you qualified as a bed blocker four days ago and that goes against our community engagement target. I wonder if we could get you home tonight? No sign of your replacement Vaccard though. Getting anywhere without that will be tricky.'

'I'll walk.' Ken didn't want to be where he wasn't wanted.

'It's pouring out there. Wettest autumn on record, they said. But then every year seems to be record breaking now.'

Even though the staff were keen, it was the next day before they could find a consultant who could release Ken. He spent the intervening time restoring his details to his new mobile and combing through all the reports of the explosion that should have killed him. Not that there was much. The press seemed to have the same preoccupation with Neo-Soviets as the police, to the point where nothing else seemed to count. Now he stood in a bus shelter in shirt and trousers that had been cosy enough for the overheated infirmary but inadequate for the chill of the damp night, which quickly got hold of him. He looked at his phone. The nurse had been right – no rides would take him without a Vaccard this close to a hospital. They would lose their certification within minutes if they took the job.

Looking at the downpour reminded him of the shores of the Emerald Sea. He and the real Candy – Candice, the one with the tail and horns, would slip away. Naomi had always been happier running the show without him. On the shores of the Emerald Sea the rain was warm. Ken and Candice would magic up a sail to catch the offshore breeze that moved off the palm-tree-covered slopes of the Edgeward Isles to the turquoise ocean. Sometimes they would skim just above the waves or hold tight as they soared up to the edge of the cloud, using the mist for cover as they made love. He felt a stirring in his trousers again and thought of Candy, the one without the tail.

'Why not,' he said to himself. He could look after her now. Money had never been an issue, but that hadn't been enough for Candy and he respected her for that. But he had been so focused on getting Naomi back he had overlooked any other possibility of happiness. Ken felt his enthusiasm grow along with a few other things. She would never have to clean or appear on that private OnlyFans site again. The rain didn't feel so cold now.

'*Huǒyàn,*' he said, and the projector sprang into life; the fast-refresh LED froze individual raindrops as they fell, creating an intricate pattern in the air in front of him. He moved the lamp around trying to bounce the light off a sail that wasn't there. As he walked slowly around the space where it was in his mind's eye, the lamp caught the driving rain, holding the drops in place. They slowed in the air as if beading on an invisible object. Then the light from the phone started to reflect off its surfaces, the harness, the sail itself that billowed out in the breeze, snapping out, shaking itself free of the water droplets that had given it shape. Ken reached out to hold it in place now that it was solid enough to contain the wind. Laughing at the joy of being able to summon again he tugged the sail towards himself and it pulled back, urging itself up. Another gust and he was hauled up into the orange sky. He stuffed the Xiaomi into his sodden trouser pocket so that he could take up the controls with both hands, and he climbed and circled until he was sure of where he was in relation to A1 Kitchens.

Below, the downward-facing lamps showed up two gangs squaring up in the street below. Scooters had stopped so their riders could watch, their headlights creating a floodlit stadium for the drama to unfold. Ken pressed on, trying to avoid the brightest lights around churches. The office blocks were mostly dark apart from the ones that had been converted into flats. He resisted the urge to sail closer, to peer in on their little lives. Tonight he was going to rescue Candy.

Ken landed on the balcony of the window he had got to know so well from the other side of the glass. The pounding rain washed the sail away and Ken revelled in the freedom to move that way again. Candy was in her room, dancing to music that made the ironwork he stood on vibrate. She performed in front of the mirror taking images of herself with her phone. She pulled off her top, taking more pictures while using her left arm to cover her breasts. Ken could see now that she was playing to the mirrors around her; that was the real audience. This young woman was sharing her solitary moments with hundreds or possibly thousands of others. Turning her back on her reflection she pulled a bra on, still keeping up the rhythm, rotating, using the bright lamps to flare out the parts of her body they were so desperate to see. That was the artistry; a full reveal would be the end of the show, the end of the fans, just one more naked body among the countless women chewed up by the porn industry every year. A grey dress was pulled from the bed and over her head. She smoothed it down like a second skin.

Ken realised he didn't have to settle for furtive glances anymore. He pulled the window up and fell in. A less elegant entrance than he had planned.

Candy screamed as he bundled in, bringing the storm with him. She looked stunned, trying to make sense of what she saw as Ken disentangled himself from the mass of cuddly toys he had knocked out the way as he entered. She went to scream again but her eyes focused on his. 'Ken? What the fucking hell were you doing out there?' The accent was pure Lancashire this time.

'Candy, I have come to rescue you.'

'Eh?'

Ken heard heavy feet pounding down the hall towards them. 'Look,' he said desperately, pointing at the bulge in his trousers. 'I'm a man again. Come away with me and you won't have to do this anymore.' The look of disgust on Candy's face hurt Ken more than the explosion had. 'I haven't done this very well. I understand it's a shock.'

'A shock? For fuck's sake, Ken.'

The door opened and the bouncer stepped in. 'You all right, love?' he asked Candy.

'Of course she's all right ...' Ken said, but a strong hand lifted him off the nylon carpet by the throat and pushed him against the wall, choking off the rest of the sentence.

'Cause if you've touched one hair of Judith's head ...'

Pale fingers appeared on the bouncer's arm. 'Not here, David. Candy, remember?' She was back in control, and with her eyes she highlighted all the mirrors and the witnesses they held.

The bouncer nodded and put Ken back on the floor so that he could breathe. 'You okay?' he asked again.

'Fine. He was hiding out on the window ledge. It will take more than a creepy old man on Viagra to throw me. Thanks, babe,' she finished brightly in her London accent.

The bouncer picked the deflated Ken up, bundled him out of the room and closed the door. 'You,' David said quietly, 'are in so much trouble.'

Ken only saw the first fist coming.

Ken peered out of one puffed-up eye onto the concrete that supported his face. He spat out blood and snot, which quivered in front of him, black in the low orange light. He had tried to find the anger he had used when fighting the angel, but all he could see was Candy's look of revulsion. It tore the rage out of him, doubled the force of each punch and kick he had received. The blows had kept coming until Ken heard someone suggest that the bouncer should stop unless he had a good idea of what he was going to do with the body. With a grunt of acknowledgement, the beating had ended and Ken was thrown out the fire exit like a bloody rag. He lay where he had been cast with his arms trapped under him, unable to move.

A couple sauntered by looking like hyenas nervously approaching a lion's kill.

'You all right, mate?' she asked while her partner scanned every approach and the sky above. Quick fingers darted round his pockets, pulling away his new phone and a wallet that he'd bought in hospital.

'Sweet,' said the other.

She slapped her companion's face lightly. Then she looked at the phone with an expert eye. 'Water damaged. This man's not been looking after his kit.' She spun the phone so that it shattered against something metal. 'Next time you come here, make sure you have something worth nicking.'

'He's not having a good night.'

They laughed and jogged back into the rain. Ken pushed himself upright, wheezing as he rested against the end of a Biffa bin among the wreckage of his Xiaomi. He closed his eyes; they didn't know the half of it. This world had achieved what the Queen of Heaven could not. He was emasculated to the point where even a waif would rather dance in front of a one-handed audience than be with Kenato Orin. Naomi had quit this world in preference to coming to his aid. After the magic he had so carelessly used tonight, another avenging angel would be on their way. The only other people he had ever cared for had already been killed by the same recklessness.

He pulled out the policeman's card, thinking he should report his mugging. But he let it drop into the pool he sat in. No human cared whether he lived or died. Not the police or the hospital staff, even the phone shop people had treated him with contempt simply because he was old. Candy and Ellie had only tolerated him while he paid them for their time. Indifference and antagonism had stalked him throughout his time here. What would they have done if they knew his true nature? He should have the grace just to die.

Ken thought of the train journey back from Scotland and how sure he had been that there was a way of fitting all the pieces together. Some way of fighting back. Naomi had given him all the answers but as usual neither of them had seen it until too late.

'We have no army,' she had said. But she had already pointed out that there were surrounded by one of the most aggressive species either of them had ever met in a hundred worlds. A species that had purged a planet of rivals before they had even invented the wheel. It gave him a nameless horde whose fury would overwhelm anything he could point them at. 'We hide our magic in the shadows,' Naomi had said, but he could make phones magic. If there were enough of them he could act unseen, a single torch in a city of light.

Revenge warmed Ken's heart and it started to beat stronger.

HOODED CROW

The Road to Hell

Chapter One

'We cannot allow this war to reignite.' Alfin stopped. He was unsure what to say after that. He looked around the cell for inspiration, but none presented itself. He put down his quill and stroked the fine grain of the maple desk, lost for a moment as he traced the scrollwork round the edge of the table. The desk glowed golden in the light of the oil lamp. There was a knock at the door and a dwarf entered. He held out a blue woollen habit folded over his left arm and carried a jug of hot water in his right hand.

'Your cloak has dried out, angel, and I thought you might want to freshen up before seeing the Chancellor.' The dwarf put the vessel down beside a polished stone basin and smoothed the gown over the bed.

'Thank you. I am only sorry we did not arrive last night as planned and enjoy your hospitality a little more. The weather is foul.'

The dwarf smiled and left with the smallest of bows.

Alfin pulled the loaned shirt off and felt the contrast between the smooth linen he was discarding and the rough wool habit, though they had washed and ironed it rather than just dry it out. Its borrowed heat was still evident, and it was softer than ever it had been. Another knock at the door. He looked at the paper on his desk with a sense of despair. Even if he'd had inspiration, it seemed he was not going to be allowed the space to follow it.

An angel entered the room. To Alfin her hesitant smile lit up the cell more brightly than a dozen dwarf lanterns.

'Alva! So wonderful to see you.' They held each other's arms for a moment in silence. 'You are well?' he asked. 'You dress like a dwarf now?'

She looked down at the padded silk jerkin and trousers though the colour matched the sky blue of an angel's robes. A thick leather belt hung around her waist with many tools and pouches on loops all the way round.

'I am well, Alfin. I have learned so much here, of their masonry and their metalwork. Oh, Alfin, you should see what they can do. The fine silverwork is like spinning moonlight into solidity.' Her smile broadened and Alfin's heart lifted.

'That is very good to hear.' Alfin paused, revelling in the pure joy of seeing the delight in Alva's face.

'But I am here to bring you to the great hall. And we do not have much time because even as I was dispatched, I thought that blood would already be spilled.'

'How is Chancellor Sindri?'

'Not good. The Chancellor's daughter Ranvaeig was site manager of the reparation mining crew. No one has had contact with her or her crew since they left Holme. His mood has become more grim with each passing day.'

'Then we must go.' Alfin glanced back at the table. There was no point in bringing the paper; hopefully the words would come to him as he walked with Alva by his side. They stepped out into the corridor. It was long with many cells on each side, and a lantern hung high in the arches above every ten paces.

'How are things in Heaven?' asked Alva as she guided him confidently through the many passages and stairs of Holme.

'They are good. The eucalyptus that we planted when you left are over a hundred feet tall now. But the rest is much as it always has been. Aileen has been planning a poetry festival with her sister. Lorcan has been trying to overcome his fear of the sea by learning how to sail.'

'Really? Is he any good?' She sounded sceptical.

'Dreadful,' he confirmed. They both laughed as they walked. 'We all miss you, Alva. I miss you.'

'Good,' she said looking pleased with herself. 'It's nice to be missed. I'll be back soon.'

Living with the dwarves had changed her, Alfin thought.

'Now, we are here.' They paused at an entrance that was taller than twenty dwarves. 'Ready?' she asked. The doors slid open, pushed lightly by the guards.

Alfin stepped out with confidence; he was the Arbiter of Heaven. He could not be awed by the mere physical things the dwarves had wrought.

The room stretched out left and right, greater than his own abbey in Heaven. But that was only the width; the length stretched out for two hundred paces or more. Great piers rose up on either side to support a two-tier triforium with intricate stonework, creating a gallery for hundreds if not thousands to watch the activity below. Above that were ribbed vaults only partly illuminated by the candelabra below. In front of him, the great and good of Holme stood as silent witnesses. At the far end, the Chancellor sat on his great throne with its dark inlay of walnut and oak worked into the maple that the dwarves prized so much for bringing warmth to any room. The Chancellor's feet rested on a rolled rug, for he was short even among his people.

Before the Lords of Holme stood three of the tendua. Twice as tall as an angel, they towered among this company but they moved with a grace that none but perhaps Alva could match. The tenduas' golden fur with darker rosettes mirrored the throne in front of them. Their bright yellow eyes reflected the lamplight as they scanned the great hall for threat. And there was plenty. Alfin could feel the tension in the hall, claws unsheathed, crossbows cocked. Alfin tried to identify the chief tendua. He thought it was Bankim, but it could have been his brother Ekavir, the Great Hunter.

'We cannot allow this war to reignite!' Alfin was pleased that his voice sounded strong in such a massive chamber. Everyone's focus was on him now. 'The war between dwarf and tendua was the most destructive the world has seen.' He crossed the last open space before the Chancellor alone, his soft shoes making little noise on the polished limestone tiles until he stopped, creating a triangle between the throne and the lead tendua. 'Every manor in Holme has empty beds because of this conflict. Every clan is diminished by the barbed bolts of the rangers. That is what brought both Chancellor and Great Hunter to the bargaining table six months ago. That is why you made an agreement sworn on what you both hold sacred.'

'It was an unfair bargain,' said the foremost tendua. He had a chipped incisor, visible when he spoke. Bankim then. Alfin felt a spike of fear that Ekavir was not here. Did that point to the tendua not taking this seriously?

'Bankim, the tendua attacked the land above Holme,' Alfin pointed out. 'Throughout, you have never made any other claim than that you were the aggressors.'

'It is our nature,' said Bankim showing all his teeth in an approximation of a smile.

'So the mining rights on your lands were given to the Chancellor as compensation for the deaths your invasion cost.' Alfin looked to the throne to see if his reminder of the deal registered. The rivers of the tendua mountains ran with gold and silver since none had ever dared work them. But the dwarf lord gave nothing away, he only stared at his enemy with absolute hatred.

'We care nothing for rocks and metal,' said Bankim.

'So why was the deal unfair?' Alfin asked.

'The dwarves started passing through our mountains and forest.'

'How else would they know where to start digging for the precious things they seek in recompense for your wrongs?'

'It was unfair to expect my hunters to allow the little people to move through without triggering a response.' Alfin was still aware of a boiling up of restrained anger in the hall. Fists curled white around axes, fingers rested on the triggers of so many crossbows, eyes fixed on the three nimble giants in their midst.

'But that was the deal, to make amends.'

'We could not let them pass. We tried and there were many fights between our clans. But it is not in our nature.'

'They attacked the prospectors.' The Chancellor's voice was so low a rumble that Alfin wondered if only he and Bankim could hear.

'We did.'

'You risk losing your souls to the wrath of Heaven,' said Alfin, shocked.

Bankim for the first time fully looked into Alfin's face. 'Our shamans have said our souls will no longer go to Heaven. We will go back to the old ways and eat our dead so that their souls will go on in us rather than be reborn.'

At this the Chancellor twitched and gestured to the courtiers at his side. A young lad still to grow a beard ran out between the speakers but despite his haste he laid a bag at the feet of the arbiter with great care. With a growing sense of unease Alfin looked from seated lord to the bundle.

'Open it,' Sindri commanded.

'Chancellor, what is this?' asked Alfin.

'Open it,' the voice repeated from the throne.

Alfin tugged at the cord and the stiff gold fabric fell away on four sides revealing a set of bones and a skull. They gleamed in the lantern light for they were still raw, having been licked clean in the manner of the tendua.

'Bankim! What have you done?' Alfin exclaimed in horror.

The tendua danced around as if he were a child caught stealing the last of honeycomb.

'He has eaten my daughter,' answered the Chancellor.

'It is our nature. Angel, you bound us to such a high standard we could not keep. Can you ask the lightning not to strike? The rain not to fall? The dwarf not to seek vengeance?' With that he turned his toothy smile to Sindri. 'Your rangers are good, Chancellor. They found the bones where they could not be found and took my brother from where he was safe. I have come for my brother. We three have agreed to offer our lives if he is freed. A hundred of us shall die to pay the blood price for his freedom.'

'No harm will come to you while these peace talks are in place, as I promised,' said Sindri. 'A dwarf keeps his promises. You can take your brother – he has been keeping my grandchildren warm.'

Bankim tilted his ears, obviously trying to make sense of the Chancellor's words. Alfin thought the war leader of the tendua would be very dangerous company for any child, even a young tendua. The Chancellor made to stand up, kicking the rug out from under his feet. As it rolled towards the angel and the tendua, the young dwarf deftly cut the loop as it passed him so that it unravelled towards Bankim and Alfin. The same golden fur with brown rosettes now covered the flagstones. The head had been preserved so that the jaws were set in a mocking smile. Bankim screamed and fell to his knees, holding the empty head in his hands. The eyes, now just brilliant yellow glass, stared up blankly into those of his brother.

The Chancellor stood up now and walked towards the reunited tendua brothers. Bankim, still collapsed, was at his eye level.

'I think we both agree there can be no peace,' the Chancellor said, carefully wrapping up his daughter's remains. 'These talks are over. You are no longer safe.' At that, a score of bolts tore into the two standing tendua. They stood still for a moment as uncomprehending as their war leader. Bankim tried to clear his eyes as they fell by his side.

'I have changed my mind. The winter ahead will be cold. I will keep your brother.'

Bankim struggled to his feet trying to look every way at once. He stopped as his search reached Alfin. 'This is on you, angel. Heaven shall offer you no safety from the wrath of all tendua.' With that he sprinted from the hall so fast that Alfin wondered if a crossbow bolt could have caught him. The Chancellor lowered his raised fist and the rangers that had stood around the galleries gave chase.

'See that he does not dally or cause harm on his exit,' said the Chancellor. 'And clear this mess away – feed it to the dogs.' The dwarf looked at the angel with hope. 'Bring my daughter back to me.'

Alfin shook his head, though he did not mean to. The optimism fled the dwarf's face.

'Can we discuss this matter privately, my lord?'

'My lord? Well, at last the angel recognises the seriousness of the situation. None of your usual clever word games? Treaties? A riddle to solve? It is simple enough. I want the soul of my daughter back. Name your price. There are a dozen women here who have already said they would be honoured to welcome Ranvaeig to their womb.'

'You know it is not that straightforward, my lord. Reincarnation is not guaranteed. First, she must choose to return. Then her soul must be found and weighed.'

'Are you saying that my daughter is not worthy? That she deserves to be punished more than she has?'

'No one is blameless.'

'She was caught up in this deal that you made. That animal was right in one thing, Alfin. You put this contract together despite knowing the natures of both parties. We had to go and see what riches could be had. They, it seems, had to hunt down their prey. Ranvaeig was an innocent miner.'

'She was a veteran of many campaigns. A soldier's life can be complicated. Her soul must be weighed.'

'Let me make myself clear. The only thing between Heaven and those monsters is my soldiers. Will you release my daughter's soul, angel?'

Alfin closed his eyes. The chancellor could only see this as a transaction. Everything had its price. But Heaven didn't work that way. You could not buy your way to reincarnation. Or threaten.

'It is not in my power,' Alfin said sadly.

The dwarf looked crushed. 'Leave Holme and my protection then. Angel, don't believe others shall come to your aid. All have seen the rewards of Heaven and the hollowness of its peace.'

'We have kept the peace for millennia – do you really want to return to chaos?' asked Alfin.

'Give me my daughter,' said the Chancellor flatly.

Alfin looked out for the other angel in the hall. 'I cannot. But even so I would ask one thing. Sindri, would you keep Alva safe here in Holme? If she wishes it.'

The chancellor looked surprised. 'Alva may stay here. She has a skill that could surpass our best, I think, if she is given the opportunity to follow her path. But should she choose it?' The dwarf turned to where the angel stood, her face a study in confusion.

'The trees will still grow,' said Alfin confidently. Despite what Sindri had said, perhaps some would help defend Heaven. The angels had been good warriors long ago.

'Then I shall stay. There is so much more to learn here.'

Alfin felt a tearing in his heart – he wanted her to cross the floor to him. But blood was still pooling from the tendua at his feet, reminding him that crossbows had been reloaded and the Chancellor was not patient. He bowed to Alva and then to the Chancellor and walked swiftly from the hall.

Chapter Two

Alfin had been exhausted by the hard journey back to Heaven. The weather had worsened, and the last four days of the walk had been made through heavy snow. Alfin hoped that no one could follow him in such hostile conditions. Soon he was overwhelmed by a sense of dread of what was behind him, though each turn showed only a tree shedding snow or a crow hiding from the wind. He finally reached the Gates of Heaven at a run, looking more behind him than in front. He battered on the gates till a face appeared in the small window.

'Lorcan! Let me in!'

'At once, Alfin.' There were shouted commands and all the while he watched the shadows gather in about him. At last the bar was lifted and the wicket gate opened.

Alfin all but fell through. 'Close it. Close the door and lock it!' he commanded. The angels looked surprised. 'Guard the walls. The tendua are almost with me!'

They looked at him, still confused.

'Get our people to the walls. Bar the door. Get the dwarves from their barracks!'

Lorcan, the most beautiful of angels, was clearly trying to find the right words. 'Arbiter. The dwarves left two days ago. A crow arrived and despite the weather they said they must be away at the chancellor's command. They would not be drawn as to the reason. The giants left with them.' Arden had joined the group by the entrance.

'Then we must rediscover our warrior past.'

'Why, Arbiter?' Arden and her sister replaced the beam as she asked the question.

'Both tendua and dwarves have rejected the peace of Heaven,' said Alfin. 'The tendua have decided the death of the war leader is on us.' There were gasps around the barbican. 'I felt sure that the tendua were closing on me as I returned – that somehow this blizzard is their doing.'

'In that at least we have good news. The storm has passed and it is now as peaceful as can be.' Lorcan led the arbiter out into the courtyard of Heaven. Above the deep snow the stars were bright.

Aileen met them all as they looked up. 'It is the eye of the storm. The blizzards will return soon enough.'

'We must look to the walls,' repeated Alfin for the third time, frustrated that they should react so slowly. Both sisters shouted orders and the angels were disturbed from their singing, their writing and their slumber. Torches and weapons were passed out from the armoury and the angels ran to the walls. Alfin joined them, sword in hand, walking along the wall, reassuring each of them by name that no one had ever conquered Heaven, even in the days of Chaos. The walls of Heaven were extensive for they encompassed the Great Arboretum that filled the land from the fortifications to the open city of the angels. Two hills were contained within the space. The eastern hill, the Dawn Mount, rose sheer from the forest, and the western hill was surmounted by a single spire upon which stood the Treasury of Souls. All were lit by starlight, bright above the snow. As torches spread around the circumference Alfin, felt his confidence returning.

Arden caught up with him and pulled him towards the lower inner parapet. 'My sister went to release the bear hounds. We thought they would be useful against the tendua.' Alfin nodded. Arden continued. 'So it seemed did the tendua. The hounds and the kennel masters are slain in their pens. No one heard their cries.'

'So they are already here!' Alfin rested his hands on the stones of the wall, the sense of safety robbed from him. 'They will be hiding in the arboretum waiting for more to arrive.'

'We must find them before the storm returns,' Arden agreed. She closed her eyes and then opened them again. 'Aileen can lead the hunt from the north. We must do the same here.' She moved off silently. As Alfin watched, the ring of fire marking out the walls of Heaven cascaded down into the parkland by the various staircases. Below, the torches created pools of bright orange among the blue-white snow, but the black trunks and boughs above the warm light resisted any illumination. The defenders gathered around the base of the great trees, casting their eyes up into the bare branches. But there were so many brands that the shadows twisted and turned so that shapes were imagined, resulting in confusion. There were shouts now from those close to the wall.

'Here!' cried two groups simultaneously. The shadows seemed to leap from tree to tree as the lights beneath shifted in response to the calls. Alfin watched the angels running, scattered as each chased what they believed to be a tendua, to the point where they each stood under a pine peering up into the dancing night, their torches giving the illusion of warmth to the golden snow around them. Alfin had stayed by the gate, convinced that here would be where the blow would fall first. From his vantage point, though, he could see the pool of darkness was growing in two places among the trees and a third from the southern part of the wall.

'They are among us!' he shouted. He dashed down the great steps from the keep and only then remembered the horn kept above the door that would have rallied the angels again. Aileen sped past, her brow furrowed, her hands tight around a bloody spear. 'They are among us!' he repeated. Alfin stopped and thought for the briefest of moments. 'Take all you can find to the Dawn Mount. When the sky lightens we can bring our archery to bare.' Aileen ran on and the torches streamed after her. Alfin looked to the east of the forest where a few lights were gathering. He came towards them, sword drawn.

'Arbiter,' said an angel. 'We are surrounded.'

Alfin paused to register the look of fear on the angel's face, something he had not seen for millennia. 'Take heart, Maon. It is we who have them surrounded. It is said that when we fought at the beginning of all things, even a seraph was not as swift as an angel. When the sun rises we shall triumph as we always have done.' The two angels with Maon looked a little more reassured. Alfin continued 'We cannot gather with the rest on the mount so we will go to the Treasury of Souls and see if we can make ourselves comfortable there.'

The band moved forward, stepping out from the arboretum into the deeper snow of the clearing. On reaching the base of the hill they started to climb. The last angel cried out, dropping his sword and torch. In its light Alfin saw a tendua, his claws buried deep in the angel's habit, blood darkening the sky-blue wool. High above the tendua's head the screaming angel rose only to be shredded and cast aside. The angels charged at the towering figure before he could disappear back into the dark. Within moments all five were bleeding into the drift, but only Alfin breathed.

The arbiter rested on his sword looking for a moment at the faces of his friends in the last of the torchlight. A flurry of flakes passed between them; the storm was regathering its cold fury as Aileen had predicted. He limped up the rise to the Treasury of Souls. As the cloud closed in, the tower stood black against the remaining few stars above and the snow below. The archway had no door but it was the only entrance. Above it, the walls rose sheer to an open roof. It contained at its centre the two trees that between them framed the misty gateway for souls returning to the world. There should have been angels here to guard the pair and guide those ready for reincarnation, but there were none, although Alfin did not feel alone.

A solitary torchbearer below ran north trying to avoid the edge of the woods. Alfin drew breath to shout but the flame threw up monstrous shadows round the internal wall of the Treasury. Vast tentacles coiled round a shifting body. Dark red eyes blinked above a fire filled mouth as it slipped around endeavouring to stay out of the light. Alfin advanced, his sword bright with blood, a notch where a tendua spine had briefly held it. The angel and the shadow danced for a moment, circling the two trees. The torch flared and died with its bearer, catching Alfin momentarily in the light as it did so.

He thought of his life as it had been, playing music in the forests or researching in the library; attempting to find a way to bring order and justice to a world torn by chaos and magic; the long-ago internecine war between angels and seraphim; how the seraphim had fled beyond the sea and perhaps beyond the confines of this world; the rise of the angels and the foundation of order through the reincarnate returning by the Treasury of Souls with a chance to begin again. Sometimes these souls walked with the angels through the arboretum seeking guidance or having questions answered before going on to begin their journey again. Occasionally their fury survived death and the angels' counsel and they would be returned again to the Treasury. By this gradual process the angels hoped to achieve accord – a progression, perhaps over many lives, to where all could achieve the harmony of an angelic life. Alfin became aware he was being observed in his thoughts as if catching someone at an upstairs window in his mind.

Ah, said the darkness collapsing in on itself as a shadow does when light approaches, although Alfin thought the word rather than heard it. A woman stepped forward. She had a fuller figure and was more moonfaced than any angel. She was as tall as Alfin but her hair was a cascade of red ringlets like a dwarf's.

'I'm not sure where I am,' said the woman.

'Are you Ranvaeig?'

'My name is Naomi.'

'Are you a lost soul?' asked Alfin.

She laughed a little. 'I don't think I would qualify as a lost soul. There are many worlds, many planes of existence, and I travel through those worlds. Usually I'm as you saw me, an insubstantial being of smoke and fire.' She looked down at herself. 'Here, in this reality, I seem to be more corporeal than normal.'

'A demon then?' Alfin remembered the fierce sometimes-allies of the seraphim.

'I am familiar with that term and them. I'll stick with traveller.'

'Well, traveller. I would return from whence you came. Normally you would be invited to our abbey at the bottom of this hill where you would find the succour you require, physical or spiritual. But not tonight.' He turned and saw his city burning through the bare arboretum. 'Not this most unhappy night.' He walked back to the open gateway and watched a black shape run towards him, unhindered by the climb. 'Flee now – my doom is upon me.'

The tendua burst through the archway, carrying the angel almost to the twin trees. Alfin's sword was useless, pinned between them while the tendua's claws tore at the angel's back. Within seconds he was a mess of cut flesh and wool. The tendua pressed Alfin deep into the ground, both paws digging hard into the muscle of his chest. The tendua threw back his head to howl and Alfin saw the broken tooth.

'Bankim!'

'Arbiter. Greatest of all angels. Your body will heal me. Your intelligence will make me Great Hunter. Your soul will live on in me.' The words were spoken as brutal poetry.

Something very heavy knocked Bankim out of sight leaving the angel staring up at the undersides of the last few stubborn leaves of autumn and the remaining fruit.

The woman put down the broken font she had wielded. A flame sprang up from the palm of her hand, and she looked at the flicker as if surprised. 'I don't have a dog in this fight but I'm sure that no one should be eating anyone at the moment.'

Bankim jumped to his feet, seeing the woman for the first time. He shook himself free of the impact of the blow. 'What are you? You smell of charcoal.' The tendua circled round the great trees and the traveller backed off a little. 'You are stronger than the arbiter. That strength will be very useful.'

The traveller drew breath to speak, her hand towards Bankim in a calming gesture, but he leapt across the gap and was upon her. Alfin tried to stand but found himself too weak. He could only drag his torn body towards the struggling pair. The woman was completely hidden by the bulk of her attacker. Alfin heard the blows landing, sounding like a prize fighter pounding a pig's carcass. At least he might wound the tendua to make him break off his attack.

The strikes and tearing stopped and only Alfin's steel scraping on the floor broke the silence. Bankim threw back his head again in triumph. Alfin, still feet away from a strike, was too late to help. There was a great snap of bone and the tendua dropped, quivering, smaller pops following as ribs failed. Alfin was unwilling to retreat, unable to go closer. Bankim tried to rise, struggling to separate himself from the woman beneath. Alfin hurled the sword but it missed and bounced off the abandoned font with a clang. Trembling, Bankim fell to one side as the traveller pushed the corpse away.

'Ha!' Alfin laughed. 'You are alive!'

The woman pushed herself up on one elbow, her face lit by the burning of Heaven behind Alfin. 'Evidently. I'm bleeding.' She was inspecting her arm where blood welled up through a dozen cuts. One pumped apparently in rhythm with her heart.

'You sound surprised.' Alfin propped himself up on the font.

'I don't, usually.'

'You beat a tendua, possibly the greatest living tendua, barehanded, in single combat. I have never heard of such a thing. What was your name again?'

'Naomi.'

'Will you join us, Naomi? We need you in our fight.' He looked over his shoulder and watched the inferno curl up around the buildings of Heaven. Now the city illuminated everything within the walls. A giant version of the torches in the woods, the abbey lit the snow below in gold and red while sparks chased the falling snowflakes through the dark sky. He could feel the heat from here. 'We have so much to do here, you see …'

'I'm going to stop you there, angel. This …' She held an arm up, apparently mesmerised by the blood falling in the flickering orange light. 'This is not my thing. Mainly though I need to stop you because if I don't get out of here, I really think I'm going to die.'

'But I need you.'

'Not me. But I know someone who would be interested. I can find them but it might take a while. Or a moment.' She laughed and there was a gurgle in her throat. She spat darkly. 'I am broken. What's your name, angel?'

'Alfin.'

'Okay, Alfin. So time moves differently in different worlds. Just like the rules – they are different too. I will find the war demon you need and return whenever that may be. I think he will like this world where he can be in his own body, experience things first hand. Be warned – I may search for a hundred years and return with him in an instant or I could find him immediately but still not reappear here for a century. You just need to keep your people alive till then.' The abbey roof collapsed and the bonfire flared unsteadily.

'But if you let me bind your wounds you can help me now.' Alfin shifted a bit to try and see Naomi's face more clearly, to make her understand. He was alone in the Treasury of Souls.

Chapter Three

Alfin had moved through the forest so quietly that he could have reached out and touched either the feeding doe or the buck guarding her. He wore a close-fitting suit into which had been woven fresh leaves and torn strips of cloth that made him look more shrub than angel. A hood, similarly camouflaged covered his hair while a green mesh hid his face. When stationary it allowed him to merge with the foliage around almost perfectly. The mayfly danced through the shafts of light created by the branches above while late spring had given everything a vivid green intensity that he had not really appreciated for what felt like a lifetime. He was distracted when a bird landed opposite him in the glade. The size and shape of a rook or crow but with a grey back and chest, it ignored the other wildlife and appeared to look straight at him. The grey crow continued to stare a long minute before inspecting the branch it stood on.

The doe snorted as flies collected round her nostrils. They were doing the same to Alfin but he didn't have the luxury of moving them on. He closed his eyes and tried to hear above the hum of silvan life. There was no clue that he and the two deer were not alone, but the hunt had led him here.

Alfin reached forward and slapped the animal. With an alarmed bark she leapt up and forward, further into the valley. A taloned hand snatched the animal out of the air and the buck took his first running step. The doe screamed as the tendua spun it towards the ground, smiling at finding the prey so unaware. Four white arrows drove into him and he threw a spear in response back down the flight path of one of the arrows. The buck made his fourth step. The broken doe, forgotten now, crashed towards the forest floor. An angel soared backwards, pinned to a tree by the wooden lance, and three more arrows hit the tendua. The buck took his seventh step as Alfin took his first towards the tendua. The tendua tried to block the angel's blow but his arm was pierced and the shaft impeded his movement. Alfin sliced down from collarbone to crotch; Alva's new sword did not fail him. The buck bounded away as fleet footed as all of their kind, likely unsure why the doe did not follow.

The only noises now came from the wounded angel and the doe. Alfin hesitated as he saw the great slash the tendua had inflicted so easily on the deer. He knelt and cut the animal's throat. There was no recovering from that wound. Two of his companions supported the pinned angel a foot above the bracken while the third, Aileen, extracted the spear. The angel screamed and then fell unconscious. They laid him down while one began to build a fire.

'I'll get some water.' They were the first words spoken since the fight had started. He was making his way towards the undergrowth, merging back into it again, when he stood still. He was being watched. Had there been another tendua? Then he was already dead.

'Alfin, I need you to come with me,' said a voice.

The angel looked around carefully but only the odd-looking crow stood at the source of the words. 'Naomi,' he guessed.

'Yes,' said the bird.

'It's been eighteen months.' Alfin pushed back the hood on his jacket, allowing himself some cooler air. The other angels were watching the exchange open mouthed. The bird glided further into the forest.

'And yet you live,' said Naomi.

'Ogan is dying,' Aileen said quietly. Like the doe, the angel was not going to recover from the touch of the tendua.

'Keep him comfortable.' He saw the question in their eyes.

'Are you bewitched that you would leave us to follow a crow?' asked Aileen.

'You need to come with me now or the moment will pass,' said Naomi.

Alfin ran after the crow as it made short flights from tree to tree. 'Did you find who you were looking for?' he asked.

'Yes. I have found him. Or rather he found one of the messages I left in a score of worlds and he came here. But he will not wish to stay long without a bargain being set, so we must hurry.' They sped along in silence for a few minutes.

'Why a bird?'

'I didn't want to look like I was on the menu,' said Naomi. 'And it seemed a good way to move around without getting noticed.'

'I noticed you,' said Alfin feeling an odd new emotion. They burst out into a clearing, a natural bowl created by the stream that had carved away a bank leaving roots and trunks high above. In the centre was a log, the remains of a great pine that had fallen many years ago. Sitting on the timber was a figure that Alfin had never seen the like of before. Physically massive, the thing sat legs spread wide, a great hand on each knee. The face was broad and flat with a pug nose and tusks pointing both up and down that escaped from a black mouth. Long hair was tied back in a top knot and spilled down his back between two horns. He wore a heavy padded jacket of scarlet and black. Great squares of stiff cloth protected his thighs and calves. The gold embroidery caught the sun and dazzled Alfin as he tried to make sense of what he saw. A huge hammer the height of an angel rested on the fallen tree. So regal did the figure look that Alfin felt the demon had transformed the glade into a royal court and the log into a throne.

'Is this little earth spirit what you were looking for, Naomi?' asked the ogre in a deep rumbling voice.

'He is the very one that requested my aid, and having seen his heart I could not refuse.' The bird flew up to sit on the end of the hammer. 'Alfin, this is Kenato Orin.'

Alfin, still dressed in his forest camouflage, approached the ogre impressed but unafraid. 'Can you help me protect my people?' Alfin asked.

'I can help you win,' said the demon confidently.

The very idea of winning was so far from Alfin's state of mind that he laughed. 'We have just killed a tendua and lost an angel in exchange.' Alfin walked away from Kenato Orin and sat on a smaller log facing him, mirroring the demon's pose in miniature. 'That was a well-laid ambush with five of our most militant angels. Even then a chance deer gave us the edge we needed. There are many tendua and an ever-lessening number of angels. From here the war does not look winnable.'

'Naomi told me of your foe.' Kenato Orin looked around for his companion. 'Are you going to be a bird the entire time?' he added in an exasperated tone. Naomi spared one eye for the ogre but said nothing. He shifted his focus back to Alfin but seemed to have trouble looking in quite the right place. 'How can I hold court with a talking bush and a conversational covid? This plane is filled with a flavour of magic that is both new to me and powerful. The tendua don't access it and neither do you. If I can bind it, we will win the war.'

'What would be your price?' asked Alfin.

'Prices,' Kenato Orin said. 'All that I ask is that I and my kind could live here in peace when the war is won. Naomi has her own bargain.'

Alfin shifted his gaze to the bird in trepidation. Land would be easy to grant. Between the three edges of the world there were many empty places. He was sure though that Naomi would request something impossible – a tear from the desert wind, the laughter of a basilisk or the sound of a shadow. And in failing to meet the request he would be binding Heaven to a demon.

'I would like a fruit from each of the trees in your Treasury of Souls,' said the crow quietly.

Alfin felt relief flood through him. 'That is straightforward, Naomi – the Treasury has been unguarded since I last saw you. You could go and claim them yourself in a few months.'

'It would be better if they were freely given.'

'Both freely given,' said Alfin and felt strangely as if the world had shifted around him. He sensed that some great magic had been released in a way that he didn't understand.

'Good, then we have a deal.' Kenato Orin clapped his knees and stood up. 'I am keen to see our foe.'

Alfin filled two skins with water and took a moment to wash his face and neck before retracing his path towards the fight scene. He was aware of the ogre crashing through the undergrowth behind him and tried to think how he was going to introduce the pair. *Hello, I have enlisted demons to help us win this righteous war* didn't sound very acceptable even to him in this most desperate state. But all doubts were brushed aside as he re-entered the glade and knelt by Ogan. His breathing was shallow, his cheeks grey and his forester suit bloody. The faces around were focused only on their dying friend.

'You will be with us again soon, Ogan. And with hope. Look – we have new allies.'

The angel managed to open his eyes for a moment. 'Seraphim?' Ogan asked.

The two angels looked up in surprise. Aileen went for her sword. Alfin too was amazed to see a pair of seraphim walk into the bloody scene of the fight. They were dressed for war with strange armour and great bows, taller than either of them, tied to their backs.

'Yes. Our lost cousins from the Edgeward Isles have come to help us,' Alfin explained.

He watched his friend try to focus on the newcomers, the angel's eyes searching without success.

The two 'seraphim' bowed low before the angels.

'Kenato Orin and Naomi,' said Alfin by way of introduction.

Aileen still held her hilt, for she was old enough to remember the First War. 'If you are to eat with seraphim, it's best to sup with a long spoon,' she said coldly. 'Are there many of you?'

'Only us,' said Naomi, removing her grey helmet with its long wide neck guard. 'Some others will follow when they hear of your plight.'

Kenato Orin walked over to the tendua, and despite their disparity in size he rolled it easily on its back. He held one of the massive paws in his hand, squeezing it so that the claws extended. He stretched both arms out in the trampled bracken, nudging Alfin's cut as closed as he could, and stood back, looking up at the four surviving angels. He spoke to Naomi and she nodded. He whistled, looking back at the fallen tendua. Kenato Orin then addressed the angels, looking to Naomi to translate.

'Kenato Orin says that our enemy is mighty,' she explained. 'We bring …' Naomi hesitated a moment, glancing at Alfin, 'seraph magic that will, with trust between us, allow for victory.'

Alfin watched the faces of his companions carefully. Even Aileen's face relaxed a little. The angels' need for good news outweighed any concern. Alfin hoped they were right, that he was right.

Chapter Four

Alfin stood with the Treasury of Souls at his back, the one part of Heaven that had remained pretty much untouched by war. The fire that had lit his meeting with Naomi ten years before had burned for days; it had spread to the arboretum so that now not a living tree stood, only blackened trunks like a charcoal drawing of what had been there, unrelieved by the spring so bright green around them. Alfin heard a voice come from the far side of the hollow tower.

'Stay here,' said Naomi to someone. 'I will call if I need you.' She appeared round the side of the building.

'Naomi! Very good to see you.'

'Alfin. Very good to see you too. I am pleased to report that I and my riders have scoured all of the great eastern plains. No tendua will escape your justice.'

'Excellent. You are the last of the heroes to testify.' He looked at her a moment. 'But had the greatest task.' Naomi dropped her head in acknowledgement. These false seraphim had become as prickly about any slight, real or imagined, as their namesakes. 'Now we can proceed.'

'The end of the war?' Naomi asked. With a sweep of her arm she indicated Alfin's return to sky-blue robes rather than armour or disguise.

'Yes. Finally. An end to all war.' They started to walk down the hill. 'You have left somebody behind?' Alfin observed.

'Only my horse. She is not one for ceremonies.' Alfin smiled. The armoured horses the demons had brought were smarter than any dog, but it still seemed odd to him to talk to a beast of burden so. So many changes in such a short space of time. It appeared that a gate had been opened and many things from many worlds had followed his 'seraphim', some openly, declaring their loyalty in return for space to live, others came in the dark, seeking out secret valleys and untrodden moors. The pair walked through the burnt arboretum. Alfin stopped beside the two great grey trunks that rose higher than all around them. He placed his hand on the scorched bark and then rested his forehead. These were the trees that Alva and he had planted before she left for Holme. Naomi paced around the Mountain Ash, her hand on the hilt of her larger sword as it protruded from her sash.

'How long before we can truly be at peace among trees again, Naomi?' Alfin asked. 'Will we recover faster than they?'

Naomi knelt at the base of the other tree, her riding trousers billowing out around her. 'If you look, Alfin, the process has already begun.'

Alfin walked to Naomi's side and saw the clusters of small brown leaves sprouting from the dark grey trunk. 'This is marvellous. A great portent of the day.' Alfin caressed the tree as he left feeling the rough charred bark under his fingers. The pair strolled up a gentler rise to where the abbey had stood. They looked around the scene of destruction. Each year tendua had returned to inflict more damage on the home of the angels. The stones were tumbled blackened granite. The earth beneath was still barren or thick with thorn-covered brambles.

'What did you find in the east?'

'A huge empty land where the grasses moved like the sea under the wind. It is a beautiful place.'

'Does it have an end?'

'Not that we discovered. There are high mountains to the south. I think when this is done and you have returned to the forest I will live there.'

'Returned to the forest,' Alfin repeated. He rolled the phrase over in his mind as they reached the edge of the burnt stone, a half arch above them both. Beyond, filling the vast space from the abbey ruins to the walls of Heaven were the tendua, each separated by an arm's length from their neighbour, each kneeling, head down as though in prayer.

'How many are there?' asked Naomi.

Alfin's lips pursed as he thought. 'All of them.'

'What do you plan to do?'

Alfin had an answer to that question locked away. In dealing with the demons he had learned that his surface thoughts were as easily read as his face. He had to bury things away even from himself so that he could stand in a demon's company and yet leave some of his views deep within the halls of his own mind. 'All will become clear.'

The pair joined seraphim and angels at a high table laid out with a banquet. Aileen was the first to greet Alfin, though she barely spared a moment for Naomi and quickly returned to her conversation with Lorcan and her sister Arden. These three above all the angels had worked tirelessly for the victory and everyone had applauded their place at the top table. Below them sat the thirty-four companions, the survivors of the one hundred and sixteen demons that Alfin had enlisted in his attempt to save Heaven. Walking between the rows of prisoners, Kenato Orin, Seraph Friend as he was known to the other angels, looked up and smiled at Alfin. The demon had revelled in war. The greater the foe, the greater the joy at each triumph. His anger was swift and his aspect terrible. Kenato Orin was to sit at Alfin's right hand during the meal and judgement, for Alfin had to admit the demon had fought harder, taken more wounds, saved more angels than any other. Kenato Orin stepped up onto the first dais, shaking hands and hugging his fellow seraphim. Aileen had moved down onto the heroes' table and was talking to the seraph Vatn. That left Arden, Lorcan, Naomi and himself at the top bench standing in comfortable silence.

'We should enjoy this moment,' said Aileen, turning back to face the higher table. She looked up at Lorcan for confirmation but Alfin saw that the most handsome of angels was lost in his own thoughts, looking from face to face of each of the Companions. A fearless fighter, Lorcan had never hated his foe in the way so many of the angels had come to. Lorcan had remained true throughout. Alfin noticed a cloud pass on Aileen's face and she returned to conversation with Vatn. War with the Tendua had brought them all together so tightly in order to survive. Alfin wondered what would happen when they were not so bound.

Kenato Orin came up to the dais and clasped arms with each in turn. He held Alfin's arm the longest. 'Archangel, all is ready.' The idea of a change in title had been the demons. It was something Alfin had grown into.

Kenato Orin appeared in Alfin's mind as he expected. He had constructed a hall there where they could meet. Some recent memories hung from the walls like tapestries that changed as Kenato Orin brought in his own mind. Here Alfin could see him as he truly was, the great ogre, and that was a useful reminder for the angel.

'I would be more comfortable if I knew what I was to be ready for,' said Kenato Orin.

'We have reached the appointed time. All that I need from you is your total power. Hold nothing back and we can save this world from the tendua forever. You will have fulfilled your side of the bargain.'

'And you will meet yours?' asked Kenato Orin. A demon could have no sense of what a bargain with an angel meant, but a little part of Alfin wished that now, after ten years of striving together, that question need not have been asked.

'We will meet ours. Your people shall be free in this world.'

'Good. You know, Alfin ...'

Their conversation was interrupted by a sound from outside the hall of the archangel's mind. They shared four eyes as they looked across to the cast-down Gates of Heaven. Coming through them was a single angel leading a great dwarf army. They had struck up pipes and drums as they entered, the drummers whirling around the pipers and each other as they beat drums each bigger than the dwarf that carried them. But it was the angel that held Kenato Orin's attention as she walked forward through the still-kneeling tendua.

'Who is this vision?' asked the demon.

'Alva.'

'Your mysterious smith that made your new swords?'

'And so much more.' Alfin was confused as Kenato Orin's desire mixed with his own delight at seeing his soulmate again after so long. He saw the beauty in her pale skin, the sun caught up in her black hair. He felt for the first time a passion for her red lips, her slim hips. The demon and Alfin broke contact. The dwarf army

spread out left and right against the torn down walls of Heaven. Their chain mail shattered the sunlight and shimmered like a great steel curtain.

'Alva!' Alfin shouted in the real world. He walked forward, conscious that he now looked at her with eyes still tainted by Kenato Orin's desire. He held out his hands which she took in hers. She looked puzzled at his smile and tilted her head a little as his silence stretched into seconds. What would it be like to be close enough to feel her body in his arms, to have her press against him? Though the link with Kenato Orin had been broken the thoughts did not seem his own.

'Alfin?' she asked.

'I am just so happy that you have joined us at last.'

'I have brought some company too.' She stood aside so that he could see Chancellor Sindri striding towards him as the pipes and drums came to a halt. Alfin struggled for a moment. How to greet this leader that had left the people of Heaven to their fate?

'Chancellor.' Alfin bowed. 'I thank you for all the gifts you allowed Alva to send in aid for our struggle.'

The dwarf stopped far enough away that he didn't have to crane his neck too hard to look Alfin in the face. 'My daughter is now a lost soul thanks to this war. I have come to see that it is ended and that justice is done.' He took a couple of steps to the side to inspect the closest tendua, who in kneeling still towered over the chancellor. A cub beside him was about the same height. 'You have bound them with magic?' he asked.

'We have, for we found nothing else strong enough to hold them,' Alfin said.

The tendua glared at the chancellor with hatred in his bright yellow eyes. The cub copied the look. Sindri drew a knife defensively but stepped closer. The tendua snarled.

'Even now when they are beaten, they would rather claw my belly open from hip to hip than accept any form of peace. It is in their nature.' The dwarf shook his head and put his knife away. He pointed at the tables built on the mound of the old abbey. 'You have food? Good. It has been a long march and since your invitation was lost we feared that we would arrive too late.' The chancellor smiled at his own pretence and walked towards the banquet. The angels had no choice but to follow him. Alfin saw them hurriedly rearranging the table.

They sat facing out towards the tendua and the dwarf army behind. When they had settled Arden, and Lorcan sat with Alva closest on his left. To his right sat Sindri, then Naomi and Kenato Orin furthest away. Aileen sat with the demons.

Alfin could barely taste the bread and wine as he tried hard to not think of what he planned while wrestling whether it was the right thing to do or not. The conversation ran around him.

'So you are the seraph that killed Bankim?' Sindri asked Naomi.

'I am, Chancellor. Though to be fair it was a close-run thing. His spine snapped just before I bled to death,' replied Naomi.

The dwarf appeared to consider her carefully before digging Alfin in the ribs. 'There is more to seraphim now than there was, eh, Alfin? Who would win the First War now that the seraphim are so mighty? Though perhaps the thought should be who could stand against the seraphim and angels united? What price has been agreed for such generous support and self-sacrifice on their part?' The chancellor clearly had years of questions building up waiting for the chance to burst out.

'Chancellor,' Naomi began. 'The deal is well known. There are many empty lands here and all that we have requested is that we build an Eden here and live in harmony. As we did before,' she added.

'All of you?' asked Sindri.

'Some have chosen to return to the Edgeward Islands. Others will join us here when word of the new peace reaches them,' said Naomi.

To Alfin's left, Alva was catching up on the news with Arden, but Arden seemed intent on trying to draw Lorcan in a discussion about what they would do now the war was over.

Lorcan looked over the other two angels and into Alfin's eyes and raised the question they had all discussed when hope had returned to the angels' campfires and war councils. 'Will you take all of these lives, Alfin? Judge their souls and cast them out of the world?' He held Alfin's gaze, and Alfin felt more interrogated than when wrestling with Kenato Orin in his own mind.

Alfin stood up and spoke so that all within the tumbled walls of Heaven could hear him. 'Will you take all of these lives? Judge their souls and cast them out of the world?' he repeated. 'That is the question I have been asked. I have been asking the same question since it became clear that Heaven would triumph. The tendua have ensured that no stone stands upon another. Our forests have been burnt, our souls consumed so that had the tendua won there would be no angels in the world. How should Heaven meet such determination to wipe us from history? In fighting a total war, is the destruction of the tendua the right response? The only response?' Alfin returned Lorcan's gaze. 'How can Heaven be merciful when to do so means its own destruction?'

The great bowl with its hundred thousand occupants was silent, waiting for the answer. Alfin called out with his mind to Kenato Orin and the demon responded.

Alfin felt the power come through him like a fist filling a glove. *'You are ready, Kenato Orin?'* he asked.

'It would be easier to say yes if I knew your purpose. But yes, I am ready.'

Alfin gestured with his right hand. 'Chancellor Sindri has said that war is in the nature of the tendua. All of you who have fought these long years, you who have buried brothers and sisters, dwarf and angel, who have shed tears into ashes, can testify to that. So Heaven must change their nature.' Alfin stretched out his arms, fingers wide, towards the bound tendua. Great waves of magic flowed through him, rippling the reality in front of him. The sun dimmed, though the sky was still clear. It darkened almost to black and the evening stars shone brightly.

The tendua screamed in fear, staring as their talons shrank to transparent nails, their teeth dwindled in size, their eyes changed from yellow to brown. Patterned fur became dark skin. The tendua now struggled out of their bonds as they melted towards the grass, their long limbs shortening, great muscles wasting. Within moments they looked around with round eyes at the furless bodies surrounding them, lifelong mates and children unrecognisable to one another.

'The tendua are gone. To speak of them is a sin. You have a new beginning. Go and find your place in a changed world. And mark my words – Heaven will not be merciful a second time.' Alfin's arms were still flung wide as the magic faded.

'Your mask is slipping,' said Alfin to Kenato Orin. Alfin shared with the demon his sight of a body slumped, nails growing long and black, tusks thrusting their way past slack lips. All focus though was on the new-found people staggering around below as the hunters, moments before so sure-footed, now struggled to walk with their new legs. Sindri stared out across the field slack jawed. Only Arden glanced back at the Seraph Friend and frowned.

'I thought you had trapped me in a spell that would undo me,' said Kenato Orin, *'and the world.'*

'And yet you live.' Alfin let his arms drop. The weariness of both himself and Kenato Orin overwhelmed him and he fell back in his chair. His head felt too heavy for his neck to support.

Alva stood up, her voice as loud as Alfin's had been. 'Praise Heaven! Praise Heaven! The war is over – feast and be merry!'

Below them the people who were no longer tendua laboured to their feet, free of the bonds, free of their nature, free to choose. Alfin felt Alva's warm hand on his shoulder and he slumped into a deeper sleep than he had known for years.

Chapter Five

Naomi led her horse up the steep final ascent of the sand dune. At last they crested the top. The sea sparkled under the brilliant sun. Hundreds of redshank and plovers played dare with the small waves. To her left the vast beach ran to the horizon and far beyond. To her right, if she had her bearings correct, it would be about ten miles before she reached the mouth of a river, though in the centuries since she had previously been here it may have shifted itself by miles in either direction. But it would still flow between her and her goal for tonight, White Mountain, and the agent who should be waiting for her. And beyond that, still at least a week's ride away, Heaven itself and the wedding she had been invited to.

Naomi gave a withering glance back at the salt marshes that stretched northwards, lapping up behind the sand like a thick sea. For nine days she had endured a continual cycle of insects that shared a thirst for blood but preferred different times of the day to draw it. Below her lay the final, most salty of the lagoons where her mount had stirred up vast flocks of flamingos up into the sky. They had wheeled around her filling the air with flashes of red and black and their goose-like call, while below she and her horse had plodded through a landscape that shifted from shallow pools in muddy land to muddy islands surrounded by shallow pools and back again. Here on top of the dunes the untrodden sand was soft under hoof, but at least an onshore breeze seemed to be keeping the biting things at bay.

Naomi arrived at the river when the ebb tide meant it was brackish but drinkable. Caution dictated that they would have to wait until it turned before trying to swim across the river or risk being swept out to sea. She shot a rabbit that seemed more curious than was advisable and made a fire. The breeze died though, and the marshes reached out with rain and gnats to remind her of the delights she was leaving behind. As the daylight softened she tucked into her meal of rabbit and biscuit and listened to the curlew and oystercatchers lamenting her departure. Mice appeared, looking like tiny sabretooth tigers with their oversized teeth protruding well below their lower jaw. They pulled the discarded offal back into the ryegrass, growling at each other as they did so. The red V-shaped band on their chests made them easy to spot even in the half light.

As the drizzle continued a great booming call bounced off the shore. Naomi stood, trying to discern the source. A song filled the air, a deep rumbling that she felt through her body, and a wonderous dragon burst from the sea. Just above the horizon, below the low cloud, the setting sun caught the water streaming off the beast's chrome scales. Another huge serpent leapt after it and soon the two were coiling around each other so quickly that Naomi couldn't be sure if they were chasing their own tails or each other's. As quickly as they had appeared they sank beneath the boiling waves. Naomi stood, mid-mouthful, wondering if this was Vatn at play. The sea exploded skyward as the dragons surged vertically until almost their whole bodies were clear of the deep. They trumpeted to each other as they slowed in their bid for flight before, outstretched, they slapped back down into the bay. The spray burst aloft in a golden curtain as the sound of their massive bodies smacking the water reached her. They and the sun were gone; just the sad birds remained.

White Mountain was not white. And it could only be described as a mountain by those who had lived out their lives in the crusted salt beds and lagoons where every dry hillock was worth fighting over. At its base the village of the same name had found root. A small harbour was crammed with boats and bored-looking fishermen fixing their nets. They all watched her approach through the last of the scrub. She carried on, climbing into the town proper through the meandering streets. Every white house seemed to disgorge at least one child determined to follow her. Some offered to make sure no harm came to her horse; some just dragged along for the want of anything else to do. They reached the central square where Naomi and her mount drank deep from the fountain. She looked up and considered that she seemed to have swapped biting insects for questioning children.

It was only then she noticed the fire-blackened iron cage on its ash bed, the unfortunate occupant still inside. The kids seemed oblivious, and Naomi decided asking questions might lead to a conversation she didn't want to have. One of the girls was shorter than most of the others but looked older. She was watching Naomi's eyes rather than trying to touch the fine silks or pat the horse.

'You, where should I stay?' Naomi asked.

The girl pursed her lips. 'Well, miss, the White Horse is the cheapest but a lady of your standing should stay in the Crown. It has the nicest beds, Ritesh doesn't water his wine and most of the rooms don't have bedbugs.'

Naomi produced a copper coin out of nowhere and tossed it to her. 'That's to take me there and another if it's as good as you say it is.'

The child made the coin vanish as quickly as it had appeared and she swaggered slightly as she led Naomi out of the square. The gaggle slowly dispersed, partly at the girl's instruction.

The inn looked respectable enough with an expansive veranda offering relief from the sunshine but many windows open to make the most of the slightest breeze. A man leant on his broom as he watched Naomi, the girl and the last of the youthful pack approach.

'I have been advised that I should stay here.' Naomi gestured towards the girl. The sweeper nodded. 'How much for your best room?' she asked.

'Thank you, miss. Five marks for bed and board. Six to stable the horse for the night.' He drew himself up a little as if ready for an argument.

'Seven if you can make a bath hot enough to cook a lobster in. I have spent days crossing the marshes and I don't think there's a part of me that isn't bitten at least twice.' Naomi found herself scratching for emphasis. She began to unbuckle the saddle.

The man's face broke into a smile. 'Meena. Go fetch the stable boy to sort the lady's mount out.' The girl ran through the wide doors to the courtyard without hesitation. 'I'll show you the way. If you give us half an hour or so we'll bring the water up.'

The innkeeper walked her up to her room on the third floor where windows to the west showed the rocky shore that continued from the White Mountain south over the roofs of the other houses to the sea, now a darker blue as the sun approached the horizon. A gentle breeze moved lazily from the windows. Naomi was stripping off her silks before Ritesh had managed to close the door.

Coming down to the bar still glowing from her bath, which would have cooked a lobster very nicely, Naomi watched Meena moving through the crowd with pitchers of light golden beer. The saloon was almost full but the landlord cleared a table by the open doors.

'You're busy tonight,' Naomi commented.

'The fishermen can't fish while there are dragons in the sea.' Ritesh screwed up his face and spoke a little more quietly. 'But this means they can't spend much on a drink either.' He placed three seared mackerel in front of her with a salad garnish, a fiery sauce and small round dumplings that she didn't recognise.

'We would normally serve tuna, but we're reduced to what can be caught from the rocks. Some wine, something stronger?' he asked.

She had intended to enjoy a bottle of wine but the frothy beer looked better for a warm summer's evening and she said so. Two fiddles and a complicated instrument that seemed to be bellows with buttons on both ends appeared and the band struck up some slow tunes to get themselves going.

A youngish man sat at the next table; judging by his jacket he was certainly more well-to-do than the fisherfolk around him. He stared at a chessboard in front of him, though as Naomi finished her meal there was still no sign of the other player. She wondered if this was her agent.

'Whose move?' she asked.

He raised an eyebrow at her. 'White.'

'Then I would take the knight,' Naomi said.

The man stared at the board a little longer. 'That's a very aggressive stance.' He looked up at her and smiled. 'Would you like a game? My partner appears delayed.'

'I wouldn't want to interrupt a long-standing arrangement.'

He started rearranging the figures. 'It's fine. We write down the locations at the end of each evening. Since Pran is late he has forfeited his place for tonight, at least.' His quick fingers had already pushed the pieces into their starting places. 'Please, if you can play at all I would relish the chance to compete against someone else,' he said looking hopefully into Naomi's face for a response to his invitation and smile. Naomi stood but her short sword caught on her table as she moved opposite the chess player. She laid the weapon down beside the board and he looked surprised.

'I'm not sure what stakes we are playing for,' he said.

'A gold coin if you can beat me. And what would you offer me?'

'I am Ajay, the magistrate. Anything in this village that takes your fancy.' He raised an eyebrow suggestively.

Naomi laughed and, still warm from the bath, wondered at the strength of the beer. 'We'll think of something,' she said.

They both moved their king's pawns out into the centre; the kings' knights and bishops quickly followed. Naomi caught Meena's eye for another beer.

An older man joined them, by his robes and clean hands a priest of some kind. A grey band of hair survived at the back of his head. 'Ajay, I can't believe you have given my chair to another.'

The player looked up from the board in surprise. 'Pran, given the choice between looking into your weary eyes for another evening or those of this beautiful lady it was an easy decision to make.'

'At least I know where I stand.' The priest ordered a cup of tea and sipped it as the game played. 'I hear you came out of the marshes and forded the river. Not many come that way these days.'

Naomi was conscious Pran watched her face as intently as Ajay watched the chessboard. 'Yes. You say these days. I haven't been this way for what feels like an age. Has something changed in the last few years?'

'The swamps are haunted by water spirits that seek to draw you into their pools. It has made the marshes much more dangerous to traverse, the traffic less frequent. The roads have fallen into disrepair,' said Pran.

'I saw a will-o-the wisp. It called to me from the reeds,' Naomi confirmed.

'Check,' said Ajay moving his queen forward aggressively.

'Most would follow the call. It is good that you resisted its summons,' said the priest.

Naomi thought of herself three nights ago plunging through the scrub, chasing the mesmerising light before falling deep into a pool. The spell had only been broken as she drowned. She had blazed in her anger then. The spectre waiting to drain her life fled in terror and she had to claw her way back to the surface. Naomi could still taste the salty water when she coughed. She took a long draught of beer and removed Ajay's queen.

Chapter Six

Their conversation and the game had pulled in a crowd. From their knowledgeable comments, chess, it seemed, was popular in White Mountain. 'But it's not just the lights in the marshes, or the dragons in the sea,' said Ajay frowning at the board. 'It's the trolls under bridges. The wolves in the forest that can open cabin doors, the shadows under our beds that try to pinch the warmth from our children. These small gods have infested our world since the seraphim returned all those centuries ago.'

'But the seraphim are tied closely to Heaven,' said Naomi hoping she sounded puzzled. The priest was still looking at her intently; there was a hint of recognition that made her uncomfortable.

'They are,' agreed Ajay, 'but in the thousand years since the Edgeward seraphim came to Heaven's aid, other things have come through the door they opened. And Heaven has no interest in anything beyond its own walls. Only this week we had a heretic, here, in White Mountain.' There were murmurs from the audience.

'Really?' She sat back. Although Ajay had a more open position, he was a queen down. Naomi relaxed a little allowing her to look at the tired faces around her. 'How did you know?'

'He confessed under torture,' said one of the fishermen.

'As I would, I'm sure,' Naomi said.

Ajay looked up from the board. 'We don't go around torturing people randomly. I am the magistrate here and there were good reasons for suspicion.' He seemed annoyed to be distracted from the chessboard.

'Which were?'

'He called the dragons by name, which made us wary. When we examined his room in the White Horse, he had papers written in an ancient script, which luckily Pran was able to translate.'

He nodded at the priest, who shrugged. 'I was blessed to go to one of the lesser temples in Heaven to study when I was young, so I could recognise the Heavenly words. But the subject of the papers was not divine – they were some kind of military report about the comings and goings in Heaven. Of strengths and weaknesses. Mostly who among the angels would not see Heaven return to war and those who wanted to cleanse the small gods from the world. Archangel Aileen was the keenest to see the world purged of evil,' said Pran, who had become more hesitant as he spoke.

'These were not religious texts but the notes of a spy gauging the strength of Heaven. So as you can see, there was a logical chain of events that led to his confession,' Ajay explained.

Naomi thought of the occupant of the cage in the square. She wouldn't be meeting her agent any time soon. 'And then you burned him,' she said. 'Was it wise to burn a heretic? If as you say Heaven has no interest in this town, who would be your defence against that man's master? How would a power that considers acting against Heaven react to hear of his servant being treated so?'

The priest was looking increasingly uncomfortable at Naomi's questions. He reached out and touched Ajay's arm. 'I must go and find a privy,' Pran said. As he all but pulled at Ajay's jacket, Naomi had the distinct impression the priest wanted the magistrate to follow. Ajay didn't take the hint; his concentration was almost absolute. With the advantage in the game, Naomi pressed her attack but, in her ire, had the feeling she was missing something.

The priest returned looking paler than ever. 'What was the wager for this game?' he asked wiping the sweat from his brow though the evening had cooled.

'A gold piece if I win,' murmured Ajay.

In answer Naomi pulled a hefty coin from her belt and laid it on the table.

'And if you lose?' questioned the priest who visibly blanched at the sight of the sovereign.

'Ajay offered me anything in the village,' Naomi said without smiling. Now it was her turn to stare fixedly at Pran.

'For fuck's sake, Ajay, when are you going to realise that words have consequences?' the priest all but shouted. 'You better deliver a bloody victory for all our souls.' His eyes fluttered anywhere rather than at Naomi while the audience looked shocked at the old man's language.

'I will,' said Ajay confidently.

'I'm going to get a drink.' Pran stood up and pushed his way through the bemused crowd.

The last light fled the scene and lamps were set about them. Flamingos called as they flew home in loose formation to the salt marshes. The innkeeper hovered by making sure that his honoured guest wasn't being bothered. As Naomi's concentration returned to the board she saw the game anew and realised that each loss of Ajay's pieces had not been carelessness but sacrifices. Even throwing away his queen had been bait. She pulled back her own queen, but Ajay moved one bishop to check her king, revealing a second check by his rook. She sipped her beer and tried to think of a way out. Pran reappeared by the magistrate's side with half a glass of wine; he now looked twenty years older. Naomi seethed. She wanted to win, to demand the justice that had been so carelessly offered. The old man's hands trembled so much he put his cup down but still managed to spill some. She withdrew her king. Two bishops pinned her king up against her own rook. Naomi closed her eyes and sighed. It was over.

When Naomi looked up Ajay was looking pleased with himself but Pran's left hand still dug deep into his shoulder. She slid the gold coin over the wine-soaked wood to a cheer from the bar. 'Well played,' she said but she could not raise a smile.

'Thank you for the game and the prize. If you will excuse me, I should have gone to the privy an hour ago.' The magistrate stood and swayed as he was enveloped by the slaps and congratulations of the village.

The saloon had largely cleared as the crowd followed Ajay to see what he would do with his new-found wealth. For a moment Naomi found herself alone looking out over the night sea under bright stars. Pran returned and sat where Ajay had. He looked exhausted, his shirt dark with sweat. Meena was curled up by the fire, fast asleep, so Naomi attracted the attention of Ritesh for a refill of her pitcher. Pran ordered a bottle of wine.

After the confused innkeeper retreated, Pran spoke softly. 'It was better that he had no idea what he was playing for.'

'And you do?' Naomi enquired.

'I think so,' said the priest. 'As I said, when I was a small boy I was sent for some schooling to Heaven. Among all the wonders of the city there was a painting I used to go and look at when I had a quiet moment.' A full jug and a bottle appeared. Naomi had to wait until Pran was sure no one could overhear before he continued. 'It was *The Judgement of the Tendua*, painted, it is said, by the angel Lorcan himself. Have you seen it?' Pran asked.

'No,' said Naomi quietly.

'It is a wonderful thing. The ruin of old Heaven, the cowed tendua. Above them the Free Companions and the high table. The angels shine as if there is illumination hidden in the paint. The seraphim from the Edgeward Islands also glow, although you have to look much longer to see it. Each has a different life within. Naomi, highest of all the seraphim save for Kenato Orin, Seraph Friend, is seated with the archangels. She has a fire like a forge within her, red and gold and black, both beautiful and terrible.'

'I am no seraph,' said Naomi pulling her hair back over her ears.

The priest drained his cup with a gulp. 'And yet your eyes flashed with that same fire tonight when you realised you had lost your bet.'

'A trick of the light. The lamps must have caught them.'

'It must be so,' said Pran, but he could not hold the bottle steady, so Naomi refilled his glass. 'For Naomi, Procurator of Eden, some now number among the fallen, who built her false Forest of Souls and misleads people away from Heaven and true reincarnation.'

'So they say. But the children of the tendua have multiplied to rival the stars above. And so many of them find the truth of Heaven hard to live up to. When predestination became dominant, forgiveness became a very rare quality. The Forest of Souls offers an alternative path.'

'For a price,' said the priest.

'There is always a price. One way or the other.' She took a sip of beer. 'Why didn't you decry me in front of the village?' she asked.

Pran seemed to calm slightly. 'They were drunk on wine and the win. Full of bravado and a sense of righteousness, they would have tried to detain you. Many would have died. Perhaps all of us. Even though you have only your little sword to hand.' Pran looked over at the sleeping girl. 'Better that you leave tomorrow and White Mountain remembers the stranger that Ajay the magistrate beat in chess for gold. Will you go peacefully in the morning?'

'Yes. The moment has passed. I would ask though that my man out there in the cage receives a proper burial. His name was Jim Hazy.'

The priest nodded. 'Because he is a criminal it must be outside the town, but I see no reason why Ajay would want to refuse my request. It makes a grisly centrepiece for White Mountain. I prefer it when they sell flowers there,' he confided taking a mouthful of wine. His hand seemed steady now and his voice more sure. 'Now you said "when predestination became dominant" earlier. That would imply that it has not always been so.'

The sky was lightening before the priest finally fell asleep; it seemed the only way that he would stop asking questions. The dragons calling from the sea through the open doors was the only sound in White Mountain. Naomi dragged herself upstairs, not wanting to miss her last chance of sleeping in a real bed for a while. When she woke late in the morning it was with a pounding head that the first jug of water did little to shift. The inn was quiet and the harbour empty, so she guessed that the chrome monsters had moved on for the moment.

Meena had packed her saddlebags with bread and cheese and an orange spicy sausage that Naomi had not seen before. 'I wish you could stay,' she said, twirling on her hips very slightly.

Naomi, already dressed in light silks and trousers, was finishing plaiting her hair by the window. 'Why?' she asked.

'You play chess with magistrates and argue with priests. And you wear two swords. I would like to be like you when I grow up.'

'I'm not sure you would like to be me really.' Naomi pulled another gold coin from her purse and handed it to the girl. 'You have a choice now, Meena. Spend this and you can live well for a while and no one would blame you for that. Or keep it and when you are older go east. If you show people that coin they will point you to the black road. At the end of the highway you will find Eden, as it is known, and perhaps, if we are both lucky, I may be there to greet you.'

'Who should I ask for?' said Meena, her face very serious.

'My name? Ask Pran when I am gone,' said Naomi, mirroring the child as she crouched. 'But no one else, not a soul.' She folded the girl's fingers round the coin and left.

When it was clear the dragons had gone to play elsewhere, the same day as the traveller, some noted, the fishermen brought in better catches than they had in years. Salt had long been gathered from the marshes and all of the villagers were put to work before the great harvest spoiled in the heat of the day. Long into the night they toiled and the next day they started early. The priest asked the magistrate if they could bury the stranger in the iron cage, but the magistrate said that there was too much money to be lost if the fish rotted, and besides, the devil worshipper wasn't going to Heaven so what was the hurry?

The priest and a small girl resolved to dig a grave by themselves, but the ground was baked hard by the summer and they were only a few feet below the surface by nightfall on the third day. They returned to the safety of the walls of White Mountain to find that all the fish had been salted and the village square was filled with barrels to be sold to the cities.

So pleased was the magistrate that he bought drinks and food for all the village and they celebrated their good fortune into the morning. The little girl who had no home but the hearth at the Crown worked serving the best wine in the house to the magistrate until she fell asleep standing up. The village dreamed of a better year ahead, mostly where they sat or lay.

As the village rose with the sun there was great consternation, for the magistrate was dead. The scorched corpse of the condemned man had freed itself from its prison and, having stepped over the sleeping girl, throttled the magistrate in his chair by the chessboard. The traveller's gold piece that he had so recently won was clamped between his killer's teeth. Its bony fingers, blunt from clawing at the iron cage, were fast around the man's neck. The magistrate could only be released when the carpenter resorted to a hammer and chisel. Seeking consultation with the priest, they buried the skeleton and the magistrate deep in the ground outside the wall, and, after some debate, the coin with them.

Chapter Seven

The hills to Heaven were steeper than Naomi remembered. A bustling town, bigger than White Mountain, had grown up where there had been high pasture. The road was wide where carters tried to avoid the heavily rutted centre which was, after a long summer, harder than stone and ready to pull wheels off and break axles. The place was swamped with merchants toiling slowly up towards the market or coming away with lighter loads and hopefully fuller purses. Such was the bustle and noise of commerce that Naomi was able to pass through without comment. Three miles beyond all the trade and she had climbed enough that the air cooled and mist draped around the tops of mountains that Naomi did not remember. She paused to pull on a heavy black samite cloak with silver threads that was welcome proof against the chill.

A great wall ran between two peaks barring the progress of the labouring convoy and people with long weapons and dark helmets marched briskly behind the ramparts. A tall watchtower, partly carved out of the westernmost mountain, dominated the pass. At its base, the open gate provided the only entrance. The carts had ground to a halt now and Naomi rode slowly up the line causing occasional comments about people too posh to take their turn. When she reached the end, she came across a group of eight soldiers, their twelve-foot halberds held upright, checking the paperwork of each merchant.

'Hey, lady, back of the queue! Heaven does not like people who try and push their way in,' said the officer looking up from a merchants paperwork. Naomi presumed he had command of these new Gates of Heaven by virtue of being the only one who could read.

Naomi rested on the broad wooden board at the front of her saddle. 'When I was last here there was a warmer welcome in Heaven. I do not remember this wall.'

The captain laughed. 'These walls have been here for hundreds of years. I think you must be confused, lady. Now go to the back of the queue and we'll say no more about it.'

'I am here for the wedding of Alfin and Alva.' Naomi stood up in her stirrups and looked back down the line of carts and riders. 'If I have to wait at the back of this lot I shall miss the ceremony, the feast and the fortnight of celebrations.'

The captain had turned purple with barely contained rage.

'All hail the Archangel Alfin of the Heavenly Host who has saved all the peoples between the snow and the sand, whose ships have sailed to the three edges of the world bringing Seraph Friends to aid their victory. All hail the Archangel Alva of the Heavenly Host whose forges produced the bright spears of the angels that dazzled the tendua, whose petal armour protected the blessed archangels in their righteous victory.' All the guards had joined in the chant as had the merchants within earshot. 'What kind of blasphemer are you that would so casually call upon the archangels' names?' he asked, stepping forward with his sword drawn.

Naomi pulled down her samite hood ensuring that her sharp angelic ears were on show. 'One of the seraphim that your exalted archangels are friends with.' She pulled out a folded piece of vellum and passed it to the officer who, unwilling to sheath his blade, took the note awkwardly in his left hand.

'It says you are to pass without hindrance,' said the captain as if this would come as news to Naomi.

'Yes,' she said simply.

The captain handed the letter back but still waved his sword at her. 'Pass then, Seraph Friend. But I would caution you with being so overfamiliar. You were lucky that I'm not one of those hotheads that would cut you down for such informality.'

'Indeed,' said Naomi. She pressed her horse forward through the crush of nervous guards who held their spears tightly.

Going under the vast bulk of the watchtower, Naomi left the caravans as they descended north from the pass. She had had enough of crowds so she followed mountains that were fresh to her to the west. Within an hour she was in high pasture dotted with unattended cattle. But then, she thought, who would steal a cow from Heaven? A mountain stream ran past a small house. Beside it an angel stood at the gate of a pen full of complaining sheep, pulling them out one by one. He inspected the animals' feet and teeth before passing them on to a woman and three men who were expertly shearing them with heavy black iron shears. She recognised the sheep-carrying angel but took a moment to put a name to him.

'Lorcan!' Naomi had to shout above the noise of the flock. The angel stood, holding the sheep easily in his arms as puzzlement swept across his muddied face. He always was the most handsome of angels, Naomi thought. Somehow his being here in the role of shepherd only added to the effect.

A beautiful smile slowly broke and he passed the animal to the shearer and wiped his hands on his apron. 'Naomi! It has been many, many years since I have seen you. You look well.'

'Thank you, Lorcan. I'm afraid I don't know your title.' His look saddened a little.

He walked towards her taking his apron off. 'Lorcan is good enough for friend or foe.'

Naomi dismounted. They stood and looked at each other for a moment. Naomi recalled the priest's description of the painting and wondered what those angel eyes saw.

'Naomi, friend, you are here for the wedding then?' Lorcan asked.

'Yes. I have been travelling for about three months now. Have I missed it?'

'No, you are in good time. Four days from now Alva and Alfin will be wed.' He wore an odd expression now, looking far away. 'Three months. Who would have thought the world had got that great. Come to my house then. It is simple enough, but I can at least give you some rustic comfort before you press on to Heaven itself.'

'Is it far? I find myself quite disoriented. You have changed the place while I have been away.'

'About twenty miles or so to the city you would know. Maybe a little more. Come. The stables are there. We have no servants here so you will need to see to the mount yourself, but he will be in good company.' Naomi scratched her horse where the bony head plate met the hair of his forelock and he followed Naomi towards the house.

Lorcan's hall itself was bigger than it looked from the outside, with a roomy central space and smaller chambers off two of the sides. An open fire in the centre kept the chill of the mountain air at bay and Lorcan stirred the contents of a pot slung above it. His contentment gently filled the room with a light that matched the evening sunlight outside.

'Mutton and barley soup?' he offered. 'We should have fresh bread soon, but you are hungry so let us not wait.' He ladled two bowls' worth out of the pot and they sat at a wooden bench beside the fire.

She looked around the room with its plain white plaster and dark wood. 'This isn't what I was expecting,' Naomi said.

'We manage a little venison sometimes but it is mostly mutton here, with all the sheep.'

Naomi returned his smile. 'No, I mean this place. I thought the vanquisher of the tendua would have some grand palace.' She looked at her wooden spoon and bowl. 'Silver cutlery and gold plates.'

'The vanquisher was Alfin. You and I played our part, but it was his war. I am happier here rather than in the city of the angels. It keeps things simple. Easier to understand. I have an important role in this place. Those four are souls that have led many good lives and now have to decide whether to go on and become angels themselves or return again to the world outside Heaven, reincarnated once again. I have found that helping with the flock allows them space to think about that next step.'

'What do you …' Naomi was interrupted by another angel entering the house. One of the two sisters, Arden or Aileen – Naomi had always struggled to tell the difference between them.

'Oh, am I late?' she asked. Lorcan jumped up and took the armful of provisions from her.

'Come to the fire. No, I started early. We started early.'

The angel looked again; she must have missed Naomi in the relative gloom beside Lorcan. The newcomer looked briefly worried at the sight of a strange woman and Naomi felt very much out of place. 'If I had known I would have brought more bread,' she said slightly defensively.

Arden, Naomi decided. She always had a thing for Lorcan, many people did, but her more than most.

'Arden, good to see you.' Naomi stood up closer to the door and the angels so that she would be easier to see.

'Naomi! Goodness, I thought you had left this world for other adventures. And yet here you are.' She looked to Lorcan for reassurance, but it was Naomi who responded.

'Chance. I was travelling to the wedding and ended up here by following my nose.' Naomi paused for a moment. 'Story of my life really.' She laughed and the angels joined in out of politeness. The three sat down with refilled bowls.

'The wedding, of course,' said Arden looking a little relieved. She clasped her hands and looked earnestly at Naomi. 'Though I understand you have been riding about and fighting wars and such, but it is Lady Arden now.'

'Ah, yes, I had sort of gathered that was the way things were going.' Naomi noticed that Lorcan's face had become unreadable.

'What do your people call you?' Arden asked, looking attentive.

The first few things that popped into Naomi's head didn't seem repeatable in front of angels.

'Guv,' Naomi said.

'My,' said Arden, who then changed the subject back as if her interruption hadn't occurred. 'Many of the Free Company have already returned to the Celestial City for the wedding, though not all.'

'It's a dangerous world out there, with wars and such,' Naomi confirmed. Lorcan hunched a little and Arden looked serious. 'Have I said something wrong?' Naomi once again found reason to curse the zeal of the good folk of White Mountain. This was what she had hoped to learn from the agent.

Arden took the loaf she had brought and broke it into three. 'No, no,' she said. 'It is just the great debate. Everyone has a view – should we go back out and help beyond the Gates of Heaven or is that interfering in fate, in free choice? It has reached the point where it seems that every meeting, every meal is dominated by variations of the same argument. It's one of the reasons Lorcan lives out here.' She made to reach out for his arm across the bench but redirected the gesture to pick up the water jug.

'Yes,' he said flatly.

'Alva is very keen that we do offer aid. It will be interesting to see if marrying Alfin can move him into that faction.' Lorcan stared at Arden who seemed unable to stop. 'We could do so much by going back out, beyond this. You live out there – what do you think?'

'Life is made harder by the small gods. It's put a new fear in the world but also wonder and joy,' said Naomi. 'It's a richer place. More exciting. But there are sacrifices, prices to be paid.'

'Like the tolls on the black road offering the forgiveness of sins,' said Arden pointedly to Naomi.

'The Forest of Souls gives the opportunity for redemption.' Naomi stopped herself from saying more.

Arden, her eyes bright, was ready for an argument. 'It puts a false choice in front of people. It creates a false equivalence with the majesty of Heaven. If you are leading people away from Heaven, surely that is a hell you are building? And what does that make you procurator of?' Arden made as if she was about to continue, but Lorcan looked like a thunder cloud in front of the sun and she sat back.

'Hopefully we will have the opportunity after the wedding for this discussion. Lorcan, I cannot recall tasting a better soup,' Naomi said.

Naomi sat on her horse and looked at the Celestial City in amazement. She recognised the walls of Heaven, though there were more and taller watchtowers than she remembered. But the city had expanded to take up all the vast space once occupied by the arboretum and having reached the boundary extended up so that Naomi thought of a loaf in a baking tin. Within the walls, each palace and lesser building was white, but the late evening light bathed everything in rose and cream. The tops were red slate or gilded domes that caught the last of the day and sent it back out golden and marvellous. A bell rang and in response at the main gate a slow procession of angels came out beyond the confines to sing as the day ended. Naomi felt herself tearing up at the beauty of their sound as it echoed off the hills behind her. Her instinct said that she should return to the shepherd's house immediately. Enjoy another bowl of that most wonderful soup, have a second night of the deepest of sleeps and then leave Heaven with these perfect memories intact.

Arden watched her from a little way on. 'How does – what do you call it? – Eden compare?' she asked.

Naomi shifted her gaze from the scene to her angel companion. Too late, the moment was already sullied. Naomi smiled thinly in response.

The Celestial City was a wonder and a maze. Naomi would have been lost had it not been for Arden, the Lady Arden, guiding her through the bustle. The towers and grand houses seemed more impressive up close so Naomi could make out beautiful detailing around each door and window. Stairs and windows were piled up like clouds. The pair reached a square where a fountain bubbled in the dying light of the day. There were three paths; Arden pointed to the east.

'You will need to be quick if you are to avoid the curfew,' said Arden conversationally. 'You'll find the other seraphim and everyone else in the Worldly

Enclave. If you go to where the Dawn Mount used to be you can't miss it.' It was only then that Naomi became aware that the traffic to her left was made up of hurrying dwarves, fairies and others while the angels milled about in a more leisurely manner, enjoying the evening.

'Where will you be?' Naomi asked feeling slightly stupid.

'I am to go to the archangels' palace. There is simply so much to do before the wedding. Hurry along,' said Arden kindly as though to a child. Naomi nudged her stallion and followed the streaming people through the city of angels thinking about palaces and wooden spoons.

Chapter Eight

The road climbed past several Fairycotes and their weaving sheds towards a looming building of featureless stone. This massive circular block was home to the seraphim and those who served them. The only apparent entrance was a temple portico with three rows of eight pillars holding up a gable roof. A frieze above the doorway showed the binding of the tendua, reminding the surrounding Celestial City why this monolithic intrusion was here. Eight jackal-headed soldiers, each twice as tall as Naomi on her horse, guarded the way in with hands resting on heavy bronze axes. They stood so still that Naomi wondered for a moment if they were painted statues and the real guards were elsewhere.

One moved her head very slightly. 'Guv. Been a while.'

'It is starting to feel like a lifetime, Maat. Is Kenato Orin here?' she asked, dismounting and pulling the tack off her steed.

'Been back about a month, Guv,' the cynocephali confirmed. 'He should be glad to see you – I think he's getting bored.'

'Never a good sign. Where are the stables?' Naomi asked.

'We'll get someone to sort that. A house has been allocated for you. Just ask one of the little blue fellas and they will point you in the right direction. But the boss isn't in.'

Naomi shouldered her saddle and panniers; she walked through the columns and into the building itself. The architect had wrapped a substantial street in a circle around a central plaza. The houses reached five or six storeys and above them, a smooth wall rose to the great arc of a patterned dome high above. None of this had been visible from the outside. The ceiling ran almost to the centre where a hole, which Naomi thought might be sixty feet in diameter, let in starlight and a hint of evening sky. Below, a group of stone seraphim battled some oversized tendua. Several of the seraphim spouted water from their mouths and hands to represent the crucial role of magic in their victory. Naomi couldn't resist looking for herself in the struggle, but she had been fighting on the steppe while history had been written here in the city.

She shifted her heavy saddle and bags and collared a kobold running across the square with a barrel of wine. 'Is that Kenato Orin's house?' The kobold nodded his blue head, his pink tongue flickering out between the hard lips. 'My name is Naomi. One of these houses should be prepared for me.' The kobold thought for a moment and pointed to a smaller building on the north side of the arc. He ran on before she could give any response. Naomi walked across the marble courtyard and through the open door. Inside, a porter sat in a small office with what looked like a rather nice fire.

He glanced up and smiled. 'Lady Naomi – how lovely to see you. I can arrange food and a drink in the drawing room. There is a gentleman waiting to see you.'

'Who?' asked Naomi.

'Lord Jasper, I believe, my lady. Or you can go straight up to your suite.' He rang the bell on the counter twice and two younger servants appeared as if from nowhere. 'Alison, go and get some water boiling for a bath. Jon, take the lady's saddle and bags up to her quarters.' The boy attempted to pick up the riding tack and panniers and failed to shift either.

'Something to eat, I think, and I seem to have developed a taste for beer,' Naomi said.

The porter stepped out of his office, reached over and rang the bell twice more. 'Follow me, please.' He led her through a wood-panelled hall and into a room lit by only four candles. High-backed leather armchairs flanked a slightly larger version of the fire in the porter's snug. Sitting in one was the elemental she had expected.

'Jasper, well, this is a rather marvellous way to end a journey.'

'Kenato Orin was quite specific about sorting this place out when he heard you were coming.'

'And there you were saying all those bad things about him,' said Naomi, smiling as she settled into the other winged chair. 'This is quite lovely – was all this made by you?'

'You know how it is. The elementals do all the work and the demons take all the glory.' The porter had sneaked back into the room with a tall jug of beer and two glasses.

He poured one for Naomi. 'The chef is rustling up some chicken, my lady, and your bath should be ready when you are.'

'Thank you,' said Naomi with a warm smile and made sure he left before she continued.

Jasper sipped his wine.

'Where is Kenato Orin?' she asked. 'The guards told me he wasn't here.'

'Ah, the Seraph Friend has special privileges and will be staying at the palace,' said Jasper.

'He is always happiest when someone thinks he's special.' They both smiled but Naomi felt badly informed. 'The agent you sent to meet me in White Mountain, Jim Hazy, was spotted by the locals.'

'Yes. I had gathered that. Very unfortunate.'

'It certainly was for Jim. Was he careless or do we have greater problems?'

'Arden and Aileen are taking a close interest in our nature, but I think it's more to see if they can tap into the same power we can. They resent being reliant on us for delivery on the complex projects – walls, towers, mountains, world peace. But in terms ...' The young lad who had struggled with Naomi's baggage appeared doing a better job carrying a chicken salad and some cold potatoes, which she attacked while Jasper continued. 'And your Forest of Souls is as popular in Heaven as chewing a wasp.'

'They just can't stand the competition.'

'I don't think it was what they had in mind when they created the one true path.'

'No, they now just filter out the very best to refill their ranks and the rest go round to the back of the queue. Ascetic to angelic is a very tough message for most people.'

'How perfect do you have to be to be an angel? Whereas we …' Jasper raised his glass of wine.

'Though this business of the sisters calling Eden Hell isn't helping.'

'What else would you call something that is not Heaven?'

'Give a dog a bad name,' said Naomi as she finished the meal and wiped her hands on a napkin. 'But we should recruit that priest in White Mountain – Pran was his name. He fingered Jim Hazy but when he heard about redemption it really engaged him.'

'I think if you start stealing their priests as well as their followers you really will spark trouble,' said Jasper.

'Well, they should pay more attention to what's happening outside these mountains you've built for them.'

'Ah, the great debate – is it the role of angels to go out and enforce the rules as to how the masses should live their lives? Perhaps to defend the people from the monsters that have come in our wake? Should we?'

'Supporting heroes teaches the people they can defend themselves. Eden gives a greater opportunity to be better in so many ways. The tollhouses are a real shot at redemption,' said Naomi, feeling defensive. Jasper went to respond but instead just smiled. It was a conversation they'd had many times, taking either side of the argument. Naomi thought of the serenity of Lorcan and his shepherds, of the processional vespers at the close of day. 'But it is not Heaven,' she added quietly.

The Judgement of the Tendua was vast. Naomi could see why it would make an impression on a young acolyte from White Mountain. Even here among the wonders of Heaven it stood out. Escaping from the bustle of the wedding she had stolen a seat and placed it far enough back that she could see the whole frame without moving her head. A jug of beer and a bowl of fried potatoes, also stolen, sat by the chair and Naomi drew from both as required. She wanted to enjoy the moment without interruption from the celebrations below so created a turn at the door to ensure that other guests would forget the hall existed or remember somewhere else they wanted to be instead. Undisturbed, she saw that Pran had spoken truly about Lorcan's work. The angels appeared to be illuminated in their own subtle brilliance, the way that Lorcan had been in that dark shepherd's hut – in a way that the angels in the city weren't, but Naomi put that down to the ambient light level.

More subtle was the means by which Lorcan had painted the seraphim. It took her quite a while to pick it out, but Vatn was the first that caught the corner of Naomi's eye. He seemed to shimmer like a stream in the sunshine, subtly in the beginning, and then stronger as though the sun had come out from behind clouds. After a while she could stare at Vatn's image directly and still see the movement. Jasper and Sandi looked somehow massive, mountainous if you looked at them obliquely. Candice darkened in dangerous desirability. Kenato Orin looked bigger than he should, as if he would burst out of his skin at any moment. And Naomi herself? Pran had been right. She glowed in a rolling orange, gold and black like the heart of a smithy's fire. She was mesmerised by the colours she had rarely shown since she had come to this world.

'You have to wonder if he knows,' said Alfin.

Naomi jumped up to bow and to look around. Seeing that they were alone, she responded, 'As I understand it only you have this knowledge, Archangel.'

'That's what I thought until Lorcan painted this. But he has never said anything to anyone. Only completed the painting and then requested that it be hung here in the high hall. A few can see the true portrayal of our seraphim but none, I think, understand what they see.' Alfin went to stand beside Naomi's chair. 'He is the best of us. The fiercest warrior. The strongest advocate for peace. The most faithful to the Treasury of Souls.'

The pair stood and watched the subtle shifting image for a while.

'He has captured our essence.'

'Lorcan created two more pictures but has locked them away. I have seen one. It is of a brilliant white figure entering through the cast-down walls of Heaven. But he would not be drawn on its meaning. The other, he says, will only be seen at the end of time. It is a shame he did not paint when the hundred companions were first assembled. Each one of you is so different. Kenato Orin tries very hard to tell me as little as possible, but you cannot share the same mind space without some transfer of knowledge. I understand that you are from various planes of existence?'

'Yes, some worlds have sentient fire, others have rocks with the life force to move. Some are more ...' Naomi couldn't think of a word other than demonic '... trouble.'

Alfin smiled. 'What he has never explained is what drew you all here, to risk all for a place to which you owed nothing.'

'Every world has its rules, Archangel. You remember the first night we met?'

'Even though it was more than a thousand years ago every moment seems as fresh as Lorcan's painting.' Alfin smiled as he spoke.

'I had existed as a spirit, for want of a better term, for an age without measure. Suddenly I was clothed in a body of flesh and blood. I could feel heat and cold, the dense fur of the tendua, the sharpness of his claws. To be here in this plane is to live.'

'And die. You did nearly die that night.'

'That is part of it. Every day has a value because you may not see the next.'

'To grow old?'

'Perhaps. Since I have come here to the city, I feel time's passage much more strongly than before, and only now I wonder if we shall weaken and fail as others do.'

'Then will you escape death? Become spirit again?'

'I don't think I can now, Alfin. I have been corporal for so long that even when I travel to other worlds I retain this flesh in some form. I now take the rules of this existence with me.'

There was a wave of laughter from the party in the lower hall, which jolted Naomi out of her reverie. 'Congratulations, Archangel. How does it feel to be married?' She lifted her glass in a toast.

'Thank you, Naomi. It feels like I have partly accomplished what I should be.' Naomi tried not to look surprised but obviously failed. 'Alva is my soulmate. In that way I am complete. But marrying me seems poor reward for all that Alva has done for us. I would do something for her, with your help. Which is why I sought you out. Will you come with me?'

Naomi felt she had little choice but to agree with the archangel, though she did look wistfully at the bowl of potatoes.

They walked out of the upper hall, into a gallery and onto the highest balcony of the lower hall. The throng of the nuptial guests were below, dancing, eating and drinking, talking and laughing. Naomi paused at the top of the great stairs, trying to take in the whole scene in all its detail. *An angels' wedding is a rare thing,* she thought, *and probably should be savoured.* Maybe she had been out on the steppe too long.

'Come, Naomi. You were first of the seraphim to come to our aid.' Alfin spoke but his words somehow rang out across the great chamber as every conversation finished at the same time and all looked up to watch them descend. Alva and Kenato Orin stood by the high chairs the bride and groom had sat on during the feast. Kenato was smiling so much, Naomi suspected he was drunk. The two archangels sat in their chairs, and Kenato Orin indicated that Naomi should stand behind Alfin as he stood behind Alva.

'We searched the whole palace for you. Even sent a runner back to the Worldly Enclave,' the Seraph Friend said quietly.

'I was just upstairs,' said Naomi.

'Eventually the archangel himself had to go and find you.'

'Ah,' said Naomi, remembering the turn she had put at the door. Her lips thinned in apology. 'Yes.'

'Hold this.' Kenato Orin handed her a delicate band of gold. The finest of tracery seemed to move as she rotated it. Forest and sea, mountain and tower rose and fell as she turned the circlet in the torchlight.

'Very nice, what's it for?' Naomi asked.

'If you had been here when you should have been you would know,' said Kenato Orin, still grinning at Naomi's discomfort.

'Friends!' announced Alfin. The great hall quietened again and people finished dancing, bowing to the partners. Some found seats while others stood cup in hand, a smile on their faces. 'Friends. You have come here for our wedding day from all three corners of the world, and for that I thank you. But you have heard enough speeches today from Alva and me. I have only one short thing to add.' He looked over at Alva and Naomi observed the love pour between them like a great waterfall. 'From the First War, Alva has been here strengthening the angels in their cause, in their defence, in their love. Her swords cut down our foes. Her armour kept us safe. What gift could we offer her equal to her gifts to us?' Alfin asked the indulgent guests.

'The answer,' the archangel continued, 'is to make her Queen of Heaven.' Naomi watched bemusement turn to guarded shock on the faces of those before her. Kenato Orin nudged Naomi and stepped out to the side with a gold circlet held carefully in both hands. Naomi did the same. The pair placed the crowns on the brows of Alfin and Alva and stood back.

'All hail the Queen of Heaven!' shouted Arden and Aileen before dropping to one knee. 'All hail the King of Heaven!' Like a wave the shout and the action swept around the hall until only Naomi and Kenato Orin still stood. 'All hail the King and Queen of Heaven!'

As if crushed by the weight of expectation, Naomi found herself kneeling too, looking up into the beneficent faces of Alva and Alfin bound in their ever-changing bands of gold. Now, Naomi thought, he looks complete.

'It wasn't my idea,' said Kenato Orin.
Naomi looked at him askance. 'Denial just makes me suspicious,' she said. Instead of giving an answer he took a swig from a jeroboam of champagne. They had brought two from the party along with a crystal plate piled high with chocolate truffles. After a bit of a drunken slither from a top-floor window they sat now on

the sloped tiled roof of the angelic pavilion. Before them was the city, the walls, above a sky that was light enough to hint of the mountains beyond. In a testament to the strength of the roofs of Heaven, Jasper, Sandi and a fire elemental called Eldrun were a couple of hundred yards along at the south end of the archangels' palace with the same idea, though they also carried guitars, a fiddle, and songs of when volcanoes met the sea.

'It seemed to have come to him while I was away. Candice and I, and a few others, went to the Edgeward Isles to make sure the real seraphim weren't going to turn up and blow our story.'

'Very sensible. What did you find?' she asked.

'A great city on the main island – something so fair as to put this place to shame.' Naomi raised an eyebrow as Kenato Orin continued. 'Stone quays that moved with the tide, temples that sang with the wind as the evening breeze came on. Great auditoriums where you could hear a whisper to the furthest seat. But all empty, though there were carts in the streets and plates on the table.'

'War?'

'No sign of it, no door split, no brazier overturned. Honey-coloured villas with children's toys left on the parquet floors. The fields fallow, the farm animals grown wild. It was an eerie place to be.'

'What did you do?' Naomi bit into a truffle and washed it down with her champagne.

'One great temple had a gateway so Candice and I followed it. We needed you there really. I'm not that good at shifting from one world to another,' said Kenato Orin.

Naomi smiled. 'You just have to slide sideways, anyway …'

'So the same again. Nice place, blue trees that touched the sky and a great white band hanging above from horizon to horizon. Neither of us had seen anything like it before. Eventually we found another temple and another gateway. A great daisy chain of castles on cliffs above a grey churning sea. Still no sign of their builders.

At that point I was exhausted, and we were worried about how long we had been away.'

'How long was it?'

'When we returned to the Edgeward Islands they said it had been two hundred years or so. While we were on our journey they cleaned out the city, planted the fields and made it their own. We stayed with them for a while as I recovered my energy. Beautiful place. Candice and I sailed among the clouds and, well, other things.'

Naomi could imagine. Candice had a clever mind, a low boredom threshold and a body made for trouble. 'But no real seraphim,' she said.

'No. For whatever reason they have moved far beyond the circles of this world and the next.'

The pair sat for a while drinking. The sun must have neared the horizon for the mountains now were darker pink shapes running from north to south, and the edges of the eastern peaks were edged with gold. Jasper, Sandi and Eldrun were singing a complicated harmony that was like listening to sunshine leaping between two avalanches.

'How are things with Eden? I hear you have built a new road,' asked Kenato Orin.

'We did. It's worked.' Naomi felt a glow of satisfaction.

'Does a road work?'

'No carts stuck in the mud, safe passage ensured by patrols, all paid for by tollhouses with clean beds and good beer. In just a few decades the children of the tendua have created new cities and roads leading from my road.' Naomi could see she had lost the demon. 'Trade generates wealth. Use the wealth to support wider education, education leads to new ideas and new things to trade. Wealth and happiness are generated.' She looked at Kenato Orin's blank face. 'Have you been to Sestola?' she asked.

'No.' Kenato Orin drained his bottle and went to lob it over the guttering but stopped himself.

Naomi held her jeroboam out and they swapped. 'You should go. There are now dozens of cities along the length of the road, but Sestola is the best.' The sun broke the mountains now so that the very tops of the city where the pair drank basked in morning while far below was still in dusky dawn. Kenato Orin passed the bottle back to Naomi who stared at the two in her hands for a moment before tossing the empty expertly through the window that had afforded their exit. There was a soft thump as it landed on a bed. Kenato Orin clapped. She would have stood up and taken a bow, except that would have sent her tumbling off the roof.

'But,' said Naomi, aware that she was struggling to think now, 'enough of Eden. What of the king and queen? Created by our hand, note you.'

'They crowned themselves. We were merely crown stands,' admitted Kenato Orin.

Naomi thought he must be more drunk than her if he wasn't taking credit for the whole monarchy scheme, or out of sorts. 'You managed not to drool on Alva,' she observed.

Kenato Orin sighed. 'And now they are bound together forever. Forever.'

'You should stick with Candice – she knows what you are.'

'Do you not think Alfin has told Alva our true nature by now?'

'Alfin said last night that the only other one who knows is Lorcan.' Naomi felt her brow furrow. 'Lorcan is worried that they will bring Heaven back to war. He wasn't there. Was he?'

'No,' Kenato Orin confirmed.

'Thought not. Shame, Alfin described him as the best of them. He is more like the angels when we first met them.'

'Being eaten?' asked Kenato Orin.

'Well, there is that. But that's the point – to win, the angels had to change, they had to lay aside peace. Some of them have gone back to poetry and contemplative sculpture. Lorcan has his flock. But they are not the same.' Naomi thought of the sisters Arden and Aileen. 'They are judgemental. There is a taste for war and glory.'

'It's not going to happen,' said the Seraph Friend confidently. 'I can't see Alfin switching to being an interventionist. Look at what they have here. What beyond Heaven would be worth risking life and limb when you have all this?' He shook his head. 'It is dull though ...'

An odd ripping noise broke their conversation. As Naomi struggled to focus it became clear that the source was Sandi sliding off the roof. He gouged out slates and rafters as he tried to stop himself following his guitar over the edge. The troubadour came to a halt with his feet dangling in the air. Eldrun burst into flames in readiness to try and slow Sandi before he dashed himself on the gardens far below. Jasper was too busy laughing to help his companion.

'Elementals,' said the demon, making it clear they weren't his problem. 'I'll hold your bottle.'

Chapter Nine

Kenato Orin pinned the bird like Exarch of the Furies to the ground with one foot. He had trapped her head between his war hammer – taller than he was in his seraph form – and the rock of the mountain pass where she had ambushed them. He looked around at the shattered kobold spearmen and dead and torn demons. He breathed hard as he tried to gather his thoughts. The attack had been so fast, so unexpected, that there had been no time for battle lines; everyone had to fight for themselves, for their own survival. The exarch tried to speak, but Kenato released a little more of the weight of the hammer and she stopped, bloody claws flexing but no longer struggling.

'Quiet. I need to think.' But Kenato Orin couldn't get past the anger he felt. It was reinforced each time he looked around at the devastation the furies had caused. He tried looking up rather than around. A bright orange speck broke off from the rising sun and raced towards the scene of carnage. *This will be Eldrun, despatched by Naomi to tell me to do something I don't want to do*. Kenato Orin sighed and let go the hammer. A sound like an eggshell breaking was masked by a roar as the fire elemental landed nearby.

'Boss. I'm sorry we were slow to respond to your call for aid. We were … delayed.' She looked around the scene, grim faced, but didn't seem surprised. Her own armour was torn and blooded, and the flaming sword in her hand was missing the last inch or so.

'The furies have attacked elsewhere?' Kenato Orin asked.

'Lord Jasper as he worked on the gates of Eden. Vatn on the Crystal Sea, and the guv at her summer horse fair on the steppe. All still live, but the losses have been heavy.'

'And me here returning to Heaven. The exarch was overambitious. If she had picked two targets she would have been successful and we would be reeling, too shocked to recover.'

'I'm searching for the exarch herself. Naomi sent me out to try and secure her capture.'

'Ah,' said Kenato Orin inspecting the gory end of his hammer. 'If only you hadn't been delayed. I fear you are too late. Did Naomi say why?'

'The exarch is the focus of the furies. She said without her they will become wild – an undirected tidal wave of chaotic anger that will spill out across the world creating many needless deaths.'

'That sounds like Naomi. A pity.' Kenato Orin tried to move away from the corpse as if it was nothing to do with him.

Eldrun stepped forward and picked up one of the fury's broken wings, revealing a scarlet tunic. 'Oh bollocks.' She sheathed her sword and crouched beside the body, searching quickly through the battered corpse. 'No letters, no clue as to what their plan was? The exarch didn't say anything?'

'It was all just despair and death from the dark. She wouldn't stop attacking me even when it was clear she had lost. I know Naomi wants everyone to sit round tables and sort out deals, but this was a bleeding nightmare. And no, I have no idea why.'

'The guv thought the target might be Heaven itself. The furies believe that Heaven is failing in its sacred duty to the world.'

'A successful attack on us would mean that Heaven has no defence.' Kenato Orin stored away the fact that Naomi had thought an attack was possible but not highlighted the risk to him. There would have to be a discussion about sharing later. If the rest of the battles really had gone as badly as this, it would be years before Eden's forces could be back up to strength.

'I'll need to warn Heaven and then get back to help the guv. It was a real mess,' Eldrun said as she stood up.

Kenato Orin thought for a moment, if there was bad news to deliver to Heaven he wanted to do it. The last thing he needed was some uncontrolled gossip unsettling the angels. Who knew what they would decide to do without his good counsel? 'You leave that to me. I will warn Heaven while you get back and help with the clean-up.' Kenato Orin tried to sound reassuring. Eldrun hesitated. 'You go straight back. I'll tell Naomi when I see her.'

'Right, boss.' Eldrun stepped back into the sky and shot off low eastwards.

Kenato Orin looked around for a kobold he recognised but couldn't see one. 'Has anyone got a horse that hasn't bled to death?' he shouted.

'Where is the King?' asked Kenato Orin as he strode into the angels' palace. He'd kept the damaged armour with the gore and claw marks across it – he thought it would add dramatic authenticity to his story. But so far, the angels had just looked disgusted rather than impressed. He was hoping Alfin would appreciate the theatre.

'The High King and Lorcan are contemplating in the Garden of Eternal Spring and left strict instructions not to be disturbed,' he was told.

Kenato Orin had been part of this occasionally himself, the two angels with their eyes closed *being in the moment*. Kenato Orin had either fallen asleep or become bored enough to overcome his fear of missing out and left them to it.

'He will see me,' Kenato Orin said, confidently pushing past an angel too horrified by the bloody hand on his shoulder to stop him. Kenato Orin threw open the doors and looked around the courtyard to see four rows each of around thirty cherry trees. They were in perfect blossom, the air filled with gently falling petals. But, as the name implied, here it was always like this. The Dryads had been furious- 'Transience was a key part of the beauty of spring,' they said. They had refused to have any part in what they described as a 'Travesty' until Naomi had a word. Kenato Orin limped as he walked up the marble avenue between the achingly magnificent trees towards a dais at the far end where two thrones had been set. Only one was occupied. Alfin sat with his head resting on his hand, his eyes closed. Had Lorcan left the king to his slumber too? Maybe Lorcan wasn't quite as dull as Kenato Orin thought. He decided to go the whole hog and prostrated himself before the throne in supplication.

'All hail the Archangel Alfin of the Heavenly Host, who has saved all the peoples between the snow and the sand, whose ships have sailed to the three edges of the world bringing Seraph Friends to aid their victory. This Seraph Friend, your most humble servant, has returned from battle with news of great import.' No, reaction, Kenato Orin was irritated that his dramatic entrance had been wasted.

Impatiently he reached out to the king's mind. *'Alfin, old friend, there have been many deaths to defend Heaven this day!'* He spoke as if to an empty room. The space within the king's consciousness where he and Alfin would normally meet was hushed. Half memories as if from Alfin's sleep hung from the walls like faded tapestries, images of Lorcan sitting beside his king prominent among them. Was he with Lorcan then? When Kenato Orin and Alfin had communicated by thought before it had been like two armed encampments carefully exchanging messengers with what must be shared. Were Lorcan and Alfin experimenting with a willing communal body? *That could be fun, if a bit scary.* Reflecting Kenato Orin's own thoughts images of Candice rippled around the empty hall of the king's mind. Kenato Orin smiled to himself. Alfin had learned a new trick then, leaving his physical self behind and sharing his spirit with Lorcan in his body. Kenato Orin looked around the quiet halls of the king's mind.

'Well, be a shame not to make the most of the opportunity.' As a demon he had possessed people before, it was part of the job. But that was always a struggle because the mind of the victim never fully accepted the intrusion. This felt far more illicit as he opened Alfin's eyes and saw his own seraph body stretched out before the king on the marble steps. He felt Alfin's face slowly stretch into a smile. *'This will be fun!'* His attempt to leave the throne was shaky but since no one could see him he stomped around a bit trying to get used to the limb length, the muscles, the skin moving under silk. Kenato Orin found it was actually quite easy when you didn't have some idiot shrieking at you about being violated.

By the time he got to the end of the avenue he had decided to find Alva, all thoughts of the furies gone. He pulled open the doors and stepped through quickly, closing them behind him, pleased at how smoothly he had managed it.

'Fool! I said I wasn't to be disturbed. Let no one in on penalty of death till I return,' said Kenato Orin, trying to suppress a grin. The guard looked shocked.

Kenato Orin was aware he hadn't got the words quite right – Alfin sounded slurred. He walked away singing one of Vatn's sea shanties, trying to get used to someone else's tongue and lungs.

Kenato picked up a bottle of wine on the way to ease his throat, it was already sore from his misuse. He used his free hand to open the door to the queen's apartments, taking in the group sitting round her, despising them all. Weak angels that would deny Alva her warrior path, surround her with lace and flowers rather than allow her to be at the forge where her true talents lay. The queen herself, stretched out on a divan wore a diaphanous golden dress that accentuated what was beneath rather than hid it.

'Why?' he asked out loud before closing Alfin's mouth. *Why dress like that when none of these angels have had a lustful thought in their long lives?*

'Why, husband?' asked Alva, looking puzzled, her eyes shifting from the bottle back to her king.

'Why have I not treated you as I should? Loved you as a wife. Worshipped you as a woman.' Kenato Orin swaggered a little as he came further into the room.

Alva flushed a little. 'We are not alone.'

'You are right,' Kenato Orin almost shouted. He waved the bottle at the other angels. 'Out, all of you, out!' He sat on her bed, unaware whether they had followed his instruction or not. Uncaring. He could only see Alva, an eyebrow raised, a small smile on her lips.

'And how much wine has brought you to this conclusion?' she asked.

'Almost none. I had some wise counsel from our Seraph Friend, Kenato Orin.'

'Now I know you are drunk.' Alva laughed.

Kenato Orin was taken aback, but pride could not trump lust. Not when he was so close he could at last feel her warmth in the air. 'For all his … bluster, he spoke some truth. That I have loved you from the moment I first saw you. I have desired you like no angel could. That the king may not just rule with the queen but would be her lover too. I will celebrate your body as your husband should. I say this truly to you.'

Alva looked deeply into Alfin's eyes and for a moment Kenato Orin thought he was discovered.

'You seem in strange spirits, but you do speak with heartfelt truth – though I had not hoped to hear such words from your lips before the world ended and us with it.' She glanced around the room. One lute player still loitered by the door. 'Out, as your king demands!' she shouted.

Chapter Ten

Naomi stood at the start of the pier looking out across the waves to check the progress of the ship beating against the wind. She looked back at its goal, the rock arm thrust out into the sea protecting the bright woodwork from the ocean breakers. All in the harbour was calm. The smell of freshly cut wood struggled with the salt of the sea.

'You've done a good job here, Jasper,' she said.

The stone elemental crouched, one hand on the granite. 'It's still ringing. The angels shall know its new.'

'It doesn't matter. And they are in shock, they might not notice.'

'I'm not convinced. And nor will they be. Why did you pick here to make a new harbour?'

'It's the closest point from the Setting Sea to Heaven. By sending the angels to the city of Meena's Mountain rather than here, it means we have a chance to find out what's going on before they do. Can you get the dryads to weather the wood anymore? That's more of a giveaway than the masonry.'

'That's the best they can do.'

'Okay. Tell them they're off the hook unless they want to hang about to meet the angels.'

Jasper went off to release the reluctant workforce. Naomi watched the three-masted caravel for an hour as the ship made her way past the islands. Hundreds of gannets dived into some unseen shoal of fish, folding themselves into giant white arrows as they pierced the waves. A sea eagle stole the catch from one of the gannets and flew onto a cliff to enjoy her spoils. At last the ship was close enough that she could hear orders being shouted from the deck to the masts. Gulls echoed the calls as they circled above in the hope of fish. Naomi glanced back at the shore where Jasper paced, his hands behind his back, unwilling to risk his weight on the newly placed wooden planks of the jetty.

A shout came from the low forecastle of the ship. 'Naomi!' Vatn waved to confirm the source and then returned his attention to the crew as they furled the worn yellow sails and with practised ease brought the *Notorious* in at a slow walking pace to rub up against the hay bales on the pier. Ropes were thrown and tied off.

'Vatn. Good to see you. May I come aboard?'

'Always.'

Naomi climbed nimbly up the netting to stand on the dark decking, despite her armour. They held each other's arms a second while the seamen continued to work around them.

'I think the coronation was when I last saw you,' Naomi said.

'It must be four hundred years or more since the Celestial Thrones were built,' said Vatn.

'You would find Heaven much changed since the last time you were here then. After the surprise attack of the furies, the king and queen are now of a mind to bring the peace of Heaven to all the world.' She searched his face. 'And then this. Can it really be true?' A great coffin of black ebony was held in place by runners fixed to the decking. White lilies had been piled around its base and birds of paradise added splashes of brilliant yellow and green.

'Come and look for yourself. The lid is not fixed, for after we prepared his body the remains have not become corrupted.' Naomi and Vatn stepped to the casket and Vatn lifted the lid. Amid silver satin lay Lorcan with his eyes closed and his hands laid across his chest. There was no doubt. Naomi felt weak for a moment and caught herself on the dark side panels. She wanted to reach in and shake the angel awake.

'Tell me what happened.'

'I was out hunting on my own far out in the Setting Sea. There was a great storm, the kind of thing you would find difficult to believe if you live on land, with waves higher than cliffs and lightning all about. Even in my dragon aspect I was being rolled by the swell and punished by the wind so I was of a mind to go deep and try to weather the hurricane below. As I took my last breath before diving, I heard a voice cry out above all the roar of the tempest. I knew the sound, of course. We all heard Lorcan rally in our war against the tendua.'

Naomi smiled at the memory but could not move her gaze from the coffin.

'So I searched among the tumult knowing that every moment would be too long for Lorcan to be in the water.'

'He feared it so much.'

'The sea can be so fickle, killing one while sparing another though they stand side by side. Lorcan sealed his own fate by knowing it.'

'How so?'

'He never learned to swim. Even in those conditions it could have given him time. Given me time. As it was, I found him just below the surface, bare, stripped by the waves of everything including his life. I held him in my mouth and struck out for shore. Orca gathered around me, somehow knowing that I could not defend myself, so I fled with the storm above me and teeth below me. For more than a night and a day I swam as hard as I could hoping that the heat of my breath would bring him back to us. But when at last I hauled myself ashore and placed his still body on the sands I was sure that his spirit would not return.'

'And how did he get there? There must have been a ship.'

'Conditions were such that I could have passed within yards of one and been unaware.'

'But you found Lorcan,' Naomi said.

Vatn smiled a little. 'Would you not find him on your vast steppes? Just as Jasper would if Lorcan were buried in the roots of his mountains? You would find Lorcan because you had to.' He looked up at the sky and took a breath. 'What is the plan now?' he asked Naomi.

'We are to take his remains to Heaven. The angels should have been here to accept him, but they mistakenly went further down the coast.'

'Still the plot weaver, Naomi?' said Vatn, guessing correctly that she was the source of the misdirection.

'I am the silk maker, Vatn, unravelling the plots that others make into something beautiful. I needed to hear the story first. I'm struggling to understand by whose hand was Lorcan slain.'

'I assumed it was you who killed him,' said Vatn, pointing at the new harbour. 'And all this was just to see how solid your alibi was before the angels turn up.'

'What reason would I have to kill Lorcan?'

'We would only find out in a hundred years when your plans slot together like some dwarfish engine,' Vatn said with a sad smile.

'Lorcan's death is so badly timed. He was loved by all as the quiet voice of non-intervention, yet still the king's favourite. There was so much riding on him being a brake on Heaven – to lose him now just seems too cruel, even for fate.'

'I'm sure "this is so badly timed" was just what he was thinking,' admonished Vatn.

Naomi pulled herself up. 'No, you're right. We mourn the loss of a friend.' She drummed the side of the coffin absently. 'There is nothing else to your story?' Vatn shook his head. 'No hint of another ship, either sunk under him or somehow leaving him behind. No magic? Was he bound?' Naomi was struggling to think how Lorcan could have been taken so far from land.

'If he had been bound then such was the force of the waves that it freed him before I found him. Or he freed himself, but to what end? Abandoned at the end of the Setting Sea? Unable to swim.'

'The only issue then the angels could have would be to explain how you were a dragon at that moment.'

'All the men of the *Notorious* are clear that we brought the body aboard at sea rather than from the shore. A day later they were caught in the same storm so crew and ship both show the marks of their trial.'

'Good, but the boat should be away from here as soon as possible. Away from angelic inquiry.'

Vatn rolled his eyes but nodded.

'They come!' Jasper's shout took Naomi by surprise.

Naomi and Vatn moved to the guard rail of the *Notorious*. Such had been their haste that the Heavenly Host had lost any semblance of formation. A great stream of white from the south scattered across the green downs like fog in the sun. The giant horses powered across the grass at a pace nothing on earth could surely match. At their front were the two sisters Aileen and Arden, close enough now for their grim set features to be seen. Naomi slapped the woodwork, frightening all but a couple of the gulls.

'No time to prepare. Everyone must play their part,' she said loudly. Then more quietly, 'It has been said that you and Aileen were … friendly, for a while.'

Vatn looked resigned rather than surprised. 'We were, but I began to realise that her interest was in the mechanics of magic. Not, sadly, in me.' One of the herring gulls chuckled. Vatn looked from Naomi to the bird. 'I stand with you and see spies everywhere.'

Another, smaller, host appeared from the north pushing with all speed towards the harbour. From the iridescent armour this could only be the king and queen with Kenato Orin trying to outrun the cavalry in an attempt to be first. But the sisters only pulled up to a walk when they mounted the pier, forcing those on the wall to risk falling into the sea as the riders recklessly advanced. Arden seemed reluctant to dismount while Aileen rested her hand upon the rocks of the pier, looking at Jasper for some hint of confirmation. In silence they vaulted the side of the *Notorious*. Both went to the still open casket. Aileen simply looked in for verification while Arden draped herself across it and wailed. Aileen joined Naomi and Vatn. Realising the race was lost, Kenato stood his ground and waited for Alfin and Alva.

'It is hard to believe he is really gone,' Aileen said flatly.

'It is a shock we all feel,' Naomi confirmed.

'Thank you for your message, Naomi, that landfall was in fact here.'

'Yes, sorry for the confusion. Meena's Mountain seemed the most likely place for the *Notorious* to seek harbour. Only later did I discover that it would make landfall here.'

'Indeed. I did not know this cove existed. Such an ideal spot, so close to Heaven.'

'Indeed,' replied Naomi. For what felt like an age only the horses' laboured breathing and Arden's crying broke the silence. The southern host was regrouping along the shoreline.

'Vatn, friend, I would know more of what happened,' said Aileen.

Vatn retold his story with a little more detail than before, his eyes never leaving Aileen's face. Naomi wondered if he was searching for some hint of affection, but certainly Naomi could see none. She wished she could be elsewhere but dared not move because she needed to be sure the tale matched the first recounting. Aileen nodded at each of the points and Naomi followed her gaze as she looked around the ship. Only now did Naomi notice that the mizzenmast was temporary, a spare spar bound to the wrenched root of the original, the gaps in the rails where things had been dragged off the side as waves tore anything mounted from the deck, the tired sailors, one with an arm in a sling, another nursing a splinted leg.

'It must have been terrible,' Aileen said. 'What fate meant that you were the closest? His Majesty has too small a presence at sea.'

'I would have it that we were closer,' Vatn said looking upset. 'To have held him with the warmth of life still in him and feel so powerless.'

The angel nodded and looked at her sister. 'It will be difficult for us all. I would speak with your crew. They shall travel with you to Heaven.'

'No, they must be elsewhere. The *Notorious* is only jury-rigged and must sail now while the seas are sated.'

'Their lives are nothing in balance with this terrible act. I must be sure of their innocence, for if they were complicit, I will hunt each of them down for seven incarnations to ensure Lorcan receives justice.' Aileen's fierce gaze swept the crew. Naomi had heard rumours of avenging angels striking down babes and maidens for some crime in a previous life. But to hear it said out loud as a natural state of affairs took her aback. Was Alfin aware of such acts in Heaven's name?

'Would Lorcan wish such "justice"? Would the king?' Naomi asked quietly. 'I doubt that such slaughter would encourage Lorcan back to this world, should he so choose.' Naomi's eyes flicked from Aileen to her mournful sister.

Aileen drew herself up, her attention focused on the elemental. 'You always sow doubt, Naomi. Ever the enemy of certainty.'

'I am no one's enemy.' A moment out of time passed as the two faced each other. Naomi saw only the angel's eyes while the sounds and sights of the world faded away. She wanted to argue about the power of repentance, forgiveness, of the creativity that divergence can spark. But she saw no room for debate and any talk of forgiveness would just be taken as a plea of the guilty.

'A ship's carpenter can only do so much,' said Vatn. 'Enough lives have been lost. I would see them safely back to the Islands of Dogs.'

'Have you made any preparations?' Aileen directed the question at Naomi.

'We have built a carriage to carry the coffin and have eight white oxen to pull it. I have two thousand deinony ready to act as escort,' Naomi said.

'There will be no need for your kobold cavalry.' Aileen wrinkled her perfect face in disgust.

'Then I shall withdraw and you can take Lorcan home.'

'No, you must come. If we cannot have the crew, you both must come to Heaven.'

Naomi felt slightly panicked. 'I cannot. I was told I would go to Heaven on three occasions by a queen of Sestola. The first in triumph, the second in joy and the third in sorrow would complete the charm. I had planned not to go a third time,' Naomi explained.

'But your sorrow has already occurred, it lies before you. There can be nothing more unhappy than this. You shall come to Heaven, wither you will it or not.'

'I have two thousand deinony close at hand,' Naomi restated firmly. If Aileen wanted a fight, she could have one, thought Naomi, losing control for a moment.

Aileen's eyes widened at the rebuff. 'But the king and queen have arrived, we should attend,' she said matter-of-factly. She went to try and coax her sister from Lorcan's side.

Naomi prised her own hand from the railing; she had crushed the wood beneath.

Though Alfin looked weighed down with grief he greeted the three spirits more warmly than either of the sisters had. The queen already looked lost in her own sadness. Kenato Orin seemed as uncomfortable as Naomi had ever seen him. These were events outside his control. If it were not so dangerous for them all she would have enjoyed the sight.

'We should walk along the harbour away from prying ears,' said Naomi.

They all nodded. Naomi led the way beside the king while Kenato Orin walked beside the queen with Vatn, Aileen and Arden following loosely behind. Jasper was hindmost of all, but Naomi alone was aware of his heavy tread along the path he had built. As the stonework curved out into the sea the difference between the wave-battered wall and the calm waters behind became more noticeable. Five minutes of silent procession brought them to a small lighthouse and as far as they could from their respective followers.

The queen spoke first. 'We found your dead mount on the road about a mile from here, Kenato Orin. You must have continued at pace to be here ahead of us still.'

'I could not contain my anguish,' said Kenato Orin solemnly.

'Or wait to see your handiwork completed.' Arden spat out the words.

'Kenato Orin did not kill Lorcan,' Naomi said calmly.

'Says the Procurator of Hell defending a demon.' Arden's voice was a higher pitch than usual.

'Demon?' asked Naomi, surprised.

'You may be able to deceive the king, Seraph Friend, but we know your exact disposition. Lorcan knew it and died for that knowledge. These demons have whispered in our ears too long. We must cast them out, destroy them! My lord king, what can I do to lift the scales from your eyes?' shouted Arden.

The queen looked shocked, though Naomi thought that surely through all the centuries Alfin had by now mentioned the origin of his seraphim – in which case she was playing the scene falsely. Naomi felt unsettled by so many departures from the norm. There was a game being played here that she had previously been unaware of.

'Is this your true nature? Has all of our friendship been false?' demanded the queen. The master of debate seemed rooted to the spot, dumbstruck.

'You were losing the war,' Naomi pointed out. 'The tendua were erasing you from history. Alfin knew he needed to change the odds. We were your only chance of survival. In our first meeting, before I became corporeal I picked the seraphim from the king's thoughts as a reasonable story to explain our presence.'

'Deception from the start!' said Arden.

'Only in our appearance, not in our intent. We fought and died by your side to save you. That was real. We met our side of the bargain, paid in blood.'

'And that should not be forgotten,' said the king. The sisters seemed brought up short by that. 'They came when we were at our lowest. Seraphim, elementals or demons, they were instrumental in our survival. Lorcan determined their true nature somehow but accepted their help and their friendship without question.'

Naomi relaxed a little.

'Thank you, your majesty.' Kenato Orin bowed low, which the king barely acknowledged.

The king looked specifically at Aileen and Arden and continued. 'Do not allow others to turn your grief into a wider unnecessary war. We are here because a life closer to us than all others has been torn from our side. We feel certain that his murderer is close to us. That they stand here in our presence. They, individually, must pay the price.'

Kenato Orin, Naomi and Vatn took a step away from the four angels in unison.

'I did not kill Lorcan,' Kenato Orin said. He looked at Vatn. 'You were always after Arden and yet she could not commit herself to you while Lorcan lived,' he exclaimed.

'No, as ever, you have the two sisters confused. Arden loves, loved, Lorcan,' Vatn said. 'Aileen and I have been companions at times without, as far as I'm aware, Lorcan's blessing or hindrance. But even so, why would I go to the trouble of taking Lorcan to the edge of the world to kill him, only then to bring him back and tell everybody I had done so.'

'It is the perfect cover story,' Kenato Orin declared. Vatn glared at the Seraph Friend.

'Vatn may be many things, but he isn't stupid,' said Aileen. She allowed herself a half smile at the hidden dragon. 'No, the most likely killer is the procurator.'

'What motive would I have for that?'

'Hell seeks to undermine Heaven at every turn. Without Lorcan, Heaven's ability to resist Hell is severely weakened. It is in Hell's interest as well as its nature.'

'Hell's interests, as you put it, are best served by Heaven staying behind the walls we built at your request. Lorcan was the greatest supporter of the status quo. There was no advantage in his slaying,' Naomi said.

'They are all guilty, my lord,' said the distraught Arden. She drew her flaming sword.

Cutlass and katana leapt from their scabbards. Kenato Orin conjured his hammer from the air. Jasper joined them, his great obsidian axe held in both hands. The queen and the angelic sisters fell back, swords glittering in the sun. There were cries of alarm from the shore.

'Peace.' The king looked at each of the demons in turn. Naomi felt a brush across her mind; Alfin had clearly learned a lot since they first met. The king was there with her in her mind asking a simple question. So confined, within her own head, there was no time for deception. Naomi had a simple and honest answer. Each of the accused stiffened in turn. 'We were mistaken. The killer is not here.' In his confusion the king looked briefly aged, while the queen seemed distraught, possibly even fearful, though Naomi could not think why.

'As I said,' Kenato Orin confirmed. Naomi saw he was trying to look hurt while pointedly ignoring the vitriolic stares from the sisters, the queen and Vatn.

'But we cannot continue as before.' Alfin nodded to the sisters. 'What you have said is true, Lady Arden, Lady Aileen. Kenato Orin shall be banished from Heaven and henceforth known as the Prince of Hell.'

Naomi felt a flush of resentment. Alfin was going beyond his remit, but there were greater wheels in motion here.

'My lord king! Do not cast aside my service,' pleaded Kenato Orin.

But Alfin held up his hand for silence. 'Do not fear, Kenato Orin, we will not put you apart, you who have proved so able against our enemies. We shall also harness the might that Naomi has so carefully and covertly nurtured. We have seen that there are now many wild forces in the world that choose to reach out and strike at our heart. The furies are but the boldest of many. As the old chancellor said all those years ago, "Who could stand against the seraphim and angels united?" Together, in our new guise, Heaven and Hell must find common cause, contrary to these small gods and new powers, and tame them.'

Chapter Eleven

Grerr didn't know what the road to Hell was made of, but it was as smooth and black as it was the day the forces of Hell had made it over a thousand years ago. That meant the horse had to be shod more often, but Grerr was happy with the extra cost because the other result was that he could work in the back of his caravan while the horse pulled him along. The animal knew where he was going, one of the reasons Grerr had hired him. The combination of the flat surface and the knowledgeable dray had allowed him to make things that he thought would sell while also making progress.

Working by the light of the rear door meant that Grerr generally didn't see people until he had passed them. The number of pilgrims tended to drop after each tollhouse on the road to Hell. It had reduced a lot after he had left Lust Tollhouse, but here with only Absolution ahead before Hell itself, there were even fewer travellers on the road. Some talked to him but rarely with much energy. At the start he had offered a few a space in his van, but after what had happened at the Wrath Tollhouse he had taken to just waving in response to any requests.

A little old lady stood at the side of the road looking at her pack in disgust, her hands in the hollow of her back. Her clothes hung loose around her, the style an echo of more glorious days. She looked up and caught Grerr listening to her stream of obscenities. 'You could offer an old lady a lift,' she said.

'I thought that wasn't the point of a pilgrimage,' said Grerr.

'Twenty miles a day for a hundred days – I now fail to see any point. Don't make me run after you.' She had to raise her voice a bit as the dray plodded on.

Grerr considered for a moment. 'The horse will want to charge more.'

'Blame the horse. Bloody dwarves, typical.'

Grerr frowned. Why would he stop? For the same reason he always bought the first round in a bar – to prove everybody wrong. He walked to the front of the van and shouted, 'Whoa.' The horse pulled a little to the left and looked back. It didn't say anything, but it didn't have to. Grerr returned and dropped the steps that folded out to just above the black road. The lady had already covered most of the distance to the caravan.

'Hey, lady, you've forgotten your pack,' he pointed out.

She reached up and patted his knee.

'Good lad.' She climbed up past him and sat down in his favourite chair, looking around the interior. 'Nice place you have here. I was expecting something with more stonework.'

'Doesn't work so well when you're on the road,' Grerr explained. 'I'll go get your bag then.'

'Lovely. What does it say on the side of your van?'

'It says anything repaired or mended.'

'Is that what you do?' she asked. She sighed as she kicked off her sandals and buried her toes in his carpet.

'Yes. Anything with leather and wood and metal I can make good. Weapons, of course, but toys are my real joy. I make models that ...'

Her eyes had already closed. Grerr dropped down the steps and made the short walk to collect her rucksack. By the time he returned, her gentle snoring was making the plates rattle in their pegs. Grerr pulled up the stairs and went forward to the driver's seat. The horse was still staring at him.

'I'll pay. Go on, don't look at me like that.' He lit his pipe and tried to relax but already the heavy breathing made him miss his own company.

A couple of hours later the sun was sinking down to the hills that become more numerous around the highway. A stream followed a wood to where it met the road, flowed under a bridge and away to Grerr's left. Having checked under the bridge with axe in hand, Grerr brought the van up and unharnessed the horse. The grass here was thigh deep and lush green so no need to break out the oats tonight. Grerr got the stove going while the lady went downriver for her ablutions. He had rice on the boil and bacon ready to go in the pan. The old lady returned and observed the evening flare as the invisible sun set, highlighting the tops of the Mountains of Hell as they stretched from horizon to horizon.

'I've not seen them before.'

'Orin's Teeth? It is said that he threw them up to make sure this road would be the only way into Hell after the High King took Heaven on its righteous war. It is also said that they are so tall the sky above is black even in daylight.'

'Is it true?' the old lady asked.

'The last bit is – I tried climbing them once. No dwarf has mined there. Imagine the riches of digging where no one has ever delved before. But even a dwarf has to breathe, and I had to come down.'

'Not really my thing.'

'Diamonds, rubies? No, looking at your eyes I would have thought something warm around your neck would have lit the room with grace in your …' Grerr hesitated.

'In my day?' she finished for him. The old lady laughed. 'Maybe I should commission you for such a necklace? If I could make heads turn now that would be a good test of your skills,' she said without bitterness. She refilled the pot for tea and climbed back inside the van to put it on the stove. After their meal she pulled a heavy blanket from her pack and arranged her bed away from the camp.

'You might want to sleep inside this evening,' Grerr said. The woman looked up at the clear sky and back and him appearing unconvinced. 'It usually rains this close to Hell. Naomi's tears, they call it. She mourns for all the souls of those who died without reaching peace.'

'Is that true?' the old lady asked again.

'It's more likely she mourns for all the sin taxes they didn't pay. But she will shed her tears tonight. I'll make my bunk up first where the bench is. You should have enough room to kip on the floor.'

As they sorted themselves out the old lady raised a question. 'How do you know so much about Hell? You're not some sort of ghost, are you? Sucking the life from lonely pilgrims. I have heard of such things.'

'Did you enjoy the bacon?' Grerr enquired. The old lady nodded. 'No ghost then. I trade. I fix things. Although the demons of hell can do many amazing acts, they still can't make mechanical items like locks, music boxes, toys for the children.'

'Children?'

The pan had boiled so Grerr filled the teapot with hot water and stirred as he talked. 'Children of all the cooks, cleaners, gardeners and soldiers. Hell is a whole city on its own.' He strained the tea and handed a cup to the old lady.

'And all enthralled to Hell. It's funny to think of all these folk, all the people I've met on the road, as bad people.'

'They must be. All the good citizens are making pilgrimages to Heaven. Are you one of the bad people?' Grerr asked.

'The standards in hell seemed a bit easier to reach,' the old lady acknowledged.

'Hell knew what they were doing when they aimed for those with low aspirations. They also serve the most fabulous cold beer there. There is no beer in Heaven.' Outside a wind had sprung up making the van, warmed by the black heat of the stove, abruptly cosy rather than stuffy. A lost soul howled past the caravan on its way to Hell. They looked at each other.

'I'll bring the rest of the stuff in, shall I?' Grerr reached for his axe as the first heavy drops hit the roof above.

'Yes please,' said the old lady. 'What about the horse?'

Grerr looked around the inside of his home critically. 'I don't think he'll fit.'

In the morning the sky had returned to its usual blue, but the fuller stream proved how many tears Naomi had shed in the night. The horse insisted on a brush down and a couple of apples before being hitched back up but refused to share what he had seen. As they made their way along the road it started to climb and wind a little through the gently rising landscape. Orin's Teeth were more visible than they had been before behind rolling hills of grasslands dotted with single trees or small groves. But they had the highway to themselves.

The old woman sat on the driver's board and Grerr sat behind her. Her shoulders and spine rounded forward so that her neck had to curve back to keep her head upright. He tried to sketch out in his mind what shape a necklace should be, but had to resist the urge to ask her to turn this way and that so that he could get a better picture of how she moved. Eventually she stood up, and Grerr heard her bones crack as she stretched as best she could.

'I would curse this old body. But I have earned it and must live with it. That is what all this is about. Acceptance.'

'Absolution,' corrected Grerr.

'I would settle for acceptance.'

'We all still feel young inside,' he said.

The old lady laughed. 'Oh, you have no idea.'

They were approaching a farm and Grerr slowed the horse down. There were a few decent-sized fields of barley, but it was the cows in green pasture that had caught Grerr's eyes. He went into the back to find a small wooden pail with a lid and a pouch of tobacco.

'I like milk in my tea and I've never met a farmer yet who didn't like a smoke.' He dropped down and started up the rough stone path towards the homestead. A muscular kobold split wood by the side of a barn.

'Good day.' The kobold swung his axe with easy strength. One blow to each log.

'Good afternoon.'

'Would you be interested in a trade?'

'I might be.'

'Tobacco for fresh milk?'

'You would need to ask the farmer. I'm just earning my meal.'

Grerr looked from the kobold to the stack of firewood piled up to the house's eaves. 'He must be expecting you to eat a lot.'

The kobold rested on his axe. 'I think he has a high regard for his food and a low regard for the hired help. "Double for a blue-skinned dog", was his position, if I recall correctly.'

'Bugger him then. Bring some of that kindling you have so ably split and you can share our supper tonight. I have some spicy pork dumplings I've been saving. And now I know why.' The kobold purposefully put down the axe and quickly reappeared from the barn strapping a sword belt around his waist and pulling on a pack. The pair gathered two armfuls of wood and returned to the van, walking briskly enough to arouse the old lady's suspicion. The kobold stopped at the sight of the wagon, reading the side then looking at the horse and the old woman.

She did not smile. 'Which have you stolen, the milk, the wood or the kobold?' she asked.

'The wood. The kobold brought himself and the tea will have to remain black,' replied Grerr as he scrambled up onto the caravan, but the dray remained unmoving.

'He's a stubborn sod,' said Grerr. 'Wants to increase the fee every time we meet someone.' The kobold put his gear aboard but walked to the front by the animal's ear. He spoke quietly enough that only the horse could hear. With a snort it shook his head and started forward.

The kobold easily pulled himself up as the driver's board passed. He met two sets of raised eyebrows. 'It is enough he said yes.'

They drove on through the rolling hills; the grass rippling silver in the wind chasing ahead of them made Grerr feel he was moving backwards. Since the view never really changed from hour to hour he wondered if they were in some sort of loop, just driving round in vast circles on the smooth black road. The kobold sat on the back footplate. The old lady seemed more drawn into herself than she had before, sitting by the stove and occasionally singing quietly.

'Well, with you two chatterboxes on board I was worried that I would miss the birdsong,' he said to the silence.

The old lady looked up and focused. 'I'm sorry. I just realised it will be a full moon tonight.'

'Is that a problem?' asked Grerr.

The old lady drew breath to answer but it was the kobold who spoke. 'Cavalry coming. We should pull off the highway.'

Grerr tried to see past the kobold's crest. 'You have good eyes. How long have we got?'

'Depends how hard their captain is pushing them, but fifteen minutes. Maybe less.'

Grerr looked for somewhere they could safely take the van onto the verge and pulled up. The kobold slid off the board and prostrated himself on the ground facing the oncoming traffic.

The squadron closed quickly. Grerr had seen deinony before, but still found their easy two-legged lope fascinating. Their arms like short wings were held out to the side for balance. All this troop had brilliant blue feathers with orange on their chests and the insides of their legs. The kobold riders wore lamellar armour of the same colours, and long lances with the pennants of Hell fluttered high above like a third vertical wing. The kobold drew his sword and left it on the road in front of him, and pressed his snout ridges hard into the earth, exposing his neck.

'Honourable sirs. Please consider releasing me from this life.' The troop swooped round the wagon and Grerr could see now the long tails stretching out far behind as a counterweight to the deinony as they ran. They whirled around for a moment looking for possible ambush before the officer came to a halt. The deinony hopped from foot to foot, those terrible claws tapping forward.

'Hadrati of the Fifty-third Lancers,' said the prostrate kobold.

The captain dismounted. 'The Fifty-third? You are Colonel Hadrati who fled his post in Heaven's war against the Nirakar?'

'I was.' Still Hadrati maintained his position, face down in the road.

'How many of your regiment died in that first engagement?' asked the officer drawing his sword.

Grerr felt the old lady stiffen beside him. 'We could do something,' she whispered.

He frowned at her. 'We could die quicker.'

Grerr found it was hard not to stare at the deinony. They had a single giant claw on each foot, and the three fingers protruding from each wing were longer and sharper than daggers. Their teeth could crush armour and bone. Deinony were hell's swift death incarnate.

Grerr focused back on the conversation.

'So, in all, two hundred and twenty-one.'

'But you survived,' said the captain.

'I did. I was knocked unconscious and my deinony carried me from the fight.'

'So why surrender us your head?'

'Lord Jasper spoke on my behalf at the courts marshal and no fault was found. But since I had asked to live rather than accept an honourable death, a condition of my discharge was that I should offer my head to any kobold officer who wished to add my crest to his saddle.'

The captain came over to the prostrate colonel. Grerr couldn't read kobolds at the best of times and both were speaking so formally he wasn't sure what would happen next.

'I remember the story. You were sent by Heaven to make war against the Nirakar, but the supporting angels did not arrive until too late. They also failed to tell you the Nirakar could change their shape.'

'They assumed we knew.'

'Angels assume a lot and then are dismissive when we fail.' The captain turned smartly and remounted his deinony. 'I have no need of your ridges, Colonel, and it is after all a holy week. But be warned – younger officers may not recall your name and will take you up on your offer. I would leave this road.'

'I seek absolution,' said Hadrati easing his head back up.

'It is less than a day's journey. You should find it tomorrow.' The troop of deinony swept round the caravan gliding as easily on the rough grassland as on the highway, and then flew east towards the Teeth.

The kobold picked up his sword and sheathed it. He walked to the front board. 'Please accept my apologies for delaying your voyage,' Hadrati said.

'That's okay. Wasn't sure if we were going to be taking you to the next tollhouse or burying you here,' said Grerr.

'You have to do that every time you see another kobold?' asked the old lady.

'Yes, that was my instruction.'

'No one would know if you didn't,' she pointed out.

'I would,' said Hadrati simply.

'Well,' said Grerr, prodding the horse. 'Let's see if we can get you safely to the end of the road.'

Chapter Twelve

They made camp while it was still light, carefully out of sight of any patrols. Since Naomi seemed to have cried herself out the previous night, they elected to make camp beside the van under the clear blue sky. Grerr and the kobold sat down by the fire to cook the dumplings, cabbage and the flatbreads that Hadrati had made that afternoon in the wagon. But the old lady couldn't settle and wandered between the griddle, the van and the stream they had stopped beside. Only when the food was served did she finally join them.

'These are the best pork dumplings I have ever tasted,' said Hadrati. 'I think it's the brush with ...' He stopped, and the flatbread used for mopping up the grease waited forgotten in his hand. Grerr was looking at the huge full moon that was rising in the south-east over Orin's Teeth into the still blue sky. Hadrati nudged the dwarf and nodded at the old lady. In the last light of the sun and the first lunar glow she seemed taller, straighter, her heavily lined face smoothed out, lips fuller, eyes clearer. She untied her grey ponytail and as she shook out her hair, it tumbled chestnut over her shoulders and back. She looked down at her disordered clothes and rearranged herself. Their new companion smiled sadly at them both. Grerr felt his heart break.

'It would seem that Naomi thought it would be funny to hold back her tears tonight. Truly she can be the cruellest servant of Kenato Orin,' she said; the reedy quality in her voice had gone. 'I'm starving – give me another serving.' She was met with stunned inaction. 'Give me another serving and I will tell you my tale.' Grerr went to the back of the van and returned with two bottles of wine while Hadrati refilled her plate. He tipped out the young lady's water, poured the wine for them all and sat down looking expectant.

'Once there was to be a wedding in Sestola. It is the most fortunate and ancient of cities with good soil and mountains all about.'

'I have been there,' said the kobold.

'Hush,' said Grerr.

'The prince of Rondoni was to marry the most beautiful woman in the princedom and it was no surprise that she came from Sestola, where all the womenfolk are famed for their looks as well as their knowledge. They had met when the prince had been travelling by the city on his way to the campaigns in the north.' Grerr shot Hadrati a warning glance. 'Here it was he saw Valentina arranging a rescue around a collapsed bridge. You see, the army had many heavy wagons. The bridge was old. Anyway. The prince had come back to find out why his forces were late and there was Valentina, soaked to the skin, organising his soldiers on what had to be done. It was said that he proposed to her then and there. But the prince wasn't stupid. He found out who she was first, her family standing, and thought that all in all it would be a good match. Then he proposed.' The lady took a slurp of her wine now and Grerr refilled her wooden cup in case her tongue would seize up for want of lubrication.

'So now the wedding was set. There were twenty bridesmaids all dressed in satin of the most exquisite turquoise. They had green garlands woven through their auburn hair, and white satin bands around their waists. As they pranced through the groves the evening light fell and they would have driven the air from your lungs with the strength of their dark eyes.'

'Amber, you see I was right,' said Grerr.

'But fairest of them all was Valentina in her white dress, a simple gown that hugged her figure, with short sleeves that showed her arms, chestnut brown after the long hot summer. Her long tresses were held back with a band of white flowers. Even among all the finery it was as if the sun only shone on her. But the prince, for whatever reason, was distracted, if only a little.'

'By you,' said Hadrati.

'Yes. By me. I met the prince in the build-up to the wedding and he was charming and funny and his eye tended to linger a second too long. On the day of the ceremony there was a time after the vows when Valentina had to go with her mother to sacrifice at the altars of Heaven and Hell. Valentina was very serious about these things and would complete the whole ceremony, both sets. You casually called those Orin's Teeth, for example. Valentina would never be so careless. She would always refer to him as "the Prince of Hell, the Lord of Elementals, King of the Kobolds, Seraph Friend, Freer of Dwarves, master of debate. All hail Kenato Orin, whose harnessing of magic has brought joy and hope to all the peoples of the world". With that in mind, all at the celebration knew it was going to take a while. Rather than allow the guests to get bored, the prince called for dancing and music and all the bridesmaids and their beaus enthusiastically agreed. Much wine was drunk, though we were yet to be called to the feast. The full moon rose above the celebration and I caught the prince's eye. This time he did not look away. He was particularly charming and we ... well, you can imagine the rest.'

'On his wedding day?' asked the kobold.

'I think princes are meant to be like that,' Grerr said.

'So Valentina returned to the meal with the blessings of Heaven and Hell, the happiest woman in the land. But her mother knew that something was wrong. Princes aren't that good at dressing themselves and the hooks and eyes on turquoise dresses are so easily missed when pulled on in a hurry. Valentina's mother cursed me that no man would look upon me with lust again as long as I live. But the prince said that was too cruel, given that he had forced himself on me. Which he hadn't. So Valentina's mother relented sufficiently that on nights of the full moon I would return to myself, as you see me now. Though if I ever lie with someone, that too will be taken from me. So an old woman fled from the feast, dressed in satin of the most exquisite turquoise, but she had lost her white band and no one knew her.'

'Hah! The man walks away free while the woman takes the punishment,' said Grerr.

'Oh, the prince is not free. Valentina made his life a torment from that day forward. And will do so till his end, which shall not be long. My sister nurses her wrath and it is terrible.'

'Your sister?' asked Grerr.

The young lady held out her hand in greeting. 'Viviana, sister to Valentina. Valentina, Princess of Rondoni, Sestola and future queen.'

They sat watching the moon clear of the mountains now, bright enough to drown out all but the greatest stars. They kept the fire going although the night was not cold.

Grerr shared out three cigars and they added three red points of light to the white ones above. 'Do you think Naomi deliberately held back the clouds tonight?' he asked.

'Tomorrow I hope for absolution,' said Viviana. 'Perhaps she knew I had to tell this tale before I could go to the tollhouse.'

'I have met the Procurator of Hell,' said Hadrati. 'Naomi is undoubtedly the cleverest of all the demons. I would not be surprised to hear that she arranged matters so.' The kobold took out a silver flask, out of which he poured a clear liquid into each cup. 'This is made from raspberries from around the orchards of my villa. You have seen why I seek absolution. Dwarf, what is your story?'

'I have none.' Grerr twitched after drinking the kobold's spirit but held out his tumbler for more.

'That is not true,' Hadrati said. 'On the side of your caravan you have written "Free Dwarf" in runes only known to those who have been to mines below Holme.'

'And I take it you have been there. Is there anywhere you haven't been or people you have not met?' asked Grerr, but he smiled under his beard as he spoke.

'I have had three hundred years, I think, to be sent hither and thither by Hell. Which is why my crest makes a tempting prize. But you, you are a free dwarf, which I take to mean that you have escaped from Heaven. At least that would explain the horse.'

'What's the horse got to do with it?' asked Viviana.

'It is a horse of the Heavenly Host.'

'Is it? How do you know?' Grerr frowned.

'The unblemished white coat. A carapace like polished quartz, the clean joints, the mane purer than the driven snow. The pride in his stance, the wisdom in his eyes. He still bears the scars where the straps for the barding cut around his flanks. Every inch of that powerful body shouts Heavenly destrier to anyone with vision to see. Surely you must have seen this was no ordinary carthorse.'

'He was big,' Grerr admitted.

Hadrati dropped his hand to his side to cover the top of his sword. 'My pommel. Describe it.'

'Lapis lazuli, I think, nicely cut. Mounted in wire that looks like red gold, but that would be too soft so probably an alloy. Something heavy to help balance the blade. Sharkskin for the grip and—'

Hadrati interrupted him. 'So you are not blind. But when you looked upon the horse?'

'He was big and willing to do the job for a reasonable price.'

'You are his perfect companion.' The kobold laughed. 'A stallion that has so clearly escaped from Heaven has forfeited his life. For who would choose to leave Heaven but a sinner of the lowest order? There would be a great reward for his return, I would guess, if you took him back to the angels. I cannot imagine another who would not consider questioning his presence.'

'I need to ask.' They both looked at Viviana. 'Why *free* dwarf?'

With a frown at the kobold, Grerr answered. 'When the King of Heaven came to the dwarves of Holme and asked for our machines of war, we charged. This is what dwarves do, and our price in gold made the Queen of Heaven very angry. Her angels were risking their lives to make the world a safer place.' The kobold laughed at that, but Grerr continued. 'They fought the giants, the Furies, the Danavas, and we dwarves made them better armour, sharper swords, engines that could tear down walls at a distance. All to ensure the angels did not die so easily. And as is our wont, we negotiated our fair due. But Heaven moved against Holme, cut down our Chancellor and enslaved our people so that the queen would never again have to use her gold for something as mundane as commerce.'

'But some escaped?' said Viviana.

'Yes.'

'How did you?' asked Hadrati.

'I made the great wheel upon which they broke Titania and wept. Naomi saw my grief and petitioned Kenato Orin that the King of Heaven grant my freedom, since the fairie were now crushed. The king was happier in those days, and drunk, and had won his war, so he agreed.'

'You are the reason Kenato Orin is called the Freer of Dwarves.'

'The Prince of Hell is prone to many failings and exaggeration is one of them. There was only one freed on that day. We should get some sleep. Tomorrow you reach the last tollhouse before the Gates of Hell.'

The three raised their cups. 'To absolution,' they said in unison.

'And a cold beer,' added Grerr.

The horse had pulled up and none of the caravan occupants thought to move him on. Their gaze followed the road as it wound down to a wide plain where the highway was blocked by a massive red stone castle with four square roofs of terracotta tiles, each rising one above the other. A single pilgrim walking towards the barbican was the only hint of scale – those gates could allow a dozen carts to enter abreast. Grerr eyed the overwhelming masonry critically; other than the crenulations around the top of the first level there was no means of defence. He said so.

'The walls don't go very far either side of the gate,' Viviana pointed out.

'We could go round and not pay the toll?' Grerr thought, out loud.

'You both have to remember who is running this venture,' said Hadrati.

It took them nearly an hour to come off the hills and approach the edifice, by which point there was no misjudging the size of the castle. Another hour brought them to the shade of the massive but terminated fortifications. There was a black sign by the huge archway that read: 'The Tollhouse of Absolution appreciates your prayers and supplication but the financial cost of upkeep of the tollhouse and the final monastery are very high. Please consider a voluntary donation (one gold coin) as you pass through.'

Grerr stepped down and put in five sovereigns, one each from Hadrati and Viviana, one from the dwarf and two for the horse. Travelling through the shadow of the massive arch they could now see the monastery with its grand nave on one side of a cloister formed by long low structures connected by covered walkways around a central well. Pilgrims and monks moved with a sense of purpose from building to building.

'Having arrived with pilgrims this time I was expecting something, you know, with trumpets and a choir, a bit of a fanfare,' said Grerr. Faced with anonymity the party shattered like a dropped pot, each member drifting out from the barbican, alone in their own thoughts.

Grerr watched as a giant of a man with a red complexion and generous belly stopped to look at Viviana. He crouched down, hands on his knees, so that he could look her in the face. 'Hello, little old lady,' he said loudly and cheerfully. His prayer beads hung almost to the ground. 'Are you lost?'

'We have just arrived. Through the gate.' She pointed at the massive tower rather superfluously.

'Oh, right.' The priest stood up. 'Did you explain to the porter you were new? Did he not give the introduction and orientation welcome presentation?'

'There was just an honesty box,' said Viviana, making her disappointment clear.

'Krin, he is a useless sod.' The priest thought for a few seconds. 'If you're hungry the refectory is that way. If you're thirsty the pub is over there. Dormitory is the other side of the quadrangle if you're tired. We can do things like the library later. This is a holiday week so things are a little bit at sixes and sevens at the moment, but we'll be running some meditation tomorrow, which should get you started on the road to Absolution.'

Viviana was still staring at him. 'We have reached the end of the road to Absolution,' she pointed out.

'Ah yes. But this is the start of your spiritual journey. And its end,' he added as if he was not too sure of the script. 'I'm new at being a monk, but if I were you I would begin with the pub. You tell Eldrun that Sandi sent you and she'll see you right. Things always look better after a beer.' He paused and looked closer at her and then around her. 'Little old lady, what's your name?'

'Viviana.'

'Viviana, greatest of the sorceresses of Sestola, sister of Queen Valentina?'

'She wasn't queen when I left, but she was never one to hang about, so I wouldn't be surprised.'

The priest looked round the courtyard. 'That would mean this is Colonel Hadrati of the Fifty-third Lancers.' Grerr felt the opposite of anonymous as the priest's gaze settled on him. 'And there is Grerr the Artificer. Well, this is marvellous. But where is Roch, the High King's stallion that famously fought for his own freedom after the fall of Okeanos?' asked Sandi.

'He's pulling the caravan,' said Viviana.

'You're kidding! No, no you're not. Okay, you guys, go to the bar – the first drink is on me. I need to send a runner to the gates.' The priest almost skipped away.

Greer and Hadrati gathered at Viviana's side.

'He said we should—' she started.

'We heard,' said Grerr.

'Everyone heard. He thought you were deaf. Or simple,' Hadrati added.

'If my hips still worked I would have kicked him. But apart from the shouting he seemed friendly enough. And you get your beer, Grerr.'

A large flock of jackdaws noisily swept over the monastery and flew east.

'Duty before all else. I will go and sort the horse out and see you in there,' Grerr said.

The stables seemed the most efficient part of the tollhouse and even had a covered area where he could leave his caravan. He walked back over to the bar feeling that this was a little more like his memory of the place.

The Pilgrims' Rest was cool and dark after the bright sun above the road to hell. A scattering of people were in the pub and one woman with flame red hair stood behind the counter. Hadrati and Viviana had picked a table in the corner and had lined up three glasses of beer. Grerr hauled himself onto the stool and sat looking at the beads of condensation running down the side of the glass. He followed them with his finger, aware that his two companions were watching him rather than starting their own.

'You going to drink it then?' Viviana asked. 'Or just watch it?'

'I am savouring the moment,' said Grerr.

Hadrati nudged him. 'We should leave,' the kobold said quietly.

'Absa-bloody-lutely not,' said Grerr with feeling.

With the smallest of movements Hadrati indicated that the dwarf should look behind him. Trying to turn casually, Grerr saw a small figure speak curtly to the barmaid. She then picked a table and sat looking around the place as if she had accidentally rested in a cesspit. She pulled off a very broad hat and laid it carefully on the wood, rearranging the chiffon ribbons around the crown. The barmaid watched the new pilgrim for a moment with pursed lips and disappeared into the back room.

'Is that someone I should know?' asked Viviana.

'Be glad you don't. That's Archangel Aileen,' said Hadrati quietly. 'She normally only turns up when there is some avenging to be done. Some poor sod discovers he's narked Heaven in a previous life about a minute before she pronounces judgement and despatches him off on his next life journey usually with a few of his family and friends for company, just in case. Which is why we should leave,' he repeated.

Grerr hunkered down in front of his beer. 'I'm a free dwarf. I am *the* free dwarf. I'm not going to spend my life running every occasion I see an angel.'

'How many angels have you seen in the last twenty years?' asked Hadrati.

The dwarf twisted slightly so he could look at the angel again. 'Including this one?'

'Yes.'

'One.'

'There you are then. You don't have to spend your life running. In fact, don't run, you will just trigger her prey response. You just have to walk away, quietly.'

'I've never walked away from a pint and I'm not starting now.' Grerr sat in grumpy silence determined not to move but no longer enjoying his beer. The priest they had met by the arch seemed to be in earnest conversation with the angel. Grerr drank from his glass and then closed his eyes.

He woke with a start. Hadrati and Viviana looked as if they had been pulled over the side of a trawler and dumped back in their chairs. Water lapped across the table towards him. His hand went to his protective amulet, a small silver anvil around his neck. Then he looked down to the flooded floor but his own feet on the bar of the stool were still dry. This was no ordinary leaky roof or flood hit room. He hit Viviana who was closer, she coughed up a mouthful of water and looked around sharply.

'Water magic? Drown us in our sleep? Bloody angels,' she said looking towards source who was arguing quite loudly with the priest now. They both tried quietly to rouse Hadtrati but without success. Grerr dropped onto the water covered floor. He could not get enough purchase to carry the kobold so unceremoniously dragged the unconscious body away with the old lady guarding his back. The other customers, closer to the angel, appeared past the point of rescue. Hadrati had been right, the best defence against angels was distance. The sounds of a full-scale fight between the angel and her demon hosts covered their retreat.

Chapter Thirteen

Alfin sat back in his saddle. He had been so focused on getting the Angelic Host across the steppe undiscovered that he had seen only threats and dangers. Now thanks to Aileen they had seized the House of Absolution, cut Hell off from any external support and still had the element of surprise. He looked around at the sheer mountains that dominated the approach to the Gates of Hell, the sky had become a narrowing band of bright blue overhead. The cliffs rang with the shouts of the Heavenly officers and the earth shook as the great host stamped their feet in response. Griffon vultures circled high above, their curiosity raised by the unexpected army taking up positions among the great pebble banks by the river.

Dominating Alfin's view though was the road to Hell itself. It was an unnatural thing. Smooth and black, it wound through the mountains and down towards the captured House of Absolution as if drawn on this plane by some great otherworldly hand. A small troop of Heavenly cavalry meandered back down the black road towards the army. They hailed the vanguard as long-lost friends and were confused that their welcome was not warmer.

'Hail, brothers. We thought not to see a friendly face in this strange and forbidding land. It is a place of confusion. We have wandered for an unknown duration and then found this angel also bewildered and abandoned on the road. We hoped to bring her to safety, though we knew not where that was,' said Bale, Captain of Horse. Alfin had despatched him only two hours before to reach the gates and herald the High King's imminent arrival. Now they milled about, looking bemused. They seemed hesitant, aware that they had somehow failed but unsure as to what the task might have been. A lady slid to the ground from behind the captain. Though she landed as lightly as any of her kind she seemed to be struggling to maintain her apparel and her dignity.

The Captain of Foot led her closer to Alfin. 'My lord. The messengers have returned.'

Alfin was aware of the whispers and doubts that clung to every shadow the army cast in this most troubled landscape. It was more important than ever to play the role of High King of all the Heavenly Host. He must appear untroubled by the petty doubts of hell. His voice was clear and loud. 'And what was the response to our demand?'

All of the newcomers looked befuddled. 'Demand? I know not, dread lord. We were travelling through these cursed mountains and became lost. Confused.'

'Even you, Lady Cora?' asked the High King.

She curtsied and looked at her feet. 'I remember talking to you, my lord, and setting off earnestly on a mission. But every buckle I had seemed to break, and with each failure the message became more difficult to grasp until I found myself bereft of all but my cloak when these good gentlemen came along and found me.'

'But could not find your wits, which seem to have been left somewhere on the road.' Alfin sighed. 'Having also lost their own.' *Naomi can still misdirect the best of us*, Alfin thought. In the silence, all became aware that Arden wept by the remains of her sister Aileen, the outline of whose body was distorted by shattered shafts of blood-soaked wood. The report was that Aileen had extinguished Eldrun but Sandi had somehow dealt a fatal blow before being dissolved by the angels magic.

All the host bowed low as if a heavy stone had been dropped onto an awning. At the centre rode the High Queen, to whom even the High King must lower his head.

'What is the result of our embassies to our goal, husband?'

'They have come to nought, wife. The web of deceit around the Gates of Hell has grown strong since the last time we were here.'

The queen nudged her mount forward. The caparisoned horse cast blue-white starlight on those who were close. The ambassadors were either dazzled by the light or too addled to remember to bow low. The queen's crop slashed a sharp red weal across Lady Cora's cheek. 'All you had to do was follow the road.'

'I did, your majesty, and it led me to your side,' said the angel in confusion. Alfin watched a single drop of blood form at the deepest point of the wound. He thought it brighter than any ruby and far more precious. A wail cut across the group. The queen looked accusingly at the Lady Cora, whose face wrinkled in uncertainty as she evidently struggled to think of proof that she was not the source of the wailing.

'What is that dreadful noise?' asked the queen.

'It is Lady Arden, the sister of the Lady Aileen,' said Alfin, who had mounted his own horse, which was as brightly bedecked as his wife's.

'I don't understand. The Lady Aileen died to ensure our complete surprise.'

'Though she slayed many spies and servants of hell, including a fire spirit, she was killed by a stone elemental in the House of Absolution. It is the first death in her house for an age.'

'Well, many other houses have not been so lucky.' The queen looked down at her equerry. 'Go and tell her not to make such a fuss. It sets a bad example for the troops. Makes it difficult for them to focus.'

The equerry scurried away and Alfin met the queen's gaze. It was difficult to think of her as Alva now. Since the death of Lorcan she had changed, become colder, more distant. But then he thought that loss had hit him harder than he would have thought possible. Perhaps they both changed from losing Lorcan, more than either would have given credit before, or admitted to each other.

'I suppose it will just have to be us. Inform your commanders to prepare for battle,' the queen said. In the years after the funeral procession back from the *Notorious* all the queen's will appeared to have been focused on solely delivering total victory to Heaven. Perhaps today Alfin would see Alva return.

'And you instruct your spellcasters to protect our minds. The walls themselves seem to be closing in around us,' he said quietly so only the two of them could hear.

The queen looked carefully at the rock horizon. 'They are not.'

Alfin and the queen detached themselves from the great camp. The road wound across the floor of the valley so that at each turn the sun caught their petal armour. Only those in the inner gardens of Heaven, or their close personal guard, could have had such a protective gift from the queen. It was said that it took the queen a year and a day to make each suit and that no weapon could pierce it to the wearer. Certainly this pair had put that to the test many times and here they rode, unmarked, sparkling like a brace of wet beetles as they wound their way up the last three hundred feet of ascent.

The two riders paused for a moment looking across the vast parade grounds that lay before the Gates of Hell. Centuries had passed since either of them had visited the gates as honoured guests. Alfin noted that the highest towers now scraped the clouds above them and went on far above, casting shadows down upon the mountains. In all this immense scale the only feature was a small canvas pavilion on the far side of the grounds. The bright colours of the fabric rippled and glittered in the restless mountain air. Beneath this multicoloured shelter sat an old woman with a neat fire, a kettle and a low table. Her grey hair was pulled back in an unruly bun, but her silk wraps were padded and looked warm. As the two angels approached, the old woman struggled to her feet and bowed low, cursing her knees as she did so.

'All hail Alfin, High King of the Heavenly Host who has conquered all the peoples between the snow and the sand, whose ships have sailed to the three edges of the world and returned with tribute or left their islands smoking ruin.' The old woman bowed again, a little easier and with less profanity. 'All hail Alva, High Queen of the Heavenly Host whose forges produce the bright spears of the angels that dazzle the enemy as they pierce. Whose swords, it is said, will slice stone as easily as flesh. Whose petal armour protects all who are blessed by the queen who makes it. All hail …' She trailed off, theatrically looking beyond the two for more angels. 'I am surprised you have come by yourselves. I would have thought you would send some heralds first. You know, some heralds and buglers, build it up a bit. Did you bring your own bugle?' Naomi returned to her seat behind the table and poured herself some more tea while Alfin tried to hide a smile. The steam curled up into the still air, which was cool despite the sun.

'As you know, we have been sending emissaries all day. They get lame or lost or forget their mission. With great strength of mind, the Lady Cora got closest, but all her clothes fell off and she was forced to return in shame,' said Alfin.

'I was pretty sure that was the look she was going for anyway. Would you like a cup of tea?' The High King of the Heavenly Host dismounted from his glowing charger and walked across the dusty flagstones to the pavilion.

'Thank you, Naomi. And speaking of doing things personally, why is the Procurator of Hell guarding the gates herself? Where are the great kobold battalions that have made this square tremble beneath their marching feet and the mountains echo with their ten thousand voices?'

'Today is their holiest of days in a holy week. They are at home with their families praying and fasting. What unfortunate chance that has led you here on this week of all weeks so that you must miss their show of strength.'

'Indeed, what were the chances?' They both smiled this time. In momentary fear of opprobrium Alfin glanced towards the High Queen but her gaze was elsewhere.

The sun was lower now and highlighted the weather-worn features of the old lady's face. Her fingers, no longer nimble, chased a biscuit round the plate, which she then offered to the High King. The eyes of his old friend were clouded. She seemed to wither in proximity to Alva's ageless beauty and vigour that time could not lessen.

'I am sitting outside so that I can enjoy my tea and biscuits in peace.' She shook the dish again to try and entice him to take a piece of shortbread.

'To frustrate an emissary of the King of the Heavenly Host carries the penalty of death,' said the Queen of the Heavenly Host from her high horse. Her gaze was focused back on the army and she murmured all the while she was not speaking aloud.

'Death?' said Naomi, projecting her voice to carry up to the still mounted rider. 'They were not frustrated, ma'am. A trifle tired perhaps after their long walk. A stone in the shoe, a buckle poorly secured. Death seems a poor reward for those that make such small mistakes.'

The queen's gaze swung round and fixed on the old woman, who pulled her shawls to her as protection against the cold, or possibly that stare.

'Tell your master that he must come beyond the gates to our camp where we have gathered all those that have laboured in the triumph of Heaven.'

'Few have laboured as hard on your behalf, ma'am, as has the Prince of Hell.'

'Which is why he still lives. But he must come to the camp and swear fealty to us both, and deliver offerings that we consider appropriate from a vassal to his lord. Even Hell must be seen to bow low to Heaven itself.'

'And if the greatest of all celestial champions does not wish to take part in this glorious celebration of Heaven delivering peace in the world?'

'Then he and all who choose to act against Heaven will pay the penalty.'

'Which I am guessing is death?' asked Naomi. The queen nodded. 'I liked you more when you were running through the woods singing and playing.'

But the queen had returned to watching her forces and muttering. 'The host is truly troubled in this place,' she said, perhaps to herself.

Alfin had watched the exchange, drinking his tea. 'You were there, Naomi,' he said. 'Millennia ago when even I was young and you were fresh to this world, unbowed by age as you are now. They were the dark days when our forests were burnt and angels' flesh eaten.'

Naomi looked down the valley to the host of bright spears and the shouts of the angels as they marshalled towers and other dwarfish equipment towards where they stood.

'And look at you now, all shiny and militant. I sense you already believe Kenato may not come.'

Alfin smiled sadly at Naomi. 'We know your champion better than we would like. He will not come,' he confirmed.

'But I must ask.' Naomi sighed, putting down her cup with shaking limbs and struggling back to her feet.

Alfin held out his hand to steady his aged friend in case she fell. Close now, he was horrified to see the pattern of liver spots on her translucent skin as it shifted without resistance under his strong fingers. He caught the smell of silks worn too many times. He took a step backwards out of the open pavilion and into the fresher air. Had they really been apart so long? he asked himself.

Naomi crouched and leapt into the air; her shawls wrapped around her as she became a hooded crow climbing up high above her camp against the great black Gates of Hell.

Chapter Fourteen

On Naomi climbed up the sheer walls that ascended taller than mountains, over the deep empty parapets where kobolds should have stood guard had it been any other day but this, and down into the tree-lined avenue of the palace. The path wound through pools in smaller mimicry of the great road outside only now bound by pink granite and marble. A crocodile snapped lazily at her as she skimmed the still surface of the rose-scented water.

The hooded crow flew through the corridors and up in an arc, her wings held outstretched so that she dived through the window of the antechamber of the Lord of Elementals without a single flap of adjustment. With a flurry of feathers and dust she landed outside his bedroom. Naomi smoothed down her shimmering green dress that stretched over a full figure and shook out her long red hair. There was no point being beautiful around angels, they never noticed. Old, though, threw them every time. The doors of Hades were carved from black marble with brass studs a foot apart rising in fourteen pairs above her.

Two cynocephali only slightly shorter than the doors crossed their great axes as Naomi approached. 'The boss said nobody was to disturb him in his rest,' said one in a voice like gravel.

'Especially if it was you, Guv,' said Maat.

'I warn you – I am in a foul mood. This was meant to be a special day. Years I have been nudging things so that four heroes would meet here, be here today. They were going to rival Meena in the great deeds that were to be done. And now that has been trashed by Heaven stamping in and demanding attention like some giant toddler breaking things that are beyond its comprehension.'

'Still can't let you in,' said the first guard.

'Look, I'll keep it simple,' said Naomi. 'Either I walk through the doors, or I pull your heads off and then I walk through the doors.'

Maat raised her axe and indicated the other guardian should do the same. 'Can you knock before you storm in, please, Guv,' she asked, clearly trying to form her face into something approaching pleading.

The Procurator of Hell hit the door with a sound far greater than that small pale fist should have generated. She knocked again then pushed the great bronze doors open so hard they continued to swing round and they clashed against the granite walls.

'Hail the Prince of Hell, the Lord of Elementals, King of the Kobolds, Seraph Friend, Freer of Dwarves, master of debate. Hail Kenato Orin, whose harnessing of magic has brought joy and hope to all the peoples of the world.'

She stepped into the gloom and in rotating her hand created a flaming brand that, she thought, set her hair off rather nicely. On top of the great bed lay a huge jelly version of the master of debate. A limb or two poked out seemingly at random. It was hard to tell how many were in there but one furry ankle and a hoof she recognised by the bracelet of stars illuminated part of the scene.

'All hail, Candice, Guardian of the Night and the terrors that lie there for the unwary.' There was a rather muffled set of hails in response. Naomi walked over to the conglomerate. The tangle of bodies quivered, some of the five or six in there were still in the throes of ecstasy. She could see the features of the Prince of Hell slowly coming into shape.

'Naomi? I didn't expect to see you here.'

'Your guards said as much at the door.'

'Are you planning to join us?'

'I think there are enough of you in there already.'

'Then why are you disturbing us, my trusted procurator?'

'There are quite a lot of angels outside buggering up my plans and they want a word with you.'

'Well tell them to get lost.'

'I have managed to lose quite a few but the king and queen are still able to walk through my misdirection with ease.'

The face became much sharper although there was still no discernible neck. 'The High Queen of the Angelic Host is here?'

'She who forges the sparkly spears, slicey swords and waterproof armour? Yes, she's here and she doesn't look very happy.'

'What do they want?'

'You to swear fealty.'

'Bloody angels! We had a deal. We delivered our side.'

'More than.'

'Exactly. He got to be king, I settled for prince. Why would I swear loyalty to them now? I'd rather die.'

'I think that's what they're counting on. They brought an army. Looks like they've trashed the Absolution Tollhouse too. I can't reach my people there.'

'How did we not know?'

'Sadly, they've taken the power we showed them and made it their own. Seems to be mostly water based. Maybe Vatn is helping them, maybe they didn't kill all the naiads. Not before they talked anyway.'

'Bloody angels,' said the Prince of Hell in a more resigned manner. 'Go and stall them while I get myself sorted out. And make it unpleasant for them in the meantime.' Like a slowly retreating tide, the body of the Freer of dwarves drew itself in, leaving bodies exposed to the air, crabs unexpectedly looking for pools. With a pop, Candice became free in her favourite guise, horns, bat wings and satyr legs, all in matching pink. She looked the essence of desirability and danger.

'Go get the kobolds back,' Kenato Orin told the newly released Guardian of the Night. She frowned her perfectly shaped eyebrows that ran back to her hairline. 'Yes, I know they won't like it, but they have grown strong and rich for five hundred years and today is the day we get our due. Naomi, go round up the hounds of hell.'

Naomi's skin grew black until only the burning edge of her was visible and her red hair burst into flames. Her torch became a long whip with three tails, each leaving a trail of fire as they writhed and twisted of their own accord.

She strode out, snapping at the two cynocephali. 'There is to be war,' she said driving all the elementals greater and lesser before her back to the Gates of Hell.

Naomi flew directly above the host as it dragged itself up the last few miles of the highway. They had to move slowly because Naomi and the other elementals were swirling around the head of the army tearing up the road and anything else they could find and hurling it at any unprotected angel. Those too small for rocks were summoning up angel-sized dust storms to blind and choke them. The darkening clouds above were lit every now and then by a blast of magic that leapt from the host. Mostly it would miss its target but it occasionally caught a slower-moving troll or ogre and tear the body in half. In return, blasts of flame from the fire elementals hit exposed angels while demons pulsed back darkly.

Naomi was impressed; every angel that could carry a weapon must have been down there. The High King had gambled all on this action. There was nothing in reserve, they had held nothing back. If Naomi had known the Heavenly Host were going to do this, she would have stirred up a lot of resistance in the less pacified provinces just out of habit.

Kenato Orin had come to the wall to see the great Angelic Host for himself. He had taken his favourite form, that of an ogre with tusks jutting both up and down, his top knot glistening with oil, a hammer larger than an angel held lightly in his left hand. The right hand rested on the stone crenelations as he looked out at the army advancing up the valley. Naomi knew Kenato Orin well enough to think he would be flattered at all the attention, hence the grandstanding in front of both Heaven and Hell. She tried to reach the minds of the angels as she had done to the scouts on this sunny morning that seemed so long ago. But the army's thoughts were closed, the only image that of a gate shut and barred.

She flew down to Kenato Orin on the wall. 'I came to find you. The angels appear to be controlled,' she said as the hooded crow, skipping sideways along the stonework. 'They seem to have mastered the full gamut of magic.'

'I have found the same. It's the High King,' said the ogre. 'I am sure of it.'

'Well, you taught him,' Naomi pointed out.

'I thought I had been channelling through him. Didn't realise Alfin had worked out how I was doing it.'

'Heaven is fighting with an anger I have never felt before. It is …' She paused. 'It is unnatural for an angel to hold such hatred.' Naomi felt her concentration break as an earwig ran along the wall. Maybe she had used this bird form too often. 'I know it's more your thing than mine, but I always thought possession works best when you can tap into the desires of the person. This is so at odds …' Naomi left off her sentence and snatched at the unfortunate insect but missed.

'Naomi?'

'What?' It really was hard to resist going for the earwig again.

'I think you hit on it. Go back and tell the demonic horde to keep the pressure up until the kobolds arrive.'

Naomi hesitated. 'They're killing us when they get a chance.'

'Keep your distance then but throw everything you can at them.' A snowflake drifted past his nose and his breath now clouded in front of his face. 'Is this you?' he asked.

'Mmmm?' said Naomi, her beak full of wriggling earwig. It was gone in a gulp. 'You said to make it unpleasant for them. The tendua always did well in the winter,' she observed as Kenato Orin gazed out across the battlefield. He was always better at this than her, being a demon, so she hitched a ride as she had so many times in the Heavenly Wars. His essence reached out, picked on one gated mind and battered its defences aside.

Naomi watched Kenato Orin look around the mind of Bale, the Captain of Horse, as casually as she would inspect a horse at a fair. The angel was dying. His body was broken, hanging among the branches of a tree. Through his eyes, Naomi saw the snow swirling around him and his blood dripping to the pavement far below. She was aware of the captain's thoughts. Bale had been working on a sonnet, and now it would never be sung. His memory was fading like the words he loved, and the poet captain wondered how he had come to this point. Naomi heard

Kenato Orin provide the answer. He had been misguided by a demon, Kenato Orin whispered, forcing him into this unnatural war against hell. The captain screamed the danger to his men below. Like the last flare of a guttering torch his life force failed, and Naomi joined Kenato Orin as he hopped to the mind of a spearman on the ground clutching to control his bright spear against the sudden chill wind. The king's possession was still there, but rather than try and override it, Kenato Orin just nudged what the angel saw, so the features of his compatriots distorted, angelic on the outside but dominated by Hellish forces within.

Naomi saw the spearman come to the realisation that his age-old companions were being marched like puppets to their doom at the Gates of Hell itself. 'The captain is right, you are all possessed by demonic powers! This is not who we are,' he cried, striking out at his comrades.

Kenato Orin jumped again but Naomi focused on a different angel and offered the same 'obvious' explanation. With each jump it became easier to seed the fear among the troops until panic gripped the entire unit and the only unified aim was to be away from each other and away from the black gates. Kenato Orin returned to the wall and Naomi with him.

Candice was at the gates with around a thousand kobold cavalry. 'This was as many as were near readiness.' The deinony looked magnificent in their bright red metallic plumage and yellow leather harnesses. They hopped from leg to leg, flexing their oversized claws, clearly keener for the fight than their riders. Candice swirled her fingers in the feathers of one of the mounts, lost in the pleasure of the moment. Not all demons were made for war.

'Go out there and smite any angel you can see!' said Kenato, eager for bloody chaos.

'Alfin is in the vanguard,' said Naomi. 'It represents an opportunity, though slim.'

'We await your orders, my dread lord.' The kobold officer looked between the prince and the procurator.

'Kattarati. Assemble your lancers in a wedge around me.'

'Where do we aim for, oh most terrifying of all the deities?' The kobold was calm. Naomi was impressed. This kobold knew he was going to take a thousand light cavalry and charge the largest Heavenly Host the world had ever seen. He must have known they were all going to die.

'For their head, Kattarati. Get me to the High King and we might win this.'

The kobold laughed, his tongue a shocking pink among the blue-armoured hide.

'Then we will get you to the High King. It is a fitting way to end my service. And they shall sing the song of Kattarati for a hundred generations.'

Naomi was thinking that that song would only be sung if they won.

Kenato Orin looked back at her. 'Procurator! You have seen what to do. Go multiply the fear.'

Naomi chuckled. Proof, she thought, that she had been working with demons too long. She flew off to recruit the more quick-witted elementals and demons to try sowing confusion further. Behind her the Gates of Hell opened and out pranced a thousand deinony, their small wings spread wide in anticipation of the sprint to come. Kenato Orin, his demons and the heavier elementals trotted with them, filling up the bulk of the wedge the riders formed.

As the arrowhead burst out of the snowstorm, Kenato and those with him would surely have died under the relentless hail of arrows, but Naomi and her sharper cohort were ahead of them, touching minds with fear and suspicion. Whereas disciplined ranks should have been pinning the kobolds to the earth with three feet of ash, all was anarchy. Lesser angels were shouting at each other, breaking into groups and in some cases rolling on the ground fighting. Only one unit stood solid though around the banner of the High King, and there Naomi could make no progress. Kenato, loping along easily with the cavalry, pointed at the ordered ranks with his hammer and shouted the charge.

The lancers parted the distracted angels like a longship slicing the waves. The deinony to the prince's left was hit by a spear that fastened rider and mount together, but they were packed so tightly that the half-dead beast was carried with them, flailing out with those terrible claws as they passed through the ever-thickening army. One of those claws caught on an angelic commander and it tore the wounded mount out from the formation. With a surge the two riders behind closed the gap. The deinony were breathing hard now.

Naomi wondered if Kenato Orin had started the charge a little too early as they slammed up against the king's guard. Kenato Orin with nowhere to go stepped up on the back of Kattarati's deinony and launched himself from above onto the guard. Kenato Orin struck his hammer with all his might and although the helmet did not fail, the neck below did. The angel seemed to pass his spear to his killer then collapsed where he stood. Kenato Orin turned the weapon in his left hand and drove it above the collarbone of the nearest foe. The bright spear glowed scarlet with angel's blood and Kenato laughed.

In reckless slaughter, the demons came into their own. Pennant lances and flashing claws were all around Kenato Orin and Naomi did her best to protect his back with a stolen lance. Kattarati had pressed on to the very centre of the formation and the kobolds around him fought with a purpose never seen before. The kobolds could now tell the song of Kattarati – how at the last even the king's own guard broke under the fearless charge and terrible talons. Kattarati's lance touched the very breastplate of the High King. Any hopes Naomi had for what might have been were destroyed as a gout of Heavenly magic torn the kobold to confetti, whisked away by the howling wind. Kenato Orin was a step behind and hit the king so hard that only the crush prevented the king from falling. As the king struggled to regain his footing, the Prince of Hell released his hammer and took on his full demonic aspect. His fiery hand reached for the High King and brought him close to the flame-fanged mouth. Even the great strength of Alfin's will failed to hold the Prince of Hell at bay. For a brief moment Naomi saw Kenato Orin in the King of Heaven's eyes, and it was terrible.

Chapter Fifteen

Naomi stepped through the destroyed gate of the king's consciousness and after the struggling pair. The hall of Alfin's mind was a fitting place for the fight before her. Vast forested arches led off to passageways of learning, each one greater than a normal lifetime could encompass. Paintings hung upon the wall showing key moments from his past that he had relived again and again in his dreams. New images played across them as Kenato Orin, Prince of Hell, and Alfin, High King of Heaven, fought for supremacy.

'Kenato. Yield!'

'Yield! I have you and you say yield?'

'My body will be safe. You cannot pierce my armour made by the hand of the queen. I am surrounded by my guards. Yield and we spare the lives of those blinded by loyalty to you. Heaven is merciful – do not have them throw their futures away.'

'And me?'

'You have laid hands upon our person and your life is forfeit.'

The Prince of Hell's laugh rang round the king's skull and Naomi saw the presence of the angel lord shrink back.

'You summoned us. You brought us into this world. We made a deal. I gave you the power you prayed for.'

'To save my people.'

'I'm not questioning your initial motives.'

'You corrupted me!'

'It's a nice lie to tell yourself. Don't forget I was there with you. I know that once you got the taste for magic you enjoyed it. Novelty value, I suppose. Once the tendua were beaten you wanted that thrill again. The cruelty you showed in Istria? That was all yours. Those poor dryads, how well they burned.'

'Lord of deceit. That was you!'

'It really wasn't, Alfin. I just gave you the ability to express it all so much more instantaneously than before.'

Naomi watched the images and the feelings washed through her and around them all like some giant animated gallery. They shared the vision of the platform high above the throne room of Holme and the death of Ranvaeig, the reincarnated Dwarven Chancellor.

'Speaking of which, how did you learn how to possess an entire army?' The angel was retreating through his own memories and Kenato Orin pursued him. 'Relinquish control of the host now or I shall destroy you.'

'I will not. I cannot. Alva, save me!' he cried and abruptly she was there.

Naomi swore but she went unnoticed as the yearning from Kenato Orin flooded them all. Since they were all within the same sphere, all were shown the prince's strong desire.

'Release my husband!' Her voice was a mountain torrent cooling down his burning passion.

'And forfeit the advantage? Alva, there is still time. A field of gold could be built, homage paid by hell, a clarification of dominions could be found.' Kenato Orin's argument fell away. By the nature of their communion, he shared his looking upon her spirit and his thought of the first moment he had loved her with them all.

The king had been playing with his new-found ability to leave his body. Kenato Orin, ever one to seize an opportunity, made love to the queen. She was amazed at the renewed desire in her husband, not realising that now he had in fact truly abandoned her. It was a revelation to Naomi how Kenato Orin changed; his opportunistic passion became genuine and was returned a dozen times over. Meanwhile the king had discovered a spiritual bond with Lorcan as they combined in his body. Just as Kenato Orin drew Alfin ever further into war, Lorcan refreshed his spirit, reminded him of how the angels had been.

Alfin had been so wrapped up in this new venture that he failed to notice the alteration in his wife. Fearing discovery, Kenato Orin had withdrawn then, leaving the queen distraught by Alfin's apparent sudden change of heart. But Kenato Orin had sneaked back whenever he was certain the king's mind was elsewhere, creating further confusion and chaos.

From Alva's reaction, Naomi judged that at least some of it was new to the queen. Her counterattack faltered as she saw the betrayal there that she had already suspected. The communal space meant that Naomi could experience Alva's anger at a court that had been so keen to tell her of the moments shared between the shepherd and the king. Naomi felt Alva's humiliation bubble up to reveal the vision of Lorcan and his doom. Naomi saw the most beautiful of angels weep, bound and weighted, being loaded onto an angelic ship, the malevolent sea waited impatiently at the bottom of the slippery steps.

At this discovery, the king cried out at the fate of his love, drowned by the queen, and the three tumbled on, all reeling from the thoughts they now exchanged. Naomi wasn't going to miss this for anything but still tried to keep one eye on Kenato Orin's presence in the real world, his abandoned hammer even now inches from the ground. The swirling snow slowed almost to a stop, freezing all life from the valley.

The Lady Arden joined them, and the interruption highlighted that there were now five in a space, however kingly, only designed for one. The Lady Arden, most adept of all the angels in the art of magic, bore the blood of her sister Aileen on her body and in her mind.

'My queen, without your protection the army is fragmenting, falling into confusion,' she said. Her statement faltered as she looked around the hall of memories, of lust and passion, betrayal and bitterness. Her own love for Lorcan blazed bright, his tragic drowning now explained.

'Go and support them until I can join you,' shouted the queen, but the Lady Arden looked in honest wonder at the tableau before her. For thoughts are not linear but roll over and over in the consciousness and so were re-presented to all in attendance with different details and emotions to the fore. All were distracted by the lovemaking scene, in which from Kenato Orin's perspective he had replaced the king with his own ogre's body. It was difficult for Naomi not to enjoy the Lady Arden's evident horror at seeing the High Queen of Heaven mounted on the Prince of Hell, the lord of deceit, master of lies, and quite clearly enjoying herself.

'How can this be?' Her sense of betrayal and loathing swept up all present. Her impression of the queen was distorted by this terrible revelation, the murder of her unrequited love and the careless dismissal of her sister's death.

The king wanted to speak but his thoughts were a battlefield and he had no control of the powers struggling within it. All saw the High King of the Heavenly Host who had liberated all the peoples between the snow and the sand exchange the purest form of devotion in the mind of Lorcan. Then they shared an image of the queen as petty and vindictive, and laughed.

Even the shepherd, thought Naomi.

'Alfin! This,' the queen gathered all the images together, soaked in anger, 'this is the shame you have brought me.'

'It's not …' was all the king could manage.

'Lady Arden, return now!' hissed the queen of angels. But Arden was fractured between the two acts of treachery, paralysed by Lorcan's casual indifference to her love, so brutally explained. How much had both sisters sacrificed in life and love in the service of their king and queen, and for what?

'Betrayer!' Arden screamed, launching her own attack. 'Weaver of deceit!'

The queen snuffed out Arden's mind like a candle. 'I must attend the host before all is lost.' With that she was gone, leaving the king's head feeling empty with only three of them there.

A question was forming. 'She left me to save the host?' asked the unbelieving king.

'You told her, didn't you,' said Kenato Orin.

'It was the honest thing to do. The right thing to do,' replied Alfin. 'She had become reconciled to our growing apart. You made her think our love had regrown, not knowing who she was dealing with behind my face – I, her eternal companion or your transitory passion? It was breaking her. I had to tell her the truth,' said the High King of Heaven.

'The truth? No, you really didn't,' answered the Prince of Hell.

Naomi left, now that the show was over, surprising herself that she did not want to witness the death of an old friend so closely.

In the real world Kenato Orin held Alfin's limp body in his arms. Naomi felt the thump of the ogre's hammer hitting the earth. Flesh-bound life moved so slowly. 'Naomi, press the attack,' he said wearily without looking up.

Chapter Sixteen

The procurator soared up looking to rejoin the battle but hesitated to watch the unrestrained Kenato Orin pull Alfin in for a terrible kiss. The flames poured into the High King's throat and burst from his eyes and ears, his fingertips and his toes. Two of the king's guard leapt through the burning scene. Naomi fastened one to a dead deinony with her flashing spear for there was no open ground to fall. But the sword of the surviving guard arced towards the demon as the demonic fire engulfed him. The swordsman cried out as his weapon sliced through the Prince of Hell. The elemental looked down as Kenato Orin bled fire and put his hand on the angel's head. Power showered down, a blinding light escaping from the gaps in that impenetrable armour until, without the angel to hold it together, it fell on top of the carcasses and wounded leaving Kenato Orin with an empty helmet, its iridescence now blackened with soot and burning flesh. He held his other fist aloft like a blazing torch illuminating the whirling snowstorm around him.

Through its beam, Naomi looked into the minds of the Heavenly soldiers around Kenato Orin. She knew the source of the anger now. Alva was back in control and the furious focus was stronger than ever. The Procurator of Hell assessed her own troops; kobolds stabbed out with broken lances, torn pennants fraying in the howling wind. A good number of deinony shredded all around them in a dance of death, but the angelic tide was rising and the blue faces were being submerged in the twisted hatred of Paradise. The High King of Heaven who had seen the first sunrise was gone and no one stopped to mourn. The brief moment when perhaps hell could have been victorious had passed.

Two more of the king's guard charged towards Kenato Orin, encouraged by his flaming wound. The Prince of Hell seemed stunned, still assuming that all the angels would throw down their weapons when Alfin's end became apparent. He stood, apparently confused that they hadn't even hesitated in their charge. Naomi scooped up a boulder and dropped it on the two angels. She landed on top, looking between the bewildered Kenato Orin and the twitching arm that protruded from under the rock.

'Time to go,' said crow.

The Prince of Demons discarded his burnt-out angel and leapt into the air, shedding his armour and his ogre form. 'The gates will hold them back,' he said.

'I doubt it,' said Naomi flying up. 'They were always intended for more show than defence.'

A ragged blast of blue magic caught the demon and the elemental as they rose into the protection of the storm. Naomi screamed as her feathers were scorched and she struggled to clear the light from her eyes. Below, the Lord of Elementals lay where he had fallen. The queen's foot pinned him there as surely as would a giant, and water piled up behind her conjuring a wave from the deepest ocean. Naomi concentrated the tempest on her so that Alva's wave froze, creating an expanding but still bound cloud of diamond dust that was impervious to the gale. Naomi landed beside the oblivious combatants, trying to break up the tsunami that now gathered behind the queen like massive wings of water and ice.

'Only now you understand,' the queen shouted. 'I assumed it was Alfin in bed with me. I believed we were in love again. It made his betrayal of me a hundred times worse. You could not have done anything more cruel, Kenato!'

'I truly loved you, Alva, you saw that when—'

With a clap of thunder the great column of water was released. An ice-laden river poured into Kenato Orin's mouth, drowning out his words, his furnace cooled. Naomi pulled her boulder free of the ground accompanied by the sucking of resisting mud and the crushed angel and threw it at the queen. She and the rock disappeared into the white tumult. Reforming her wings, Naomi swept past the still prostrate prince who was coughing water dejectedly in the middle of all the carnage.

'Enough of the desperation,' she said soaring into the swirling sky.

The Host of Heaven had drawn up in the valley undaunted by the snowdrifts building up against the Gates of Hell. Angels did not feel the cold, but the ropes became frail, the wooden arms of the catapults brittle, steel shattered. Nevertheless, they were managing to prove Naomi's point – the Gates of Hell were indeed mostly for show. Previously, those attempting to breach the gates were lost souls trying to get out rather than any organised attempt to get in. From the battlements, Naomi and Kenato Orin watched another flaming ball arc over the top and down among the remnant forces.

'If they had concentrated with rocks on one part of the wall they would be in by now.'

'The queen was right – how fortunate I am to have you by my side,' said the Prince of Demons.

'When did Alva say that?'

'When I last saw her, before this.'

'What did she actually say?'

'If it wasn't for Naomi …' He paused, looking up from the battlefield as he tried to remember. 'No, it was "the worst thing we ever did was pick you rather than Naomi".'

'And you only tell me now. Are you offering me a raise then?'

'They're building some sort of battering ram,' said the Prince of Hell, changing the subject. 'Those bloody dwarves, I told them they should have stuck with me.'

Naomi watched with Kenato Orin in silence for a couple of minutes. The storm was causing the angels problems; it was so cold now there was no flowing water, limiting some of the angels' magical capability. Flesh froze to iron and siege engines failed, but still the host were unrelenting in their attack.

'You can have the whole place if you like. How about that for a raise? There you go. Hell. It's all yours,' he said.

'Terrific,' said Naomi without conviction. 'You broke it and now you give it back to me. We could mount a counterattack, though we need a way to nobble the queen first. Any ideas?'

'No. We would have to squeeze the life out of every angel and even then I'm not sure it would stop them. The moment has come when we should leave this world. It's been fun. But all bad things come to an end.'

'I'll go and tell Jasper and the boys at the other tollhouses that we're leaving. How long is it likely to take you?'

'Building up a coherent idea of where to go will take hours. So I shall simply create a random tear in the fabric of reality and everyone will have to take their chances.' Three rocks smashed into the southern end of the stone curtain. When the arctic wind blew the dust away one of the great gates sagged dangerously.

Kenato Orin looked meaningfully at Naomi.

'What? She couldn't hear me from there. They were bound to figure out how to break them eventually. You start. I'll buy you some time,' said Naomi stepping off the wall and rising into the granite sky. She descended behind the army at the edge of the Tollhouse of Absolution. Dark flames licked up into the winter air from a huge pyre constructed in the centre of the courtyard between the refectory and the dormitory. Two angels stopped at the sound of her landing. They dropped the body of the monk they were carrying and ran back into the whirling blizzard. Naomi picked up a heavy dark scorched timber frozen in the drift, tapping it against her hand. She thought of Eldrun and all the others who must have died here. Angrily she threw the cinder in with the remains of the travellers and acolytes.

The door to the Pilgrim's Rest was open and she stepped over drifting sand and snow into the main bar. She had designed it herself, brass and wood, the snug in the corner sunk slightly with a protecting rail around it. Three glasses of unfinished beer sat abandoned on the table. Her whip curled out to smash the cups, the table, the building, but she pulled it back to her side where it hissed and coiled around her feet, begging for destruction. This was not how the day was meant to end. She reached behind the countertop and pulled out a smart red tin, tucking it away. She paused briefly trying to process what she had learned from the fight in Alfin's mind, then pushed it back; there would be time for that later, hopefully.

Outside, the wind had changed direction and the grey smoke and white snow spun, making it hard to see to the gatehouse. Blood on the stonework and fire in the sky provided the only colours in the frozen landscape. The two angels returned, their bright spears glowing as blue torches held in front of them. But Alva's hatred was not with them and they hesitated as Naomi approached, her whip tracing crimson lines in the air about her.

'Have you killed them all?' she asked.

The two angels seemed unsure how to answer. 'We have purged all the sinners, procurator, in every tollhouse,' said one sounding puzzled. 'As the High King commanded.'

'Alfin is dead. Alva leads you falsely against her lover the Prince of Hell.'

'Lies!' said the other, advancing with her spear.

'And yet you know it isn't,' said Naomi as she strode towards them. She shared with them her vision of Arden's denouncement of the queen.

'Betrayer!' Arden screamed in grief against the backdrop of Kenato's lurid thoughts. 'Weaver of deceit!' And then the Queen of Heaven destroyed her most loyal servant and abandoned her husband to his fate. The angels stood stunned. Naomi's whip snapped a lance from one angel's slack hand and passed the weapon to its mistress. Free of the queen's driving scorn and faced by a vengeful procurator, the angels threw themselves to the bloody paving. Uncaring of the two prostrate figures, Naomi walked towards the pyre trying to make sense of the damage that had been done. The fire seemed to leap to her, lighting her features from within like restless lava.

Her voice boomed off the walls of the priory. 'I lay this doom upon you – that Heaven will not know peace from this wrathful act.' With that she jumped into the air, skirting the top of the storm where the sky was black and the stars shone around the sun before returning like a red meteor to the frozen river where the crocodile had tried to eat her this morning.

Kenato Orin stood in the now frosted gardens, his hands held wide, breaking reality the way that ice would break stone. The world fractured in unexpected directions. The denizens of hell scrambled through the gap in space–time. Candice stood beside him in a pink dress to match her wings, her hand resting lightly on his arm. Naomi could see that Kenato Orin was already diminished, pouring his power, his being, into keeping the gateway open while the mass of his people escaped. Candice was taller than him now. He faltered, his arms sagged, the portal shrinking. Candice bent to kiss his forehead and leapt into the unlight with a final flick of her tail.

Naomi caught up some of the demons that were too damaged to run and threw them bodily over the threshold as she passed. A blast of air pushed her as the Gates of Hell behind her finally collapsed. It took moments for the howling gale to clear the dust away, but the High Queen of Heaven was first through the gap, climbing over the debris, flaming sword in hand. Naomi's stolen spear ricocheted off the queen's breastplate and hit her captain in the throat. The force of the throw knocked them both back out of sight. Using the precious seconds, Naomi reached Kenato Orin, who had slumped onto the pink marble, an old frail husk who could no longer bear the weight of his own arms. Now untroubled, order restored itself and the hole began closing rapidly. Naomi scooped Kenato up and her flames scorched him. She handed him the red tin with a castle above a lake painted on the front.

'Shortbread, you'll need to recover your strength.' Naomi paused as the queen regained the top of the rubble where the Gates of Hell had fallen and unleashed her fury across the intervening space, picking off the remaining stragglers who were blocking a clear shot at Naomi. The Prince of Hell, the Lord of Elementals, King of the Kobolds, Seraph Friend, Freer of Dwarves, master of debate, the harnesser of magic whose arrival to this world has brought joy and hope to all its peoples whimpered in the crook of Naomi's left arm and hugged the biscuits. Snow and ash raced past the last two survivors and up into the vanishing void. The Procurator of Hell reached up with her left hand and, catching the closing edge of the rift, pulled herself up, rolling out of reality. The snow followed her into the void along with the sound of the Heavenly Host singing with elation that the triumph of Heaven was complete and that all angels should rejoice and praise the High Queen who had laid Hell low.

Hooded Crow

BE DANGEROUS

Chapter One

'Obstruct~~ing~~ the doors ~~can~~ cause delays ~~and~~ be dangerous.' I looked at the glass on the train door again. Somebody had taken the time to very carefully scrape off the *ing*, *can*, and the *and* in order to exhort their fellow commuters to anarchy. Not that it was very likely with this lot. Maybe you couldn't run down the streets screaming outrage for the failure of capitalism when you were so heavily weighed down by electronics. Or perhaps Samsung and the other mobile products were more effective at isolating us from reality than either religion or opiates had ever proved to be.

Thinking about it, the only reason I had read the message from a former inmate of the commuter train was that I had dropped out of my personal bubble. Messrs Bragg and company were covering the life of René Descartes when, with a bleep in my ear, the phone part of my pod had announced that it could take no more and would like to shut down. I was abandoned back into the real world of my fellow commuters, the crushing overcrowding, and the smell of Quavers. My ears were the last to readjust, abruptly exposed to the sound of three girls nearly wetting themselves with hysteria. It wasn't clear what the source was, but it was obviously unsettling the tired-looking businessmen around them. Had I ever found anything that funny? If I had, it was long ago.

My mobile, freed from the task of enlightening me, was now optimistic about its ability to continue. I lifted it, looking around the carriage with Chorus to see everyone's status floating beside their heads. There was an art to looking through your phone without making it too obvious, but then that was why people flagged – so other folk would look. You just had to not look like you were looking.

#standing room only on the train again!!!# Does something that happens every day need three exclamation marks?

#I've left him#

#Looking @ Lesbian Porn# I bet every man in the club was trying to change her mind last night. Shame she forgot to update her status this morning.

#I have a very small penis# Bingo! Well, that explained the three girls laughing. The danger of having a son who knew more about Chorus than you did. Or a wife? At least it wasn't me they were mocking. My screen went dark. Meh. I was back in the carriage for good. I thought about charging it but was struck by the idea of proving I wasn't an addict. Which I wasn't.

A woman in a black business suit was shouting down her phone. That her clothing was holding itself together was a credit to whatever thread M&S were using for their office outfits three years ago. But I knew there hadn't been any signal for five minutes, there wouldn't be until they got to St Albans. There never was!

'June is bustin' out all over,' I sang tunelessly. Was that *Oklahoma* or *Carousel*? If my Apple was working I could have checked, and I wouldn't be reduced to singing it myself.

'I need this deal, Simon. So what I want you to do is put together the presentation we talked about. I have the slides here so I can talk you through them. You don't have to do anything, you just have to listen to me and we can land this. The largest contract, the largest client we have ever penetrated. And we can do it, Simon. We don't have to involve anyone else.' But she wasn't even involving Simon. Did she know? Had she already lost her job and was just talking to a dead phone to cheer herself up?

'That's enough reality,' I said to myself and fished for a power supply in my oversized handbag. A Twix treacherously washed up to the surface as I pushed past the lipstick and wipes, and its gold and red packaging sparkled as it promised three minutes of happiness. I looked at June, who was as stressed as the seams on her suit, and pulled out the plug instead.

'Can I borrow that?' Before I had focused on the source, the person continued, 'Please can I borrow that charger? Please, I really need to charge up before the train stops.' The voice sounded as if it came from someone my age – still young as long as the lighting was right. Nothing apart from total darkness would save this guy though. *Tramp* was the first word that sprang to mind. Lots of hair, mostly grey, a face that it would have given Tommy Lee Jones a run for his money. But it was the lack of mask that marked him out as an outsider. Some folk thought the second wave only happened to other people. He wore a long green combat jacket with bulging external pockets. It was out of one of these that a mobile was being pulled. An iPhone XX, probably, it was still wrapped in hankies and string and other things that had less obvious origins. The white technology wonder bar bubbled out into his hand, which was no cleaner than his beard and held out to me.

'Could you charge this, please? I have lost my charger. I have lost a lot of things, but I need to charge my phone before the next station, please.' He was standing a little behind me, beside the door. Every seat was taken and there was the usual line of people trying to stand and read. Or stand and work. Or just stand and listen to something that would take them away from the crushing reality of being trapped in a tin can with three hundred sweaty strangers, some of whom were clearly mad and shouty and standing next to me. This man had created slightly more space than was usually possible.

He wiggled his mobile a bit. 'Please, you could be saving my life.'

'Why not. It's the railway's electricity, not mine.' I took the phone off him with a wet wipe and tried to get the attention of the passenger in front of me – eyes closed, Bose over-ear speakers doing their job of producing perfect isolation. Bastard. I poked him with the charger and waved and pointed at the socket in the wall marked 'not for public use' behind his unconvincingly cool backpack.

With an overdone sigh he shuffled out of the way and I was able to unite outlet, charger and mobile and put the sticky mess down in the gap where the fire extinguisher should have been. I pulled some gel from my bag and washed my hands until they dried.

'Thank you.'

'No problem.'

'It's nice to actually talk to somebody. You don't get to talk to most people now. Just a casual conversation. It's nice.'

'No.' I had automatically put my earphones back in and only then realised that escape route was closed. Grumpily I stuffed them back into my holdall, the Twix mocking me now. Bose managed to convey that I only had myself to blame with a raised eyebrow before returning to his microscopic copy of *The Economist*.

I tried to skewer June with a look but she was crouching slightly to allow her to stare out into the middle distance. 'So on the third slide it's very important that we get across that we have totally restructured. All the old team have gone. They were bloody useless. Not that you can say that ...'

I guessed June had spotted the tramp next to her and clung to the call for safety. If only she had thought as carefully when she had got dressed. There really wasn't enough room for her and whatever series of supersized snacks were in that suit with her.

'You have an XX as well.' The beggar was looking at me. Well, when I looked up he was looking down my front but then he was looking at my mobile. I glanced down myself. My red jacket had pulled down the neckline on my matching jumper. From here it looked like I had just come out in a bra and coat. I half expected drops of drool to appear on my tits.

'Did you get a good look?'

His hand went half up to point at my bag. 'Your phone.' He looked like he was going to cry. 'I just thought you might have played *Under Avalon* on it.'

I had, most people had. Clever game using augmented reality, where they overlaid the game's graphics onto the real world, the same way Chorus did, only with more chain mail and less social comment. You had to solve puzzles, find places, and then they would overlay some dungeon portal onto a participating tavern where you could convert your virtual gold into a pint of Guinness. One mission we did as a pub crawl after work – a dozen of us walking around shooting demons, smashing up virtual furniture for sovereigns and drinking a lot. It had been fun. Maybe that was the last time I had laughed like that.

'No.'

'It's just that the application stays live and it broadcasts to other players if you know how to look. But with you …'

'I thought I'd deleted the sodding thing.' I have done, several times.

'You probably did, but the agreement says it can reinstall itself at the next reset and keep itself updated just in case you change your mind.'

'I didn't know they could do that.'

'Did you read the agreement?'

'No. Nobody does.'

'There you are then.'

June had stopped talking and was watching me now. Tart with no top chatting up the tramp. Bloody brilliant. I'd have to get this train again tomorrow while he would be rummaging through his bin of choice. I looked at his crumpled face, all bright with hope at a real conversation about something he really cared about.

'You do play it then?' he asked. It was a neat trick, look as disgusting as that and yet still enough of a hint of Andrex puppy not to get slapped.

I sighed. 'Used to. Not done for a while though.'

'How far did you get?'

'Just the Quiet Man.' Actually I'd had a Level 72 Master Player status last year, got all the way to the siege of Meena's Mountain, but I wasn't going to tell him that.

'Where you have to go round all the Irish pubs hunting leprechauns.'

'That's the one.' Despite myself I smiled and though I knew I would regret it I found myself asking, 'How far did you get?'

'Ever heard of the Nuneaton Nine?'

'Yeah, they were the first team to finish the game.'

'Not quite finished. Made it to the Hall of the High Queen.' If his smile had got any broader the top of his head would fall off. All those black teeth made me try another shuffle back into the commuters. But then the grin vanished, the face crumpled. 'I'm the only one left now.'

'Everybody else stopped playing it then?'

He frowned, eyes disappearing into his folding countenance. 'No, they're all dead. Don't you remember?'

The Nuneaton Nine. If I'd had my phone I could have googled it for the details, but I remembered the highlights well enough. The first serial murders played out on Chorus. They had got further than any other clan, won a prize, appeared as costumed cannon fodder on a couple of chat shows, and then Princess had been found on the Shard. Well, most of her. Act of bestiality gone badly wrong, the papers said. But that didn't explain why she had been nailed to the glass. The next was that huge lad, Thrud, or whatever his gaming name was. He had been spreadeagled by somebody with a working knowledge of Vikings and what they did to people they didn't like.

'No.'

'I was the Wizard of Under Avalon.'

'I thought you'd drowned?'

'I thought you didn't remember?'

He had me there. But that still didn't let him off for trying to look at my boobs again. I gave up and pulled everything up self-consciously. He looked embarrassed, which made us sort of even but not really, not really at all. The carriage swayed across some points and picked up speed. I looked out the window at buildings I didn't recognise and let the minutes pass.

'I have no idea where I am,' I said. I'd never really looked before.

'A couple of miles from St Albans, I think, although there's one more station before it. I better get the phone back. I'll need that when the train stops.'

Everybody around me seemed to be typing away like mad. Had something happened or were they always like this and I was too busy on Chorus myself to notice? I tried to see what was on Bose's screen, but he had turned slightly so that I couldn't peep. I felt a little empathy for the Wizard. Not a lot.

'I have to ask what happened to you. There were stories of terrorists, the software company that launched *Under Avalon* was shut down. People dying on the Underground. What was going on?' For a moment I thought I could see the man as he must have looked a year or two ago. He looked right into my eyes; his were blue, and his jaundice only threw the irises into sharper contrast.

'It was real.'

I screwed up my face and he hid his behind the wrinkles again. 'There were a lot of players who said that but come on? All that leprechaun schmaltz was real? Begorra?'

'Most of the introduction stuff you saw wasn't. But as you got into the later levels you realised the phones were showing you another reality. Did you go to the Bridges of Sestola?'

'Saw it on a friend's phone. It looked amazing.' I miss Tim, that Tim, the Tim I got engaged to. We had been walking through Elephant and Castle really but in the game, through our phones, we saw Sestola. We had fun on the bridges.

'They said they had upped the graphics but they could never be that good. What you were seeing from then on was real. Well, not real, you could only see it through the screen, but it was there. That's why it looked so believable, so detailed, because it was as genuine as what's going past the window now.' His face furrowed more than before. He had pulled the mag mount off the mobile and was powering it up. 'I'll show you. I just wish the start-up on this hadn't got so long.'

'No, that's fine. Even if it is real, which it isn't, why would that cause all those deaths? Not just you guys, the Nine, but all the other people.'

'We were bait, we think. By getting into the palace we triggered something. By getting so far in the game we could interact with the world. Not just see it. I don't know what, but we let something loose or just really irritated the elves enough to come and get us. We were never too sure.'

'Elves? Don't they just float around in nighties speaking Welsh?'

'Evil little buggers that would stab you as soon as look at you. Never leave a live elf at your back, the Princess used to say. She was right.' His face was illuminated blue from below and he didn't look so human. 'Here we go.' He did a quick pan of the carriage. 'All clear. I've had a couple of close shaves while recharging. If I had the money it would be good to have a spare phone. Of course, back in the old days you could swap—'

'Power!' I snapped the free charger lead onto the back of my Apple. It lit up a comforting start-up screen too.

His fingers were waving over the mobile, shrinking and growing icons. 'All done.' A collection of musical chimes ran up and down the train.

'Done all what?'

'I have upgraded all the *Under Avalon* accounts on the train. Now they have access to all areas. They can see all the world around them without having to complete all the quests.'

'Including mine?'

'Oh yes. I assumed you would want to since you play the game.'

'Played the game.'

'Last session was at one fifteen this morning. It was on your Chorus flag before your battery failed. It's why I picked you, why I was sure you would help.'

'I just like to watch the Forest of Souls. And sometimes—'

'You see things moving through it and you wonder what they are and where they're going. And you want to follow them.' He was nodding in rhythm with the carriage.

'Yes,' I said dreamily.

'Don't – that's how people get killed.'

'Why?'

'They don't like being watched. They certainly don't like humans wandering around their world. It's why they destroyed Starflame Graphics – to try and make sure nobody could come back.'

'The elves mounted an attack on their own software company?' I asked.

He shrugged as if the strangeness of the statement proved it as fact.

I thought for a bit. 'If you're the Wizard, how did you manage to stay alive?'

'You keep moving. You're safe on a train, you see. Even when they know where you are. In order to get on board, they have to match speed with us and then cross over. Which is quite hard since we're as unreal to them as they are to us.' His fingers swirled over the screen again. 'I have seen them charging across an empty field leaping from the backs of their horses out of existence. Of course, some miss and break their necks.'

I resisted the urge to stand closer to look over his shoulder; the smell of wet dog was pretty strong and helped me stay where I was.

'How would they know where you are?'

'They can read your mind.'

'I don't … Is that true?'

'Elves often confuse story and truth. It's difficult to get a straight answer. But I believe so. Not details and stuff but a good idea of what's going on. So you have to watch what you think.'

'Is that possible?'

'Yes, but you tend to start feeling a bit mad.'

That killed the conversation for a bit. The question 'Are you sure you're not mad?' kept putting itself forward as the obvious next line.

'Why don't you just shoot them, with guns?' I asked for clarification.

'They wear petal armour that no missile can pierce. So it means … Shit! They're close. How can that be?' He pointed the phone at me. 'You look human.' I tried to say that I was last time I checked but the real fear in his voice threw me. 'Are you working for them?'

'No.' I pulled my chin in. 'I couldn't do that because there isn't anyone to work for.' Probably. The train was slowing down. 'Are we at St Albans?'

The Wizard was saying the same thing, looking out of both sides of the carriage. A guard was trying to make his way down the crowd towards us. The tramp looked around for somewhere to hide. Everybody else was looking at us. That was very creepy. I tried to think of a brick wall just in case. The Wizard was doing something else with the phone, holding it up to the guard and back down again.

'Excuse me, sir, do you have a token?'

'No. I meant to buy one at Stevenage but the ticket machines were broken. I'm happy to pay.' He returned to fumbling through his pockets again. The guard didn't look like he was going to accept anything out of there as valid payment.

The railway man brought up his own PDA, a heavy grey industrial thing that looked like it was up to hammering a few nails if required. 'According to complaints received, you got on at Bedford. Lying to a representative of a train operating company is now a criminal—'

'Complaints?' I said. 'From who?'

'Chorus has been going full chat since you have been identified as Mr Phillips. I'm afraid your reputation precedes you and I have to remove you from the train. You will be detained at the station.'

The coach was quite definitely slowing now. A small platform that somehow escaped the Beeching axe by being entirely forgotten came into view.

The tramp was scanning it constantly with his phone. 'You can't drop me off here. It would be murder.'

'Is that a threat, Mr Philips? We at British Railways take threats to staff very seriously.'

'No, not you, me,' said the tramp.

The train stopped; the guard pressed the '><' button and the door hissed open. 'Please, Mr Philips. We get a huge amount of abuse on Chorus already on this service, and we're trending very badly. If that lot want to, they can get me fired before I get back to the depot.'

I looked at the people around me, transformed from commuters to virtual trolls capable of throwing the unworthy off trains or out of work all by the power of the capacitive touch screen.

I watched the guard expertly ease the tramp from the overcrowded carriage. The old man scanned very carefully up and down the platform. He stepped out onto mossy gravel, phone in his left hand, his right deep in his holdall pocket. He looked back into the carriage. The driver was revving the engine a little; diesel smoke curled down from the roof past the window.

Philips looked up and said, 'You clever bastards.'

Alarmed, the guard moved back towards the train but seemed to leap into the air instead, missing the door and bouncing off the side of the window. He lay face down, his shirt slashed open at the back, blood flowing freely from the fatal wound, black against the blue shirt. I saw a blade in Philips's fist, a Bowie knife, the kind of thing you saw in films for skinning raccoons or, it would seem, railway staff. But the steel was clean. Whatever had cut the guard, it wasn't the wild-looking man. The Wizard circled back towards me holding the phone and the weapon up protectively the way Mulder and Scully had taught a generation. But when he got around the body of the guard to the door it was closed. I looked at my fingers on the close button, surprised. I wanted to let him in to decimate the screaming trolls behind me, but then I was there too. Would I bet my life that blade was bloodless? The engine revved as the panicked driver started moving the train on. I tried to look sorry at leaving him behind but even I wasn't convinced. The Wizard was framed now by the words on the window.

'Obstruct the doors cause delays be dangerous.'

'No.'

Chapter Two

The police interviews had taken an age since they were determined to go through every person on the train. Given my fellow travellers' enthusiasm on Chorus to label me as an accomplice to the Wizard, the interviewers kept coming back to me with new questions thrown up by each successive statement. New pictures kept appearing that the passengers must have been taking as I talked with Mr Philips. Each one made me look more of a tart than the previous one. I will never wear that jacket again. Hardest to prove was that I hadn't known the Wizard before getting on that train. The only saving grace was that no one could prove that I had.

It was six o'clock in the morning before they finally released me from Islington Police Station. At least they let me out of the car park door on Tolpuddle Street to avoid a couple of determined reporters at the front entrance. I walked through the Sainsbury's car park in the rain trying to figure out if I should ring Tim or my work first. I wasn't sure of a warm reception from either, so I sent them both an email saying I wouldn't be in to one and that, despite everything it would be good to catch up, to the other.

I circled west and walked down to the Angel Underground and then on down the A501. I had my phone in my hand and had fired up *Under Avalon* without really thinking about it. That was what had driven Tim nuts. Initially it had been appealing – his 'game-playing girlfriend'. I was a big hit with Tim's friends. Later it had driven him nuts. But the Angel was where it all began. The original beta version of *Under Avalon* had mapped the City of the Elves under London, so you had to move around the Underground to play the game. And the Angel was ground zero.

'Welcome back, Elebereth,' said the AI-generated non-player character – or NPC – that appeared by my side. I had meant to correct the spelling of her name, but they charged so much for that option it was easier just to live with it. You could only see her on the screen; she was part of the augmented reality that had made the game so popular. She was the usual teenage male fantasy of what a female elf should look like. At least this one had a full set of clothes. Sadly, that was optional. 'You are at ...' there was a fractional pause '... the Angel building. The next part of your quest to defeat the fallen elves is at Regent's Park. Would you like me to guide you there?' she asked, and a line of flowers sprang up on the pavement in front of me, running down the road and adding a stripe of wonderful colour to the drab London landscape. I stood looking at my screen, remembering why the game was so beguiling. It brought the extraordinary into my life in a way that only Class-A drugs could have matched.

My walk took me past King's Cross and the detailed facade of St Pancras. In between I could just see the old Google Buildings where Starflame Graphics had been based. I'd gone to an open day there once, before the Nuneaton Nine made the headlines. And the vengeful elves shut it down, I found myself thinking. Regent's Park was busy with lots of people trying to get their daily exercise in before the rain intensified. I checked my phone and it showed dark clouds coming in from the north with an estimated time of arrival of just under an hour. Lots of rain.

I looked around the park using my mobile like a letterbox to peer into the world of *Under Avalon*. The closer it was to your eyes the more you could see, but the more stupid you looked. It was why a lot of folks had gone for the various glasses you could buy now. I did have a pair of Xiaomi, which were a fraction of the price of the Apple glasses. The overlay colours were a little bit garish sometimes and every now and then it would drop back into displaying Chinese characters. But Sofia would reset them for the price of a cappuccino, the only occasion her learning Cantonese had earned her an income, she used to say. Then Tim had sat on them, which was beyond even Sofia's ability to help. My fault for leaving them on the arm of the chair, apparently.

So I stood in the park looking at a house that didn't really exist. It was a hall with some sort of complicated walled enclosure beside it. But the gates had rotted away leaving fragments of wood. The spaces between the walls had silted up with earth and, from the green tinge, sheep poop. I looked around. Mountains stood high behind me in bright sunshine, and forested slopes ran past the structures down into the valley. The wall that had stopped us before was behind me. I had never been this far. Now thanks to the Wizard I could progress. The house had such an abandoned look I thought it had to be a trap.

The spells in *Under Avalon* were driven using the forward-facing camera for gesture control, words, the position of your eyes on the screen, and even facial expressions to interact with the world of the game. I cycled through the menu looking for my best distance spell – invocation for a fireball. It was the usual Harry Potter mock Latin, or possibly real Latin, but I had renamed them as I had played. Sadly the Wizard had been so right about me and *Under Avalon*. I looked up at the forest on the edge of the clearing for target practice. Well, there could be something lurking in that mixture of solid and virtual trees.

'Take that, you fiend,' I said quietly.

A flaming green light leapt from Elebereth's overlay of my fingers across the open pasture, smacking off a tree. The pine went up like it had a hundred-gallon tank of petrol at its base, as did a good ten either side. A deer, scorched and blinded, staggered forward, illuminated by the flames that climbed upwards to the blue sky above. The doe shook its head, getting ready to leap free of the devastation, just as a burning trunk collapsed on top of it. I swore I could feel the heat from the fire as I brought my phone down just to check there weren't any dog walkers caught in the blast. I must have left that spell on full power after the last session. My mana indicator showed empty. No more magic for an hour of real time.

I recovered what I could of the now cooked deer as simulated food for Elebereth and walked back down to the house. I paused, looking at the carving in the grey weathered wood. It had split slightly along a picture of two dragons wrapped round each other. The attention to detail was astonishing. This was the reason it was a fun game to play even when you weren't on an actual adventure. Just to walk through these places was a joy. So much better than the real thing.

I pushed open the door. The hinges had failed and the wood scraped over the stone and juddered to a halt, forcing me to go in sideways. I had my virtual sword in hand and waved it around a bit. Briefly I thought of how stupid I must have looked in Regent's Park as I squeezed through a door that wasn't there, but really, I was long past caring. Inside was quite a spacious area with rough wooden furniture around a central fire. If there had been food left here the rats had made off with it long since. I broke up a chair and a stream of cybernetic coins shot up to the money score on the phone screen. No one knew when this had become a thing, but one of the simplest ways to get in-game cash was to smash the right stuff up. It was always hard to guess where the money would be, so you ended up trashing everything in the room just to be safe. It was also very therapeutic.

At the end there were two trunks hidden behind a false wall, one that I couldn't open and one that I could. I put down my sword to pick the lock. Inside were some armoured and enchanted trousers, though at least one American software developer in the team had insisted on calling them pants. If you were playing in a raid, the line 'I'm going to put on these magical pants' would be the cause of much hilarity. Every time. I walked around once more checking each of the rooms and kicking the broken furniture, knowing that I had missed something but not sure what it was.

Coming back out into the sunlight from the house I had that sense of leaving somewhere cold. I could smell the sheep poo; I must have been getting really tired. There was movement where the deer carcass lay trapped. Someone stood up looking directly at me. He was referred to as a fallen elf in the game, but other than the pointy ears he looked very different from Elebereth. This guy was all angles, accentuated cheekbones and chin, deep-set piercing eyes, almost pigeon-chested, but still tall and beautiful, only in something of an alien way.

'Poltergeist! I see you,' he shouted. 'As you torture my life so I will destroy yours.' The elf drew his blade and charged down the hill towards me.

'Take that …' I said before recalling that I had already toasted that particular Bambi. I went for my sword but remembered that was by the chest. The elf was on top of me now, sabre flashing as I backed away screaming. I fell, dropping my

Apple, and landed staring upwards at a well-established dog-rose bush that had lacerated me as it caught me. Very carefully I reached for my mobile trying not to do any more damage. One cut on my left arm welled up and blood ran down my wrist in volume.

'Miss? Do you want some help?' enquired a man in his fifties accompanied by a small Papillon with huge fluffy ears. Both looked concerned while several others showed mirth and one kindly filmed me on their phone. I went to say no, but the bright red barbs lurking maliciously around me suggested otherwise.

'Please,' I said.

I walked back home, stopping off at Boots to get some wound-cleaning wipes and some clever little sticky clips that held my battered skin together. I ran a bath and lowered myself slowly in, hesitating as each cut reported in. There seemed to be quite a few I hadn't spotted earlier. I kept my left arm out of the water because I'd only just got it to stop haemorrhaging and I didn't want it to start again. It was only then I remembered that I had 'left' Elebereth being cut to bits by a dark elf on a hillside. But the image that came to my mind was the poor guard bleeding out on the abandoned platform as we pulled away. I missed Sofia then; sometimes you just need a best friend to talk to. I did cry a bit at that point.

Given that it was Thursday there was no sense in going to work on Friday so I called in sick, reassuring my boss that I would be fine by Monday. It was clear even from the low-quality video call that she wasn't really interested in my near brush with death. I thought this was particularly galling in that if she had allowed us to work from home I wouldn't have even been on that stupid train. But, as she never tired of saying, 'If your Vaccard is up to date the government says it's perfectly safe to use public transport.'

I called Tim forgetting that he was on a Vancouver time zone with his current contract so that was a fairly short conversation. Which left me with Netflix and a Deliveroo that was heavy on the cherry brandy luxury ice cream.

Chapter Three

On Saturday I felt okay and the forecast said it wasn't going to rain till three. So I set off to recover Elebereth. I didn't want to leave it too long because there was a chance that another player would come across the little shrine that the game set up where a character died and help themselves to my magic pants.

When I got to Regent's Park I looked around carefully for the dog rose of death. I could make out the place I had flattened and then where the man had had to break a few branches at some risk to himself in order to allow me out. My left arm still throbbed from the biggest cut I'd picked up. I walked back north a few paces, sparking up *Under Avalon*. Through the window of the game I could see Elebereth, with her pants still on but otherwise definitely dead.

'You can resurrect Elebereth with all her powers for two-and-a-half-million silver marks or £25. Or you can create a new character?' Smashing up the house had only brought my current total to a hundred thousand marks so I reached for my debit card as they knew I would. Some people played *Under Avalon* as a free game. They tended to be the ones hanging around like carrion crows hoping that other characters would die so they could nick the stuff they were too mean to buy.

I checked she was restored properly then remembered the sword. It was a good one – the Dark Queen herself was meant to have made it. It could slice through almost anything and I'd been through quite a lot of trouble to get it. I prepared my spell casting so that I walked back into the house with my left hand wreathed in green flame. The sword was gone though, as was the box I couldn't open. I returned outside, furious with myself for being such a wuss. *One elf waves something pointy at me and I forget everything and die.* I looked at the destruction seething in my palm and released it back at the hall. The bolt flew through the door, exploding against the hearth and taking all the windows out in the initial blast. Fire took hold quickly and the rafters collapsed, sending sparks and smoke up and out. The haze made it quite difficult to see and it was hard not to cough even though it was all on screen. I set an overwatch on Elebereth so that she would defend herself on the way back and closed the game. Despite what the government said, I decided to walk home.

Since the drizzle seemed to be holding off I headed south rather than east. I wanted to avoid going anywhere near Islington again in case the police had thought of some more questions since the last time they saw me. My meandering brought me to Hyde Park. It was good to get away from the whine of the scooters; the incessant beeping sounded like some mad flock of sheep swirling beyond the railings. Since they had pedestrianised the bridge across the Serpentine a dozen coffee vans and street-food shacks had sprung up. I bought a long German sausage in a bun and a flat white and slowed to look at the art for sale under polythene sheets. One painting caught my eye; the architecture was so distinctive it could only come from one place.

'That's the Empty Palace on the Edgeward Isles.' The man standing behind a spread of his work looked delighted at the recognition. 'You have really captured the way the sunlight makes the place float in the air.'

'Thank you. You've been there then,' he said.

'I was one of the beta testers – we were allowed to follow the Wayfarer when he sailed there,' I said. I'd hung a couple of pictures in the flat. It was a nice feeling being handy with a hammer.

'I used to do a lot of these when *Under Avalon* was a thing. I thought I'd bring a couple out now that it's back in the limelight again. You going to go after the prize then?'

'Prize?'

'Starflame have put up a bounty to find the Wizard. It's been all over the news.'

'I've been avoiding the feeds for a bit.' I could see the guard when I drifted off to sleep. I didn't need to see him on a screen as well.

'After he killed that chap in the train they reckoned the best way of finding the Wizard is through the game. He always said he lived there more than here. So the developers have put up a fifty-thousand-pound reward for the player who finds information that leads to his arrest.'

'Ah.' I felt a bit weak all of a sudden. The idea of all those people flooding back into *UA* filled me with fear. *The elf charging towards me with murder in his eyes. The smell of the burning house.*

'It's a smart move. I hear they made more than the fifty k in reactivated subscriptions in the first hour. You obviously know the place better than most. You might be in with a shout. You interested?' he asked.

I shook my head before I realised he meant about buying the painting. 'No. It's really good, really good. But if I have that on the wall it's only going to give me nightmares.' I turned to walk away and his face fell. I half turned back. 'I'll think about it.'

I felt edgy now. I was pretty sure it was just the idea of the players coming back to *Under Avalon* that had unsettled me. I started to watch my fellow pedestrians more closely. In the park, gamers tended to use augmentation less often, so someone using their mobile to look around would stand out. I took my own phone out and fired up the app, though I felt like an addicted gambler sneaking back into Coral for a harmless flutter on the three twenty-two at Chepstow. Elebereth was there, smiling and ready as she always was.

The buildings slowly faded out. The trees became a forest, the pedestrianised road a wide dirt track through the woodland. Elebereth's sixth sense was going off so somebody was watching me, to the south of where I was heading. My right hand went to my empty scabbard and my left conjured up a fireball. I dialled it down a bit. I didn't need to recreate *Apocalypse Now* in the middle of Hyde Park. I kept walking forward as if I was unaware. There was some movement behind a row of poplars and I lobbed off two fireballs, one where I thought he was, the second where I would be if I had ducked back in. I ran forward now with a heavy dagger at the ready and my third and last 'take that you fiend' ready to go. I reached the place I had hit but there was no sign that I had done anything but scorch the virtual trees again.

A party of three was coming towards me from the south edge of the park, numbers floating above their heads – one 29 and two 30s – so they probably played as a group to have stayed so close in level. Normally I would have chatted as we passed but I was pretty strung out now and just wanted to get home. I waved in what I hoped look like a friendly manner and carried on to Kensington Road. Elebereth's threat indicator was still going off so I ran to the next bus stop and pulled on a mask as I jumped aboard a Number 9 to Aldwych. I sat down upstairs, watching the park entrance. There was someone there who really looked like the elf from Regent's Park, staring at the bus. But it must have been a player who wished he'd run for it too.

It was good to be home. It wasn't much by any standards other than London, but it had one bedroom, my office stroke living room, a galley kitchen and best of all a bath. It was the bath that sold it to me. Well, rented it to me. Even after the housing crash I still was far from moving into the buying market. The outside of the building had a nice Art Deco look though I didn't think it was that old. Was mock Art Deco a thing? Being on the second floor I looked out onto some other renovated flats, but a room with a view came at a cost.

I locked the door and looked at my shaking hand in puzzlement. Even though it was still only mid-afternoon I felt washed out, exhausted. I put the telly on and dialled in some news, but it was just the usual wars and various footage shots of the death of the guard on the train to St Albans. I watched for a bit until they started repeating themselves. Looked like until they could find Mr Philips there wasn't much more to be said. I looked at the DVD box of *The Great Escape*; Sofia, Tim and I would huddle together with it under a duvet on afternoons like this. I couldn't watch it on my own. Not yet.

When I woke up it was dark. That put it after curfew when they killed the street lights, but other than that I had no idea how long I had been unconscious. Somebody was running around in the flat above. I listened as they ran from the outside wall to what would have put them in the stairwell. Then whoever it was came back, but the steps kept going down the skin of the building. I fumbled for the light switch but, still confused with sleep, I missed. The sound came back only along the bricks above me. At the third attempt I found the light. The lamp, a steampunk pipework little man with a fake filament bulb for a head cast his golden glow, dispelling the gloom. The footsteps stopped midstride. I looked at the white plaster above the bed expecting to see footprints but there was nothing. I retrieved my phone – three thirty-two. I'd left *Under Avalon* on, which had nearly flattened the battery. I plugged the phone in and tried to make sure I was awake.

The partition separating the bedroom from the living room was made up of bull's-eye glass tiles, the kind you saw in Ye Olde Shoppe windows. Someone walked between me and the TV. The heavy tread on the wooden flooring followed after. I shouted and leapt off the bed, stumbling through the curtain into the blue-lit apartment. There was just me and the news anchor there. I ran round past the kitchen to the corridor that led to the front door. The footsteps seemed to circle round back into the bedroom. I stopped and went to the galley, pulling my biggest Kitchen Devil from the faux granite block, and dashed to the front door.

'You can fuck right off,' I said trying to sound scary rather than scared. I don't think I would have convinced anyone. I opened the door and stepped out into the stairwell. The automatic light kicked in and it shone back into the hall and my bathroom. I stood trying to think through my options. I could run away. I couldn't call the police because my phone was still in the bedroom. I looked at the other doors on the landing, unsure of what reaction I would get waking them up in the middle of the night with a knife in my fist. They must all have heard me and Tim shouting at each other when he came round to drop off my stuff. Which brought me back to running away. The light went out and I had to wave my arm to get it to switch back on again.

It shone on the cupboard, which I opened with my left hand. Nothing but vintage coats and unloved shoes. Next door along, I switched on the LEDs in the bathroom. All good in there. Now it got tricky. It was grandly called a walk-through wardrobe but really it was a connecting corridor at the back of the kitchen that had a bit more cupboard space. The switch for the bulb was in the bedroom though, so leaving the front door open I walked down the hall switching every light on as I went. Still just me in the living room. Kitchen was empty, bedroom. I held my knife as tight as I could and took the step up past the glass wall. Nothing. Finally the corridor back to the front door. I was tempted to run back round the other way but the presence was gone. I felt I was on my own now and wondered if it was just that I was more awake.

I closed the front door and put the kettle on. Found a teabag, the old-fashioned ones with the string. Pulled a carton of milk out of the fridge. I was doing everything one handed and forced myself to put the carving knife back in the block. The shakes kicked in and I had to go into the living room and pace while the kettle reached its crescendo. Shaking myself, I went back in, filled the mug, put the milk in – Tim hated me not taking the teabag out first – and then stared out of the window for a moment trying to reassure myself it was a dream. Teaspoon in hand I squeezed the bag and pulled the tab out. Only then did my brain catch up with my fingers and I realised I was pulling a tail out of my cup. I continued until a very dead mouse hung over the sides of my teaspoon. I looked at the tea-soaked red 'V' on its chest, but it was the sabre teeth, which no mouse on Earth had ever sported, that gave the game away. This tiny Scrat lookalike, despite the tea dripping off its paws, belonged to *Under Avalon*.

Chapter Four

The news had picked up on the Chorus articles around what they were calling the 'Return to Avalon.' They were interviewing some folk dressed up as their characters who were then trying to explain how an augmented-reality game worked. I felt the cosplay just added to the confusion. The reporter seemed to assume that the Wizard had somehow physically escaped into Avalon, or under it, presumably, and the players were going in to pull him back out and hand him over to the police. I found myself shouting, 'That's not how it works!' at the TV before turning it off.

I still felt quite uneasy. If all these people were going back to play, would they end up in the same position as me – haunted by an elf who was now leaving mice for me to find, well, a mouse, like some giant supernatural cat. It was hard not to pull the rodent out of the freezer and look at it again, just to prove that that bit had really happened. I decided the best thing to do was to have a bath. Maybe nobody would run through the flat tonight and in the morning Scrat with the big pointy teeth wouldn't be tucked between the peas and the sweetcorn in the freezer. I could put the whole thing down to PTSD and take another week off work. I was going to need a doctor's note.

I must have dozed off and awoke with a splash and a scream. The splash was mine, but the scream was my elf with a knife in one hand and his dick in the other. I had lashed out with my left hand. Not a punch, if I'm honest – more of a reflexive flail. My engagement ring did catch on his privates though and that released a surprising amount of blood. I was surprised. He looked horrified. Dropping the knife, he ran wailing from the bathroom cupping his bleeding member in two hands. I scrambled out of the bath, pulled on my dressing gown and chased him into the living room. I felt the grass underfoot and the twigs from the trees above. I stopped. *I should put something on my feet before going into the forest.* It then registered there was only woodland behind and in front.

'I'm not in Spitalfields anymore.'

I tried to walk back but after twenty paces I gave up. My flat was not that big. This was clearly going to be something I could not just stroll casually back out of. Above the pines was a lovely light blue evening sky. The sun must just be setting. The way the light fell, the night calls, all felt so familiar, but now I was seeing it with my own eyes, not through a screen. I looked down at my body rather than Elebereth's. It was really me, in a bathrobe, in an enchanted forest. *I wish I'd picked up the knife.*

A bird sat on a branch watching me. It was one of those grey crows I had seen when Tim and I had gone to Inverness. Grey and black. It cocked its head to one side and called, then floated off to the next tree. It looked again and cawed.

'If you think I'm going to follow a strange crow into a magical wood you have another think coming,' I said to the bird. It croaked again and did a slow glide to the next bough and waited. I thought about what I had said and realised I was wrong. I set out rather gingerly among the moss and pine cones and the crow kept about two trees ahead of me.

A camp by the edge of a drop became visible as the undergrowth thinned. Beyond, cloud-filled valleys stretched away like ripples on a beach. The scale was vast. Behind everything towered a great line of mountains veined with snow, one with an overhang to the north that I recognised as the Anvil. There was no doubt I was in Avalon. It would seem this is how it works after all. I crept forward hoping that whoever was by the fire would not be able to pick me out beyond the flames. An old woman and a dwarf, as in a game dwarf with a beard and a waistcoat, appeared to be waiting for something in a pot to heat up. They looked very comfortable in each other's company and were sharing a joke.

I crept forward in a crouch until a sword reflecting the flames came to rest lightly against my chest. The arm that held it was blue. A real kobold. Really here, really threatening to stab me. I was so excited I forgot to be frightened.

A voice spoke very softly in my ear. 'They're wondering why I'm taking so long to go to the toilet.' I drew in a lungful of air. 'Don't scream. There are things about that I would rather didn't find us. Come to the fire and we will discover if you are one of them.'

'Do I have a choice?' I asked.

'No,' said the kobold, still very quietly. 'But I would rather share my meal with you than kill you, if that helps.' Rising together we stepped into the circle of light. The dwarf pulled an axe from somewhere and the woman's hands were wreathed in scarlet flames. She accompanied the magic with some very industrial language.

'What have you found in the woods, Hadrati?' enquired the dwarf.

'She found us. The old woman is losing her touch,' said the kobold.

'Bugger off,' said the old woman.

'This, whatever this is, was able to walk through your maze directly to us.'

'Hello, I'm Elebereth,' I said; it seemed right.

'Viviana and Grerr,' said the kobold. 'And I am Hadrati ...' He looked like he was going to say more but stopped himself.

'Are you a sorceress?' asked Viviana. 'I don't get any sense of magic. How could you beat my guard?'

'Maybe Hadrati is right. Old age doesn't come alone,' said the dwarf.

The old lady was looking quite crossly at me now as if it was my fault her stupid spell hadn't worked. Her tiny fists glowed brighter.

'A bird,' I said. 'I followed a bird and it led me to you.' I hoped it didn't sound quite as mad to them as it did to me.

'Describe it,' said the old lady

'A crow, only grey.' I waved my arms about. 'Mostly grey – its wings and its head were black.'

The woman stood a little more erect, her flames extinguished. 'The procurator led you here? To us?' Viviana sounded confused.

Grerr went back to the pot. 'The stew is ready. Come and share our meal, friend of Naomi.'

'What about the elf?' I asked.

'Elf? There are no elves here that I am aware of. But we do like tales. Tell us yours and we shall make of it what we can,' said Hadrati as he sat gracefully by the fire.

Grerr doled out the casserole, which was delicious, and gave a chunk of bread to each of us while I explained as best as I could how I had got here.

Grerr did most of the laughing. 'The angel was going to kill you but got distracted,' he exclaimed. Viviana spat.

I pulled my errant dressing gown together. 'Angels? I'm imagining glowing beings with wings who hang around in Heaven,' I said looking for confirmation.

'They have never had wings. Most have been corrupted by their long association with hell. The ones that follow the queen no longer glow, even on the darkest nights,' said Hadrati.

'I believe they're smaller now,' said Grerr.

'Wishful thinking, dwarf,' said Viviana 'But their decline has accelerated since they won the war with hell. The queen is the most distorted of all. They had become reliant on demons to provide the magic to allow them to prosecute their peace,' she added by way of explanation to me.

'And kobold lances,' said Hadrati.

'So what you have met is a lesser angel, a petty angel,' said Viviana.

'The queen has conquered all, for her host may be petty but it was invincible. But your guide, Naomi, laid a doom on them for what they had done so they would know no peace. And so it has proved to be. All the world rebels against the queen's arbitrary rule, but none were powerful enough to defeat her. We were all caught up in a conflict without end,' said Hadrati.

'Were?' I asked.

'About two years ago, poltergeists began to attack wherever the angels stood. Strange assaults without any sign of strategy,' he continued. 'The ghosts would appear, destroy a palace, an outpost, a stable. Kill any angel they met and then fade away.'

'The angels have no answer for them. They could dispel individual ghosts, fight them off for a while, but then the same poltergeists they had fought so hard to crush the day before would be back as strong as ever, breaking and killing everything. And the poltergeists would leave nothing whole in their wake. Once they had their victory, everything would then be broken, despoiled – chairs, latrines, curtains, doors, everything would be smashed in their attack.' Grerr shook his head in confusion.

'Ah,' I said. 'I might be able to help you on that front.' I was distracted as I struggled to hold the spoon Grerr had given me – it seemed to slip through my hand. I laboured to my feet.

'She is becoming less substantial!' Viviana shouted.

'She is a poltergeist!' cried Hadrati, sword appearing as quick as thought.

Grerr pulled a necklace from around his neck and threw it to me. As I fumbled to catch it, he said, 'Find a way back to us.' Then they were gone. Or rather I was gone.

I stood in a fenced-off football pitch just off Thrawl Street; the artificial turf felt rougher under my toes than the pine needles had done. In the security light I looked at the necklace, a tiny silver anvil on a broken leather thong.

'Not mad then,' I said to myself. I curled my fist tight around it. 'Now. How am I going to get out of here without getting arrested again?'

I moved the chair into the middle of the apartment. Since I knew the angel could move through walls, sitting in a corner didn't seem as safe as it normally would. I took the mirror down from the bathroom wall and put it opposite the seat so I could see if he was trying to come up behind me without constantly having to turn round. I unpicked the knot on the leather cord and retied what was left around my neck. It sat a little high, just below the round collar of my T-shirt, but that was fine. The knife, the angel's knife, was big enough to look like a short sword on me but it did feel much more the part than anything the kitchen had to offer. I turned all the lights on and settled on the chair watching myself in the mirror. I looked awful. It was going to be a long night, so that was not going to get any better.

As the feeble autumn sun started to illuminate the low rain clouds I'd had a lot of time to think. The wizard had been right. This world of the angels, kobolds and super-aggressive old ladies existed separately from the game. I had just physically been there, eaten the food, breathed the air and returned with an actual object in my hand. *Under Avalon* was just a portal to view it. The other side could use that same window to see you too – not just see you but reach out and stab you, and that seemed like a really bad idea.

I had checked Starflame's website in the early hours when I was less frightened and more bored. It was clear that they were back in action. They were offering fifty thousand to find the Wizard. They also seemed to be running a bunch of side quests with real cash as prizes. I looked in the Reddit commentary to make sure this wasn't just in-game coins. The company offer was British Pounds Sterling deposited in your bank account. All you had to do was add your bank details to your Avalon ID and they would send you the money as you played. I had filled it in on automatic pilot as I'd looked at some of the tasks and they weren't hard. Besides, if I couldn't get a doctor's note, I would be needing some sort of income to tide me over. At last, with the sun up, there was something important I had to do. I had gone through my arguments, rehearsed the conversation. I was going to be clear, concise and reasonable. First stop, the freezer.

The reception was a bright, airy place – lots of white marble and warm wood including a big swooping desk with a cheery-looking couple hiding behind it. They were being cheery to each other, not the courier who had come in with a box the same size as she was.

'This is for Starflame Graphics,' I said trying to sound as bored as I could.

'Leave it there,' said the woman, vaguely waving her hand at the end of the foyer.

'I need a signature. Are either of you Starflame employees?' I asked, knowing that they would be working for the building not any of the companies in it. I looked at the wall behind them where a dozen businesses were listed. 'Fifth floor, yeah?' The woman had already gone back to her fixation with her colleague. I could have tap danced the rest of the way to the lift and it wouldn't have registered. The elevator pinged open and I thought for a moment I had overdone the box – I had to put it in the lift first and squeeze in behind it. The doors closed and I blew out a breath.

'Be cool and groovy,' I told myself.

When the lift opened I was opposite a double-width door with a security panel on the right-hand side.

'Parcel for Ken Austin,' I mumbled into the speaker. There was no response but the lock clicked and I pushed my way through without waiting for instruction. The Starflame office was smaller than I expected. It was open plan with lots of empty chairs and monitors crammed together with the detritus of abandoned workplaces strewn across the tables. An orange cat curled up on one of the window ledges watched me over its tail. I guess Starflame weren't quite back up to strength yet.

A woman with short white hair looked up from her screen and pointed at a neglected desk opposite. 'Just leave it there.'

'This is marked for a Ken Austin. I'm assuming that's not you. My instructions are to get a signature.'

The woman sighed, pushed her chair back and hit the wall of a side office too close behind. 'Ken! A delivery for you.' An older man appeared, possibly in his fifties. In my mind's eye I had got Ken and the Wizard confused, but this was no rheumy-eyed tramp desperate to be believed. Age had treated Ken Austin more kindly. He had worn well as opposed to being well worn. When I had seen Ken doing launch interviews for *Under Avalon* I'd always thought he looked Japanese. Now, seeing him in the flesh, I didn't think that was right though I couldn't say why. Despite all my preparations I was thrown by the simple fact that I was in the same room as *the* Ken Austin, creator of *Under Avalon*.

'Mr Austin – I was told you would want to see this.' I put the box down and started opening it.

'I haven't ordered anything, Ellie,' he said looking hesitant.

'It's a gift.' I'd had the whole speech planned but I couldn't remember it and open the box simultaneously. It was mostly just packing paper, but I pulled out a shoebox, took the lid off and slid it across the four feet or so to Ken and the woman. Lying on top of the tissues was my evidence from the night before.

'That is an animal that only exists in Avalon,' I said trying to sound calm.

'It's just a dead mouse.' He looked at me as if I was mad.

'No, look – the red stripe, the teeth. There's nothing like that here in this world.'

Ellie had picked up the tiny carcass and looked at it. The cat watched intently, its tail twitching. 'She's right – that mouse is from the game. Why is it wet?' Her accent when she said *mouse* sounded German.

'It fell into my tea. It is very real,' I said. '*Under Avalon*, that is. And the mouse. Everyone was always amazed at how realistic *Under Avalon* looked. The breadth and depth are like nothing else.'

'It is a big instance, but it only exists in the cloud,' said Ellie.

'You remember the Wayfarer and his crew sailing to the Edgeward Isles in real time? They found mermaids on an island in the middle of an ocean. There was no shortcut there. No one would ever have gone there if they hadn't tried that pointless adventure. Well, I say pointless, he got his own YouTube channel out of that stunt. Did you put them there? Why would you put sentient mermaids in a place where no one would ever find them?' I asked.

Ellie shook her head. 'There were many developers involved in the project.'

'This mouse is proof,' I said. 'Proof they're really there.'

'The mermaids?' Ellie asked.

'All of it.'

'You know you wouldn't be the first person to say this,' said Ken.

'The Wizard.' I nodded.

'Who is now wanted by the police for murder,' said Ken calmly. He seemed to find me amusing.

'Yes, I'm aware of how it sounds. But this is more important than whether you believe I'm mad or not. Your hunt for the Wizard has got thousands, tens of thousands back into the game. But that has put them all in danger.'

Ken laughed at that. 'How could that be?'

'The angels have found a way of reaching back into this world. You remember what happened to the Nuneaton Nine? The angels were trying to cut off the attacks at source. And they're going to do it again only this time on a much bigger scale.'

'Miss, I think you better leave now,' said Ken, any trace of laughter gone. 'Ellie, you should call the police, at least for trespass.'

Ellie still held the rather sad-looking mouse. 'This could just be a prop. The kind of thing you would get at ComiCon. Do you have any other proof?' she asked.

There was a long pause as I thought through pulling out the angelic knife and waving that around to see if it qualified as evidence. Or telling them how tasty Grerr's stew was. My fingers went to pull out the anvil from under my T-shirt but the anger in Ken's face made me just cover it with my hand in case he could somehow see through the cotton.

'No, no I don't,' I admitted.

Ellie did a double take at Ken's expression and took a step away from him.

'Because there is none,' he said, his voice tight with tension.

Ellie put herself between Ken and me. 'So, I think you should go. Ken had the vision of the game, we built it, you played in it. It should stop there.'

'Okay, I'm going. But you should shut it down. If you don't, thousands of people will die.'

'Leave!' Ken shouted. I held my hands up and backed up against the exit. Ellie had to press a button to release the doors again.

I found myself in the lift, shaking, annoyed for not making it go the way I had planned. Not even close. Ellie had obviously been in that discussion a dozen times before, but she had seemed surprised at Ken's sudden fury. As I stepped out unseeing into the heavy rain of the London street it hit me – it was the word *angel*. That was when he had changed from patronising to barely suppressed rage. He hadn't corrected me because he knew.

Chapter Five

The Underground train emptied at Wembley Park. The light then seemed a little harsher without the entire football crowd to absorb it. The banter had been mostly good natured, but there was always an edge to it. A hundred people all crammed together and no one sure where the tripwire for violence was. The masks made it harder to guess who the nutters were. They had gone now. It was just me, a mirror and the yellow poles. The poles belonged to TfL but the mirror was mine. A hundred-and-sixty-centimetre one from John Lewis with a wooden frame. The bathroom one had too many sharp edges. The mirror had a stand when I took it with me from the house but that had broken at some point. I liked the Metropolitan line, very open; you could see all the way from one end to the other on a straight stretch. Made it very hard for someone to sneak up on you, even an angel.

The mirror helped too. Made it difficult for somebody to p … I stopped my thoughts there. A tricky thing to do – not to think about the things that you don't want to think about. I looked up and realised I wasn't alone. Somebody had got on.

'The next stop is Harrow on the Hill. Change for National Rail services.' I had missed a bit there. I thought it was happening more often, but it was difficult to tell. The doors opened and some way down I did notice two more people had got on. No cats, just a man and a woman walking slowly up the train and staring at me. Given that she was wearing a chain-mail bikini and he had clearly stepped out of the *Name of the Rose*, I didn't really feel it was appropriate for them to stare at me. I should have been staring at them.

'I'm sorry,' said the monk. Face looked familiar.

I tried to grab the memory, but it danced away laughing. 'Bastard.'

'I am sorry?' he repeated.

'Not you. My mind. Plays tricks on me. It's hard when you don't get enough sleep. I did when I was at home. My home, that is, but it wasn't safe there anymore.'

The chain mail caught the neon lights. Sparkled wouldn't have been the right word. Glistened? The journalist had sparkled. But then she had been wearing sequins. I thought she must have been going to a party but she said she'd come to find me about a story that she had heard. Wanted to see if it was true. Who would want to come and see me on the Underground? I nibbled at the ends of my fingers, where my nails had been. The two people had sat down opposite me. They looked expectantly at me, waiting, but I wasn't clear why.

'Can we talk to you?' 'Maybe we should go,' they said simultaneously.

I wiped my face with my hands and pulled the rope on my jacket a little tighter. 'No, you should stay. Be nice to have a real conversation. Anyone dressed like you shouldn't be out on the streets anyway. You'll be safer here on the Tube. Now that we're past Wimbledon, anyway.' They shuffled their feet. The woman's sword swept newspapers, my last meal and one of my cups off the seat and onto the floor. Hardened food spun away as far as the other detritus would allow.

'I'm sorry,' said the woman this time. She attempted to pick some pieces up but the armour hampered her movements. The mail kilt rode up, exposing a bit more of her arse than I'd bet she realised. Did people never look at themselves before going out? I caught myself in my mirror. Hair mostly escaped from a badly tied ponytail, and my vintage Barbour jacket had passed the lived-in look a while ago, cheap shoes that leaked after my nice boots had been stolen, along with my engagement ring. Although with the ring I should have thrown in the Thames long before, or sold it, or thrown it in his face.

'Not a good look.' She stood up and pulled her armour back into position. She had a midriff like a hundred-metre sprinter; how much effort in the gym did that represent?

'I was just trying to help.' She looked cross now and I recognised her.

'You're June.'

She looked baffled. 'Dione.'

'From the train.'

'Yes, I am from the train when the Wizard came on board.' June was speaking slowly as if I was special. 'And this,' she pointed at the monk, 'is Bernard, also from the train.'

He pulled his cowl back and I saw the profile of Bose. It looked like he had a short red-dot sniper sight strapped over his left eye. Fancy over-ears had been replaced by a single earpiece. A lot of serious players had initially ditched their phones for full immersion with VR Headsets. They tended to be ones who died in road traffic accidents.

'Okay. This seems a little weird. That probably means it's time for a cup of tea. Would you like a cup of tea?'

June looked around for a buffet car and settled on my thermos flask. It was obvious she was weighing up the chances of being poisoned versus causing offence. 'The station staff are brilliant – they wash and fill it for me every morning. They aren't meant to, and you mustn't tell or they'll get into trouble. I have some paper cups somewhere.'

June brightened. I checked the flask for dead mice and poured the tea into three clean cups on the seat beside me. Short measures, but it was getting towards the end of the day. After I'd finished I checked again very carefully. I could see in the mirror that they were arguing about something. That was what the mirrors were for. Not to see me, but what was behind me.

'I'm sorry?' June shouted over the sound of the accelerating train.

'Oh, nothing. Just talking to … myself.'

That was what had made me leave the house. I had packed up what I thought I would need and started moving. It seemed my angel liked to taunt me first. Break me down before they killed me. Or, possibly, it was to build himself up to killing. It seemed better to make a move before they did. I had got the mirror after that, gone back to get it, to try and make it harder for them to do that kind of thing again.

'I have Marvel if anyone would like milk. Not quite the same but you get used to it.'

'Black's fine,' said Bose, making a show of drinking his tea fearlessly.

I was losing track of what I was saying out loud.

'Are you on your own?' asked June.

'I am.' I looked at her. She had lost a lot of weight since I had seen her on the train to St Albans. Must have really worked out to get those arms too. How long ago was a question of time, though, and I had been really struggling with that. 'Lately.'

'Lately what?' asked Bose.

'I've had a lot of visitors.'

'Have you?'

'Well, two, three if you count you two separately. Or are you together? You laugh, but it had obviously crossed your minds too. You were both on the train though, if you're not together, that is.'

'We aren't together now, in that sense. We're just trying to … to stay alive, and working as a team, having somebody to guard your back is a good idea,' said June.

'Was it you who left the flour-tray traps?' Bose asked.

'You've been to my flat?'

'Tim let us in to have a look around. He contacted us. He hoped we could find you, hoped we could help.'

Tim. Difficult to follow that particular line of thought. Tim had been the man in my life. Before he … Bose was a man. I felt self-conscious but I couldn't remember what you did to make those feelings go away. *Should I ask him to leave?* That would certainly have done the trick, but it didn't seem the right answer. I tried to tidy up my hair back into the bun it hadn't been in for days.

'It's true then,' said June.

'That I should ask him to leave?' I answered a question with a question.

June looked thrown for a moment but then pointed at my head. 'The ears – you had your ears done to look more like an elf.' She sat forward. Now I felt really bad. I really didn't want to think about angels. The Wizard had said they could read minds, and thinking about them might help make them more real.

'I think I should maybe invite you both to go,' I said, trying to be firm but polite.

June sat back, hands up in surrender. 'Sorry, it's just a shock, that's all. Why did you do it?'

That was a hard one. There had been a good reason but it was dangerous to get back to that train of thought now. I'd had a plan. But if the angels could read your mind then holding that plan in your mind meant you were already beaten. They would know what it was as soon as you started. So the whole thing had kind of fallen apart. A bit like me. They both looked really puzzled. How much of that had I said out loud?

June was looking at her phone again. That seemed rude.

'I am here,' I said to remove any doubt.

'I was just checking what Anne Holloway put on Chorus tonight. "Maybe if I looked more like them they would leave me alone" is the quote.'

'Is that what I said?'

'It's what she said you said.'

'It's probably true then. Why would she want to make anything up? If she was just going to make things up, why come here and risk a cup of tea?'

I went to pick up the cups – Bose's empty one and June's untouched. My sleeves were a little short and I could feel them both staring at the scars on my wrists, some old enough to be white, some still healing. It had been tough and sometimes I thought I would end it. Oddly my angel had stopped me once. Like a cat with a mouse, they didn't seem to want the fun to end, no matter how cruel. 'Is that why they put mice in my tea?'

They looked at each other over my arms. 'Maybe we should go,' suggested Bose.

'Why?' I asked.

'It is getting late, and—'

'No. Why are you here? Why did you come tonight? This isn't where you usually are. You said you came to find me. Why?'

'We saw Anne's initial tweet and then her substack in Chorus. We had no idea you were still alive until we saw her article. We had promised Tim that—'

'Still alive?'

'Yes – the three of us are the only *Under Avalon* players still living that were on that train when the Wizard was forced off at the station and disappeared. He's being blamed for all the murders. But we know it's not him. He gave us the tools to protect ourselves.'

'I remember him sending the bloody passcodes out. When it happened I didn't think too much of it. After that though it all went to hell,' or heaven. 'What tools?' I asked.

'He gave us access to all areas of *Under Avalon*. We can visit anywhere in the game. But we've been fighting raids and they are fighting a war. So while we hold them in check on their world, they're hunting us down in ours. We have to take the fight to them or they'll kill us, one by one. We've formed the St Albans Army and we need to get to their reality, to step beyond the augmentation interface.'

Bose was quite excited but June jumped in. 'That's why we're here. In the Chorus roll, Anne says that you've been into their world, if only briefly. If we could borrow your mirror …'

I laughed. 'And you want me to tell you how to use it.' I looked down the empty carriage. The cups that I had forgotten bounced across the deck of the train, tea spreading black across the floor. I had seen that before but not in tea – the guard lying face down on the platform.

'How? The tweet doesn't say and we need to know,' June demanded again.

'I had fallen asleep in the bath.' They both looked around the carriage. 'This was when I was still at home. Next thing I know he was right there. Eyes out on stalks, playing pocket billiards.' I mimed but they had the picture anyway. June tried to stand up and stay still at the same time.

'Shite,' said June in sympathy and disgust.

'What did you do?' asked Bose.

'I punched him.'

'You punched him without it being part of the game.'

'Well, lashed out really. I think I caught him in the balls with my ring. He screamed loudly and ran off. Into the woods.'

'Woods?'

'What did you do then?'

'I was angry. I wanted to get the little bastard and went after him, but it all started to fade. Maybe as the blood dried out. I don't know.'

'But you were there, you could see without using VR?'

I was tired now and the conversation had followed the one with the journalist so closely that I was having trouble working out how far we had got with this one. I stayed quiet for a bit to see if there was a clue. I was pretty sure I hadn't mentioned Viviana, Hadrati or Grerr, which made me feel better. I fumbled with the anvil under my shirt. On the floor of the train the cup still lay on its side, bleeding.

'Not the mirror then. That's why we supposed you carried it around. So that you could move between worlds.' I scratched my head. 'Anne, the one that wrote the article, called you Alice, you see. So we assumed you were going through the looking glass.'

I could sense their disappointment but I had no idea what to do. 'I think she was joking. My name's not Alice. Or maybe it just makes more sense as a story,' I said.

'We should go.' June had stayed by the door of the carriage since I had told her about the angel and clearly didn't want to come back to where I sat. Anne hadn't given up so easily. She'd even drunk all her tea. Tough lot, journalists.

Bose exploded. 'That doesn't help us!' He seemed quite angry. 'We've done as much as we can through the game and it's not enough. We need to be able to take the war to them. Are we meant to bring our own excitable elves along? Or do we hit a blood bank before we attack their world? I have more than a thousand volunteers – we've gone over the maps the Wizard gave us. She was our one chance.' He pointed at me but looked at June for the answer.

'Or you could stop playing the game.' I shrugged. 'It occurred to me that maybe they just want us to stop. So if we stop, they stop.'

'This revelation was before or after he used you as a real-world version of Pornhub?'

'After,' I said knowing how weak it sounded when you said it out loud.

'I don't know what the driver is but I'm not sure they will stop, even when all the players are dead. And how many tens of thousands is that?' June said.

'Hundreds of thousands now with the hunt for the Wizard. And Starflame are about to launch a new release. They've done a deal so that the first level is built into the next update of Android,' said Bose.

My throat filled with vomit but I swallowed it back down. The acid bit at the base of my nose. 'But he knows what that could do,' I said almost to myself.

'Who?' asked Bose.

'Ken Austin.'

'Well, he knows it's great business, certainly. It's the Nine all over again, but this season they get to watch us die in real time.' June waved her phone at me. The screen shone brightly with a headline. 'Starflame rises from the ashes.' Underneath was a picture of the man who got cross at mice, Ken Austin. The office I had met him in made up the background of the shot but full of people now. I noticed the cat was still in the window.

'A wall.' Keep thinking of a wall. Push the idea from your mind. Neon orange suburban England rattled past, so at odds with the image in my head that I was trying so hard to forget.

'I'm sorry?'

'So am I. Look, Mr Bose, I am not going to be the pin-up girl for your war. I've done my best to forget about Chorus and tweets. It had seemed so important once to be part of that great hybrid consciousness. Now it seems so exposed, so dangerous. Bet you all wish you hadn't been so quick to drop the Wizard in it. He was safe on the train till you had him thrown off.'

Bose had no answer. He made a show of standing up, hands on knees as he did so. I was worried that he was going to leave with some quote from the game.

Instead he just nodded, walked past the disabled seat and stood by the door waiting for the Metropolitan to stop.

'Goodbye,' said June. She looked relieved as Chalfont and Latimer slid into view. She stopped to check herself in my mirror and then stepped out onto the darkening platform.

I sat and listened; they were still in the station arguing about what they should do next. I couldn't really make out the words, but it sounded like the hope of humanity had run out of ideas. I stood by the disabled seat looking out of the windows at the harsh sodium lamps gathering speed outside, trying not to think. I knew a part of me was disgusted at what I had become. That successful woman I used to know, with a life. But that girl had chased things through the woods looking for something to castrate. She had lived for a fortnight with dried blood on her body and a necklace in her hand with the vague notion that they would somehow transport her back into a magical land for vengeance. Now being dead didn't seem such a terrible thing – better than this. Despite me acting surprised at what June and Bose had told me, I had seen what the angels had done to the first two off the train. What the TV didn't show you, Chorus sure did. The words #slow death# had trended for days. Maybe mortality wasn't so bad; it was the transition that was tricky. My lovely Underground had kept me safe. But that wasn't enough anymore. Not now June had shown me that picture of Ken's recruiting poster and the millions of unprepared people he was putting at risk.

I was in the bathroom; both taps were running, bubble bath foaming, steam bellowing out into the hall. My picture hanging hammer lay hidden at the bottom of the bath. The house, unoccupied, had grown too cold for a couple of hours of central heating to make an impact. I shed my clothes like a lizard's skin but I still looked filthy in the mirror. I threw the near-empty bottle of whisky in my hand at my image and both shattered, showering the floor in a dangerous frost. I hadn't been able to find my razor but nature would always provide a way. I picked up the bottom third of the jagged glass and slid into the bath.

Heavy steps ran overhead, somewhere in the roof. As I sank beneath the bubbles I wondered if June and Bose had continued their argument on Chorus. *You might as well give the angels a call and tell them what you had in mind.* I had learned that much. That's why I'd posted on Chorus that I'd had enough and I was going home to die. I checked, Tim had blocked me. Only my arms were above the brilliant white clouds. I cut one arm; it hurt more than I'd expected, the soap stinging instantly in the bright scarlet slash. The footsteps ran down the wall. Too late for anything other than some necrophilia. I scratched down the length of my left and it spouted red. *Is that because I'm hot now?* Forgetting why I was there I thrust both limbs down into the water to finish the job.

Something crying? Laughing? Thin, pale fingers fishing in the bubbles for me. *No fun if I'm dead then.* I brought the hammer down on his head and we collapsed on the bathroom floor.

'You took your fucking time.' I felt quite weak so I hit him again just to make sure.

Chapter Six

The internet is a wonderful thing. You could find out how to do anything as long as you didn't mind your search history singing like a canary to the powers that be – a phrase I had always assumed meant the government, but I realised now included angels. Take waterboarding, for example. Everything is there to tell you how to do it, though they underplay how strong the rope has to be once you get going. When somebody believes they're in the process of drowning they can exert a huge amount of force to try and get free. I wondered if they had skipped that bit deliberately in case somebody was mad enough to give it a go. He'd broken one arm free from the waterboard before I could hit him with my trusty hammer again.

When he came to and realised he had been reattached to the board he broke. He would do whatever it took not to help me with my Waterboarding for Dummies course again. As I was on a water meter, I hauled him back into the living room and propped him the right way up against the couch. He dripped on the boards, making them slippery.

'How did you get into this plane of existence?' I asked.

'Somehow when I fought you by the farmhouse you were wounded, not by my blows, but the bleeding made you more real. I cut you then.'

'Yes, I remember.' I touched the first of the many scars on my arm.

'That brought me into your world. But I had to be cautious.'

'Why?' I asked.

'I have seen the great magic you can wield. You have the destructive energy of a demon. Of course I was cautious.'

'Ah,' I said, trying to give myself some thinking space. 'Yes, I have, haven't I? Why didn't you let me succeed when I was attempting to kill myself?'

'To see a life lost is not easy. It is much harder here, where I am not guided by the queen's will. I was no longer afraid of you though. Then you left your familiar here and disappeared.'

'Familiar?'

The angel nodded towards the phone on my table. 'It gives you power but it allows us to track you. To know what you are communicating.'

'Ah,' I said again. 'You can't read minds then. Just WhatsApp.'

'The queen can read minds. Also the Lady Arden could, before the queen killed her.' The angel looked sad then rather than fearful.

'I need to know more. Start at the beginning.'

The angel explained to me then about a different heaven and hell from the one I was used to – a plane of existence where spiritual beings are made flesh. About the terrible wars against the unrighteous, which seemed to be just about everyone that wasn't an angel. The queen eventually brought peace to the world. But that had gone wrong somehow and they found they hadn't brought peace to anyone, especially themselves. The angel explained the influence of the queen's wrath on the angels and Naomi's doom on the queen. It was a good feeling that I could get some of the references.

The day was settling into the afternoon when we finally finished. I didn't have all the answers, but I had as much as I could cope with. I made a lunch for myself and fed him bite-sized pieces of a cheddar sandwich and sips from a cup of water. He shrieked when I came back from the kitchen with his knife.

'Please, I have told you all I know!'

I looked with surprise from the blade to him. 'No, no. I just need to get back. Back to your world. I need to find some guys who can help me.'

'Who?'

'I think it's safer for everyone if you stay innocent.' I laughed. 'Just in case. So I'm going to take some of your blood. Not a lot, just enough.' I advanced on the struggling angel, but I was fairly confident those new knots would cope with anything he had to throw at them. 'You need to be still though. This is very sharp and it wouldn't take much to cut something important.' He froze in terror. 'Don't worry,' I continued. 'You've made sure I've had lots of practice.'

I sat in the great hall with the great and good of the league that had been built against heaven. That I had helped build. It had gone pretty well, all things considered. On the plus side bringing players in directly rather than through the game had made a significant difference to their effectiveness. On the negative side it had really increased their casualty rate. The blood brought them here physically, but the phones still gave them access to their gaming powers. Their chance to be a warrior wizard for real. It was an intoxicating offer. Given the choice of being hunted down at home or coming here to fight and take their chances, most people were going for the latter, even if it probably meant not getting home alive.

'So we are agreed then. We begin the final attack on the Celestial City in three weeks. Does anyone here have issue?'

The Council, as it had called itself, fell silent as everyone looked at everyone else. Jasper, the stone elemental, said that would give him time to weaken the walls in preparation for the assault. June, Bose and the rest of the ghosts were keen on waiting till the Wayfarer was back from his current trip in the Mediterranean. He would bring a tight, experienced crew with him and the Wizard had said if we could get the Wayfarer on board, as it were, then he would join the raid too. I wasn't so sure that giving the highest-profile players in the world nearly a month's notice of our plans was smart and had said so. But the mood of the Council had gone against me; I was sounding paranoid. And given the last time I'd seen the Wizard was through a window as I left him to die, even I couldn't be sure that wasn't colouring my view.

Irrespective of my own feelings, the fact was that the kobold colonel had turned ghosts, rebels, and hell's heroes into a surprisingly effective fighting force. If he was happy, then everyone else should be too.

'Thank you all,' said Hadrati. 'As convener I call this meeting closed. For those of you who can stay, Grerr has managed to put some food together – it should be ready in about an hour. I think he was anticipating a longer discussion.'

The people in the room gathered into huddles. I had said my piece so I left the hall and began walking up some steps just to see where they would go. Maybe I would find some furniture I could break up for old times' sake.

The air got colder as I climbed past lots of smaller quarters used as bunkrooms and for stores. Eventually the staircase opened out into an open plaza, sitting half on top of the tower I had come up and half carved out of the mountain. A great full moon rose in a clear frosty sky. Spindrift washed across the flagstones, filling up the gaps where mortar had failed, and collected under an abandoned iron stove. There was no rail at the edge, which made me slow to go and take in the view. I resisted the urge to shuffle forward on all fours. Below, a great wall ran from this peak to the next like a great heavy curtain draped between two poles. To the south was the merchants' town we had ransacked a couple of days before, cutting off the Celestial City and seizing three angels. Now that Hadrati was running the show we really were functioning like a proper army, executing plans, capturing and holding strategic points, bleeding prisoners. To the north, far down in the valley, lay the city of angels, a few lights twinkling like stars at the edge of my sight. I stood for quite a while shivering, but reluctant to leave.

Someone came up beside me – a youthful lady, well dressed, an amber necklace around her neck that seemed to bathe her in gold when all around was silver.

I recognised her eventually. 'Viviana?'

She smiled sadly and the effect was stunning. 'It's a long story,' she said. 'When I was young I was cursed to look old, apart from once a month when I would look as you see me now. Now I am old and am blessed that once a month I get to appreciate the power and beauty of my youth.' She stretched and did a whirl and the snow came off the mountain to dance with her. She stopped and laughed. 'Nothing hurts – you tend to forget how much pain you live with.'

'Yes,' I said in agreement.

'What will you do now?' she asked.

'Fight. I'm still one of the strongest ghosts in the team.'

'You are. But I foresee you shall lose your life if you fight again.'

'Can you see the future, Viviana?' I asked.

She looked serious – fabulous, but serious. 'Yes.' Then she snorted. 'No. My sister Valentina can. She knows which bridge must fail. Which is why she is Queen of Sestola and Rondoni while I sleep in hedges.'

'Oh. So I might be alright then?'

'Might be? You can die a real death here. How many times have I saved your life?'

I was confused for a moment by the dusky young woman and then recalled the fierce little old lady pulling me out of the way of a charging giant. Or when she deflected a blue blast from the forces of heaven when my mana was exhausted.

'Twice?'

'Thrice. And Eldrun probably the same.'

I remembered the fire elemental burning the angels' arrows as they flew towards me.

'I know and I'm grateful.'

'It's not a question of being grateful. Your companions were careless of you, even when you were their only gateway into this world.' I hadn't considered it in those terms. 'How much more reckless will they be of you now that they have their own angels to bleed?'

The air around us grew warmer and Eldrun walked through the arch and onto the platform beside us. 'I heard my name.' She looked at us both and then around the monochrome view. She had backcombed her red hair and was wearing a flowery summer dress. 'Grerr asked me to round up the stragglers for a meal.'

'I was trying to persuade her that she should be more careful in the next attack,' said Viviana.

'For sure,' Eldrun said. She sounded Nordic but I hadn't had a chance to get to know her because she was always ferrying messages from all the disparate fronts of the war against heaven. That, and the angels' heavy reliance on forms of water magic meant it was difficult for her to get involved in the fighting. For the same reason, the army had learned to love waterproof mobiles, ideally with an IP69K rating or better.

'I feel I have to fight,' I said. It was the thing that had kept me going – the notion that at the end of all of this there would be an actual end. Perhaps even victory. But mostly just an end.

'Yes, to fight, but you don't have to die. Join us,' said Viviana. Eldrun nodded.

'If that would be okay,' I said.

'Good idea. It will be easier to keep an eye on you,' Eldrun said. We stood in silence for a moment looking at the moon and the frozen world beneath. I had stopped shivering now that Eldrun was beside me.

'Thank you both.' It was nice to feel wanted for no other reason than people wanted to. As we walked back towards the stairs, I allowed myself a little pirouette in diamond-snow-filled air.

I liked sitting on buses now, especially at the front where it was easy to imagine TfL's finest as a red whale coursing through the sea and all the scooters swirling around it like shoals of whining mackerel. The image was helped by the sheer volume of water in the sky and the great pools that had formed above the blocked drains. The drivers, conscious that Chorus was their omnipresent deity, edged through the floods trying to avoid swamping all around them. The view was hampered by the condensation on the inside following lines scratched in the glass, overflowing the black rubber seals. Funny how much more you noticed when you didn't carry a phone. My Apple was just for war now.

It had always been an escape. On the night I tried not to think about more than most things I tried not to think about, I was upstairs playing *Eve* on VR goggles and headphones. *Eve* was an all-absorbing game of spaceships, pilots, and a vast galaxy to explore. My clan were in negotiations to stop a huge Russian fleet from wiping out our space station in Null Sec. It wasn't going well. I shut everything down and sat furious that a world that someone else had built was as stupid as the one we actually lived in. On *Eve* nights I set my alarm for midnight so I could still say goodnight to Tim rather than sneak in when he was asleep. It was a bit of a shock to realise it was only just after ten. No point in sitting up here moping, I told myself. I'll have a cup of tea and we can watch *Newsnight* together.

As I came down the stairs I heard Tim and Sofia laughing. Funny how that sound always carries so well. I decided I would ask if they both wanted a brew.

As I reached the bottom of the steps Sofia said, 'This is a terrible idea. What if she comes down?'

My hand was on the door handle.

'It will never happen. Wednesday is *Eve* night with the clan. If they have some big job on, I've seen her still playing when the sun comes up,' Tim said.

And we've had that argument, which is why I now set an alarm, I thought. I was feeling very hard done by at this point. 'Well, that's not fair,' I said pushing open the door.

Only the steam punk lamp above the bookshelves was on. Sofia and Tim were facing each other on the couch so intently it took them a few seconds to react to me coming into the room. Sofia grabbed her bra and that thin knitted cardigan that always had the top button pop loose. Tim looked around hopelessly for his T-shirt.

'It's hanging off the TV,' I said.

Tim looked horrified. I was so focused on him I was oblivious to Sofia, so I couldn't tell you her reaction.

'It's not what you think,' Tim said flatly.

'Seriously. Is that statement hardwired into men?'

They exchanged glances and laughed again, nervously. After that it got shouty and breaky. Which was why I ended up in a one-bed apartment and played *Under Avalon* a lot. Although in my darker moments I often wondered if it was really the other way round. Since that night, despite being the one to break it off with Tim, I kept trying to pull him back into my life and somehow hating him for it.

The bus gingerly pulled up at another flooded bus stop and sank to its knees. I heard people hopping on board to try to avoid having to stand in the puddle. A serious-looking young woman climbed up the steps. She was wearing a cream cable-knit top rather than a rain jacket, though the beaded water hinted at some sort of waterproofness. Aran was the word that sprang to mind, but I couldn't be sure if that was Irish or Scottish. She smiled at me, confirming that she wasn't a local.

'Sorry,' I said, 'I was just admiring your jumper.'

She looked down in surprise. 'This old thing. My mum knitted it. It's been everywhere with me.' She pulled off her rucksack and put it between her feet in front of her. We sat side by side for a while. She didn't wear a mask either, which I usually associated with angry young men, but she seemed the opposite. She radiated calm in a way I had only seen Grerr or Hadrati do. Calm or capable? Whatever the world was going to throw at her, she looked like she could cope.

'I'm pretty sure you're the one I'm meant to be looking out for,' she said finally. 'If you are, then I have a message for you.'

'Me?' She didn't look like the usual Avalon fan girl. No rubber sword sticking out of her backpack. And I had left my phone at home. No one would recognise me without my Elebereth overlay. 'That seems unlikely.'

She looked me in the eyes. Hers were grey under a straight black fringe. They looked directly into my soul. I wished I had eyes like that. 'Yes.'

'Okay. What's the message?'

'It is that in this coming final battle you shouldn't play their games.'

'Is that it?'

'Yes.'

'Could it not be a bit clearer?'

'No.'

'Does that mean I should just skip the whole show? Or that I should go but not take part? Or is it that I should try and stop the Wayfarer takeover? Or the Wizard? Or are we just fighting the kobold's war for him without any idea why? We're taking on angels, after all, and that would usually mean we are the baddies. Look, there's a lot going on at the moment and some clarity would be really useful.'

'I think it's meant to be unclear. It's all about your choices, your free will. She's really keen on the idea of self-determination all of a sudden. If she tells you what to do it won't work, although that has never stopped her telling me what to do. Anyway, don't have a go at me – I'm just the messenger. Literally, in this case. That's it. I've done what she asked me to. Don't play their games. Got it?'

'Yes. Got it. I just don't understand it.' I paused, thinking I should make the most of this Delphian audience. 'Is there any chance you could tell me who sent the message?' Although I suspected I had already worked out the answer.

'Nope.' We sat again looking out the front window, swaying almost enough to touch despite the aisle between us. 'Where are we?' I noticed she rolled her 'r's, which made her sound Scottish.

'Hyde Park Corner. At the back of Buckingham Palace,' I said, wiping a bit of the condensation away to confirm.

'I've never been – is it worth it?' she asked, sounding more the age she looked now.

'Not a lot to see really. With night coming on they put on the gas lamps, which makes it quite pretty. If I were you I would carry on to Trafalgar Square. That's more touristy. The National Gallery is always good. You could walk up to TKTS on Leicester Square and see if there's a show you fancy. It's a good way to make the most of the time you're here.'

She smiled again. 'Good luck,' she said as she climbed back down the stairs.

'*Danke*,' I said, though I really just wanted to take her home and add her to my useful supernatural people collection.

Chapter Seven

I had spent a week trying to figure out which game I shouldn't play. It seemed there were an infinite number of options, but in the end I decided it was simply *Under Avalon*. So, no phone, no powers. But I really believed I needed to take Viviana up on her offer. That had made me feel wanted for the first time in so long. If I was still going to go, which I was, I should bring something offensive. The ghost army of St Albans had tried recommissioned pistols, but they were not effective. Someone had even got their hands on a couple of AR-15s, but though the angels were knocked down by the US number-one gun for mass shootings, they weren't knocked out. The round was just too light. The queen's armour was indeed impenetrable. Hence the raiding parties were stuck with getting very close and personal plus heavily reliant on magic.

But I'd done physics at school so I was pretty sure that a big soft lead ball would transfer a lot of energy to whatever it hit. So the armour might stand, but whatever was behind that plate would get a thump. I knew a couple of Sealed Knot people from before Tim. Lovely lads who smelled of woodsmoke and wished they had been able to fight for king or parliament. They never could resist a girl who wanted to play with their muskets. Having seen what the ball did to a reproduction breastplate I really felt I was going in the right direction, but it took too much skill and effort to arm the muzzle-loading flintlocks. Talking about raw stopping power, one of them suggested a KSG Bullpup shotgun (look it up on Chorus) and that brought me back to Bose's St Albans army and a friend of a friend who knew someone out in Buckinghamshire.

The train to Aylesbury went through some picturesque countryside. It made me realise how long it had been since I'd been outside London. Stepping out in Aylesbury reminded me why I hadn't. The station itself looked like a survivor of the old country town, but around it was a mass of huge modern sheds, brick office blocks and failed retail outlets that had been turned back into housing with mixed success. Rubbish had piled up in the narrow walkways and the few people I saw made Londoners look friendly. A couple of the houses on my left had been boarded up long enough to attract a lot of low-quality graffiti. The rain slumped into drizzle while I looked around for Mangrove Jack's, the pub I'd been advised to go to. No Vaccard check on the door told me all I needed to know about the place. I had left my phone behind at the station as instructed so I had no choice but to go to the bar and order a drink. The bloke behind the taps was the first affable face I'd seen all day. I picked a table and waited.

'You don't look like my usual clients,' said a voice behind me. It was hard not to turn around but given that there was some sort of game being played I thought I should try and look cool.

'That's probably a good thing,' I replied. An unremarkable man came into view, very compact, Daniel Craig when he has his shirt on. His wide nose looked like it had been thumped more than once but not recently. Dense blond hair on a number-six cut emphasised the Bond look.

He sat his pint of bitter down beside my lager. 'Interesting choice of gun,' he said with a smile. 'You expecting to have to kill a lot of people in a hurry?'

'It's happened before,' I said.

He looked at my eyes and grunted with surprise. 'You a spook?' His look shifted; nervous would be too strong a word … cautious.

I laughed, which I didn't think helped. 'No. Not in that sense. No government connection. Or anti-government for that matter, I promise. The money is in the holdall as you asked. And it's the type of bag you specified. I didn't expect to get questioned on my morals.'

He drank from his pint and played with his zippo lighter. He didn't look old enough to be missing being able to smoke in pubs. The design was a plane. Swept wings. That old grey and green camouflage the RAF used to use. Tim would have known.

'We all have morals. It's just the mad dogs that don't, and nobody wants to work with them.' He closed the lid of the lighter with a flick. 'You're new, so I wanted to be sure that you weren't going to go on some sort of random spree.'

'And are you now?' I asked.

'Revenge, I reckon.' He glanced behind me for the briefest of seconds and then stood up. 'But whatever it is, it won't be random.' He finished his beer and left.

'Is that a no?' I demanded of the empty chair. I alone sat in Mangrove Jack's watching the bubbles' short rise in the last of my lager. I sighed. This had been the one hope I had of getting a modern gun. Without this it was going back into heaven armed with nothing more dangerous than a Brown Bess. I put my drained glass beside his, got up and picked up the bag. It was heavier than when I put it down. I resisted the urge to look inside and tried to walk out of the pub as calmly as possible.

A few people were scurrying from bank to betting shop in the triangle that made up Kingsbury Square. The rain-soaked flagstones looked golden in the feeble sunlight that seemed bright after the gloom of Jack's. There was no sign of the man with the squashed nose. No one seemed to spare me a second glance; no one cared. I really wanted to throw the holdall in the bushes and run but I didn't. Lives were at stake, mostly mine. I pulled on my mask and walked back to Aylesbury Station as slowly as I could manage.

Body armour proved to be much simpler to source. I contacted a company on the internet who were brilliant when I explained what I needed. There was a bit of hesitation when I said that crossbows were a possibility and they suggested ballistic plates that would fit into their bulletproof vest – just to be sure. They had told me how to take my measurements so when the thing turned up it fitted like a glove. Once I was all kitted out the New Model Army let me practice with my gun as long as I gave them a try. When we saw how much damage the twelve-bore slugs did, one of them asked if I was going elephant hunting.

Then the army of St Albans adventure pack turned up with instructions on where and when to be along with an invoice for £100. At least someone had written 'Complimentary' over it. There was a ten-millilitre red capsule with neat pictograms telling you to keep it in the fridge until needed and then smear the contents around the inside of the band at the start of the raid. The wristband was some sort of ecologically sound bamboo thing with the words '*Under Avalon*: Final Battle' embossed round the outside and a groove for the blood on the inner. I tried not to think about the three angels they had captured. I checked in on my supply; he seemed quite happy with Netflix and two tubes of Pringles.

'You be careful,' he said as if I was going to the shops. He had worked out that he could escape weeks ago but said he wanted to see how *Mad Men* finished. He seemed a lot happier in himself and glad to be out of all the hatred and craziness. That was where I wanted to be too, but I wasn't there yet.

It was odd being back at the tower when it was full of people. As the evening wore on the raiding parties and clans were coming in piecemeal and organisers in *Under Avalon* tabards were busy with sheets and flags trying to make sure everyone got to their right mustering point. There were quite a lot of muscle-bound high fives and more midriffs on show than at a beach volleyball tournament. Adding to this was June, looking magnificent in her cut-down chain mail, sword slung across her back, black hair cascading down her back in tight ringlets. She spotted me and came across, flipping through her tablet. She looked above my head for my handle, which wasn't there, and then down at my face.

'Alice?'

'Ju … Dione. All ready to go? You've done an amazing job here.'

'Yes, I think we've only got about twenty per cent no-shows, which is better than we were expecting. Some attendees just wanted the wristband.' She looked me over carefully. 'No phone? I had you down as one of the support magic users.' She used her iPad to point at one of the pop-up banners with 'UA LB M2' written on it.

'I had a change of heart since the last raid. I'm with the Pathfinders tonight.'

'The kobold's lot?' Dione sounded surprised.

'Colonel Hadrati, yes.'

'That's a pretty dangerous slot. Is that why you've gone for the tactical squad look?' she asked.

I smiled thinly. 'Too many near misses while I was gadding about in a gown. And I brought this for close encounters.' I patted the shotgun. 'I'm not sure it will help but we shall find out. Good luck, Dione.'

'You too, Alice.' She stepped back into the crowd of new arrivals still in the 'this is really real' stage. Quite a few adventurers were just feeling the stone walls and running their hands through grass and going 'Wow' They also tended to be the ones who jumped when they saw me.

'Sorry, officer,' said one kid who didn't look twenty. His eyes were as large as saucers as he gawked at the assembling army.

'It's okay, I'm not police,' I said trying to reassure him.

'Are you like a marshal, making sure everything's fair?'

The penny dropped – I knew what my messenger on the bus had meant. 'This is not a game. There are no marshals here. Nothing about this is fair. If I were you, I would take off your band now and keep walking that way …' I pointed south past the abandoned town. 'Until you find yourself back in, where are you from?' I asked.

'Nuneaton.'

'Ah, home of the Wizard.'

'Yeah.' He nodded like a dog on the dashboard of a car. 'It would be like so cool to be here, to see the Wizard in action. For real.'

I patted him on the shoulder and pointed behind him again. 'Nuneaton,' I reiterated.

The stars were fading out, obscured by unseen clouds above. I walked out of the crowds to where a small group had formed on the north side of the wall. With everyone concentrating on checking their kit it was much quieter. Grerr was there with six dwarves all dressed in chain mail with shields, crossbows and axes. Next to them, Hadrati stood with ten other kobolds in samurai armour and two big dinosaur-bird things. I hugged both the dwarf and the kobold, which embarrassed them quite a bit, once recovered they introduced me to their teams. I found myself edging away from the killer birds. They were the same size as horses but moved as fast as cats.

'Don't worry, we couldn't have deinony in the fight – they wouldn't know who to eat first. They are here to see if we win or lose and will take the message to all the free peoples.'

'Very reassuring,' I said.

Viviana came out of the tower, saw us and waved, but it was a minute before she was close enough to talk. She wore the necklace she had worn that night on the platform and somehow it carried a reflection of how she looked under the moon.

'Hello, Viviana.'

She went to respond but instead an amplified voice cut across us all.

'Ladies and gentlemen, boys and girls! Thank you for coming to the *Under Avalon*: Last Battle event.' Cheering and whooping broke out from the other side of the wall. 'But first I thought we should take the chance to meet the person who has made this possible. The one who showed us how we could really get to this world!'

I felt my stomach fall away; I didn't want any recognition. Viviana did her best to support my arm as I staggered.

'Ladies and gentlemen, boys and girls. I give you the Wizard!'

Now I felt betrayed. 'What about me?' I said mostly to myself.

Viviana looked puzzled. 'What about you?' she asked, having to raise her voice among the cheering.

'We plan to move off in half an hour, folks. That's half an hour, so we have time for a short Q&A before we do. Anyone got a question to kick off this truly unique event?'

The locals moved off down the hill away from the noise. As we walked, the valley in front of us filled with mist.

'Ah, Naomi's breath. It will hide us from the angelic arrows as we approach the city.'

'You know, for someone who isn't even in the area she gets a lot of credit for what goes on,' I said.

'It shows how powerful she is. Even in her absence she still gives us support and succour,' said Grerr looking satisfied with his argument. 'Anyway, why are you joining us tonight rather than taking your usual position in the ethereal army?'

'Viviana said it would be easier to keep an eye on me if I was here.'

'Three times I have saved her,' Viviana said.

'Once,' said Grerr.

'Same here,' said Hadrati.

'Thinking about it, is it a good idea to have you with us? Based on your track record we should be insisting you're as far away as possible,' Grerr said as we walked through the mist. He turned to me; it would usually be difficult to spot a smile through a beard in the dark, but not with this dwarf. I could hear it in his voice. 'What gave you the notion to stop being a ghost?'

'I am fairly sure a little bird told me,' I replied.

'You see. Naomi is with us.'

'I bloody well wish she was,' said Viviana with feeling.

Chapter Eight

Closer to the city than the tower, the party stopped by a long barrow where the fog seemed less thick and the air smelled sweet. A thousand flowers bloomed on the top of the mound. At the northern end was a great stone that looked like an entrance. Everyone bowed their head for a moment.

'Who is this for?'

'Lorcan,' said Grerr. 'The best of angels, loved by all. Killed by the queen's will.'

'Why?'

'Oh, it's a long story,' said the dwarf sadly. 'I'll tell you when all this is done.'

We pressed on into the thick fog, concerned that we would fail as vanguard if the angels had set up a screen to discover us. But we reached the boundary of the Celestial City without a problem. The tops of the walls were invisible in the soft absorbing grey. We backed off a hundred yards so we could talk quietly, though the mist seemed to swallow all noise as well as light. The dwarves sat closest to the enemy, their crossbows cocked.

'We have been lucky,' said Hadrati. 'On a clear night the angels would surely have seen us. Then the ghosts would have had to advance through star-guided arrows all the way to the wall. We would have failed before an angel fell.'

'Na—'

Viviana silenced Grerr. 'If we're all spared to be here at the end you can thank her then,' she said fiercely.

'You know what she said when you summoned her, Viviana,' said Grerr. 'She was clear we had to sort it without her, or she would just set herself up as another queen.'

'It's all about free will,' I said. They all looked at me in surprise. 'I got the same message and I didn't think it was very helpful either.'

'We have to have faith,' said Grerr confidently, and the Pathfinders grunted agreement with various degrees of conviction.

I had expected to hear the raiding party long before they reached us. In the last couple of fights someone had brought a serious sound system and insisted on playing a backing track as we fought. Maybe they had played Robbie Williams one time too many. I was taken aback by the discipline on show. One of their vanguard passed me in the fog.

'I don't think I've heard you guys be so quiet before,' I said.

The scout looked back to the hundreds we couldn't see. 'The Wizard said it was really important that we keep the advantage of surprise.'

'Did he say anything else?' I asked.

'Yeah, he said with the amount of firepower we can deliver tonight we should wipe out the elves before sunrise. Oh yeah, and that nobody should go full Leeroy Jenkins.' I smiled; that meme must be older than some of the kids here. If it's still on Chorus it will be in the archive section 'When the walls fall, the Wizard will lead us in.'

The timing was perfect. As the army drew up in front of the wall a gust of wind tore the fog to shreds. Jasper, having burrowed beneath the city, pulled out whatever keystone he had created and the masonry collapsed in a great roar. The Wizard walked forward into the clearing dust and mist, his full game aspect shining bright with the power of his phone. I had actually forgotten how high a level the Nuneaton Nine were.

The Wizard stopped at the top of the rubble. 'It's time for that favourite quote we used to do as the Nuneaton Nine when we rocked Under Avalon. 'It's Ezekiel 25:17' The Wizard seemed to grow as he spoke – Bose and June were bathed in the white light he was generating. Even the Wayfarer beside him looked a little in awe.

'Is this some sort of benediction?' asked Grerr.

'Sort of,' I said. I had to smile; all the ghosts were grinning at this shared instant of madness, this cinematic moment. Everyone, it seemed, had their phone out recording the scene. A thousand phones and the Wizard was finally where he wanted to be, sharing his triumph with his players. No longer the broken man, no longer grey, but white.

'... and they shall know that I am the Lord, when I shall lay my vengeance-' No one saw the bolt. It must have come from directly within the city, but it hit the Wizard so hard that he didn't even move. There was just a ball of red haze that expanded out among and above the raiding party until gravity kicked in and Mr Philips settled on his brothers, and sisters, like fine rain. There was complete silence other than the sound of fingertips and toes striking off shields and helmets as the last of the Wizard came to rest.

'Fuck me,' said Viviana.

The Wayfarer, now half scarlet, drew his cutlass and shouted, 'For the Wizard!' He charged through the gap. With a roar all the raiders followed him.

'Your warriors are fierce,' said Hadrati.

'Oh, these aren't warriors. Most of them would be farmers or merchants in this world,' I said. The kobold looked shocked. 'I'll bring you a book on Stalingrad. That will give you a better idea of what we're capable of when we put our minds to it.'

We picked our way into the city that was already bloody and chaotic. By not paying enough attention I ended up in front. Three arrows hit me in the chest hard enough to lift me off my feet and throw me back among the dwarves, who returned fire while the rest took cover. All the air was knocked out of my lungs and for a moment I couldn't breathe anything back in. I stared stupidly at the white shafts sprouting from my front and gasped like a newly landed fish. Grerr pulled me back behind some rubble using the grab handle on the yoke of my vest. Crouching beside me, he felt for wounds, and looked down in surprise when his hand came back clean. He grasped the three fletchings and cut the wood off, leaving the tips embedded in the nylon weave of the jacket.

'Two,' he said.

'Oh no,' I wheezed. 'That was the flak jacket.'

The dwarf patted me on the head and went forward with his crossbow. I pulled out the front ceramic plate, which had been snapped by the impact of the arrows. I felt a mixture of terror at what would have happened without the armour and delight at still being alive. I joined the fight a minute or so later once I had persuaded my lungs to work properly again. The roar of the shotgun proved very useful for making everybody keep their heads down. Grerr kept looking at it enviously though it reminded me I'd forgotten my ear defenders. The angels withdrew and we advanced into the city itself. In the middle of the street we discovered around twenty dead ghosts and two or three angels. It was hard to be sure how many because they had been torn apart by the ghosts and the parts scattered.

Eldrun dropped down among us, a flaming jet breaking her descent. 'I have found the queen and her close guard. They're in her old palace,' she said looking around at the devastation in horror.

'Good,' said Viviana. 'If we can destroy Alva we can bring this madness to an end. Her hatred still drives the angels. Eldrun, if you can find the Wayfarer, tell him that's where he must head. You may have to lead them.' The fire elemental nodded and thundered off into the night.

The abandoned city was so sprawling that pockets of angels and ghosts would come upon each other from almost any direction. I came round a corner and nearly bumped into an angel armed with a glowing spear. He hesitated as he looked at me, my ears, and steered his weapon through the kobold beside me. I fired instinctively, hitting the angel's shoulder, which exploded in a mass of shattered bone and flesh, leaving his left arm attached only by skin and jacket. As he reached for me, I shot twice more and the angel spun down the street and slid to a halt. Most of our party were scanning the streets while two tried to save the life of the kobold. I stared at the bloody mess that had been so inhumanly beautiful a few seconds before and threw up.

'We need to go,' said Hadrati, lowering our companion to the cobbles. I struggled to follow what was happening. The confusion of the city fighting overwhelmed me. At some point I got turned around and fired at some ghosts. Luckily, I still couldn't see straight after being sick.

Viviana pulled me into a doorway. 'Breathe. Clear your sight.' I felt a calmness come upon me, wash through me, and go. 'Are you with us again?' asked the little old lady.

I nodded. 'Yes. Thank you.'

'Four,' she said and shuffled off after the Dwarves who were taking the brunt of the incoming fire.

'That definitely doesn't count,' I croaked and followed her to break up the poorly armoured archers.

Eldrun had done a good job of rounding up the ghosts as some three hundred of them fought their way up the wide steps and into the main hall. At the far end we could see our prize. The Queen of Heaven and her bodyguard, the Queen's Rangers, stood at the bottom of the grand staircase. The air in between was filled with arrows, bolts and blasts of magic while the hand-to-hand guys tried to close the gap. Viviana sent a red ball of destruction at the queen who deflected it and ran up the stairs. The fireball tore off a chunk of marble from a pillar, showering all about with shards of stone. The rangers were dressed in the queen's petal armour. I had been told that it took the queen a year and a day to make each suit and that no weapon could pierce it to the wearer. But after this war with the poltergeists it all looked battered and dented. The rangers too looked careworn, tired. But the armour still worked and still they fought and died, and the ghosts died by the score with them.

Eldrun landed beside me. 'The queen is escaping,' she said, 'and I cannot fight her.'

'Take me,' I said without thinking. The fire elemental picked me up and we leapt to the balcony some sixty feet above. A coiling stream of water engulfed Eldrun, and her fires extinguished. She tumbled into the maelstrom of death below leaving me teetering on the balustrade. Managing to fall forward, I shot four times in quick succession, hitting the queen in the leg with the last slug. She spun, trying to recover her feet, but I fired again. The KSG could hold fourteen standard rounds and I'd been reloading as I went. I put three more into her before she stopped moving. I switched magazines and moved forward, crouching slightly, the stock of the gun tightly against my cheek. The lead slugs had created bright streaks across her breastplate where they had ricocheted off. She was lying on her back, breathing hard; twice she tried to spin her left arm and twice I shot it. She screamed in frustration as I closed over her and put one round into her leg and another in her chest. I put my kneepad on the dented metal and rested the hot barrel on her forehead. Her bloody petal armour was not going to save her now.

'Do what he has trained you for.'

'I'm sorry?' I was conscious that I was shouting. Firing the gun so often in confined spaces had made me deaf.

'Kill me. If you don't, the next poltergeist will.'

'No, you said "he" has trained me,' I said.

The queen looked over to my right. She would have pointed but I think I had broken her arm. The wall was dominated by a huge painting – sort of a last supper only with forty-odd guests. I recognised the queen straight away. I spotted Eldrun and Jasper in the picture too, which I hadn't expected.

'Kenato Orin, the Prince of Hell,' she said. I must have looked blank. 'The demon on the far left of the top table.'

I looked at the scene again. Going left from the queen there was an angel that looked like an angel should look. A dwarf deep in conversation with a woman I didn't think I had met, and then a young Ken Austin staring into the distance.

'Well, that all makes more sense,' I said, although I was still trying to put the pieces together. I'd been fighting the angels because they seemed determined to kill me and a lot of other people I knew. It hadn't really occurred to me that I was fighting for someone else. Especially if I had taken the trouble to tell that someone that thousands of us were going to die and the bastard went ahead and did it anyway. 'Ken Austin created a game in my world that brought us here to fight you.'

'You kill people and destroy everything in your path and call it a game?'

'Ah, yes. But initially we didn't know it was real.' Not the greatest defence of humanity I had to admit. I looked at the painting again. It was clearly a big celebration, lots of food, lots of wine, smiles. 'You all look like you were getting along just dandy there. What happened?'

'Kenato Orin and Alfin took my body, my love, me. They corrupted me and laughed. They laughed at my pain.'

'Yeah, it's the laughing that hurts.' I stood up but the KSG was still in her face. 'Why not just kill Ken then?'

'We hunted him through his magic, through Chorus. But he knows that and now is always on the move. We cannot find him. When he started to send you poltergeists we no longer had the resources to discover him, fight you and everyone else.'

'Call off the war,' I said. She looked confused now. 'Call off the war and I'll get you your demon.' I could see her arguing with herself, but this was definitely the best offer she was going to get today. Alva defocused her eyes, looking oddly like Ken in the picture for a moment. The echoes of battle from below in the great hall were tailing off.

'It is done.'

'But you understand this is over. I get you Ken, and you don't get to be queen anymore.'

She focused absolutely on me. 'I understand, poltergeist.'

Hadrati, Grerr and Viviana came into the room and took in the scene, though the latter two were distracted by the painting.

Hadrati walked over, his notched sword still at the ready. 'They have all stopped fighting. I thought you must have killed her.'

'No. I think we ghosts have done enough killing. She has a broken arm though and I'm guessing everything else must be shattered under that armour. She is having trouble breathing.' The kobold was using his left hand to hold an abdominal wound tightly. 'Are you okay?'

'I've had worse,' said Hadrati, but he was clearly in a lot of pain.

A dwarf and a kobold came into the room shouting. 'Colonel! The ghosts have started to bleed the angels as they surrender.'

Hadrati sat down at that moment beside Alva, his blue skin fading to grey.

'Grerr!' I shouted 'These two need your help. Viviana, with me!'

I reloaded shells into the KSG as we ran back to the main hall. Eldrun sat in the fireplace trying to dry out. Two angels hung upside down with buckets underneath them. The Wayfarer, soaked in gore, was wildly shouting instructions at those around him.

I had to put the barrel of my shotgun up his nose to get his attention. 'Get the wristbands off, Wayne. It's time this army went home.'

Chapter Nine

I put the angel's knife and the stab vest in a locker at King's Cross, walked across to St Pancras and got on the 16:24 to Sheffield. The war was over; I wouldn't be needing them anymore. I'd given the KSG to Grerr in return for a promise he would make me a necklace like Viviana's. First, though, he had to make a tomb for Hadrati. They say 'no one cries when a kobold dies', but the colonel proved that wrong.

The electric door hissed shut behind me; inside all seemed very bright and shiny. I made my way to the quiet carriage. I purchased a paper, going for *The Times* since it was the only one that didn't have someone with a bikini on the front, and the worst cup of coffee since the last time I'd been on a train. I settled down to see what the world had been up to while I had been away saving it. In the business section I saw that Ellie Chassagne had left Starflame Graphics, denying any speculation around links to the many deaths associated with the game. The piles of bodies randomly appearing should have stayed at the top of the news, but the lack of non-game players made it look more like an internal gang fight. Chorus interest in the slaughter had finally faded away when the German papers discovered that Starflame had also been behind the creation of the deep fakes of Kate and Boris. The view being if they could make those films look that convincing then the footage of *Under Avalon* Last Battle was just a very impressive endgame sequence.

I heard the whistle some minutes later and the train revved up, pulling out of the station. A few were still making their way up the carriages as we went through Cricklewood. It was raining cats and dogs beyond the glass, the hard-hitting drops cutting short horizontal lines along the window. People on the platforms looked betrayed as we hurtled past them. Around me passengers were setting up their personal area networks in a subtle struggle, the various electronic kit being the pieces and the tiny tables, the board. The game continued invisibly as the various wireless standards fought just as viciously for bandwidth, each PAN fighting to maintain a decent connection between itself and the outside world. I hid behind my paper as capacity and congestion drove commuters through the train looking for space both physical and ethereal.

'This is ridiculous! I can't get connected,' said a woman who sounded like she was used to saying 'Do you know who I am?' a lot. Another passenger just smiled weakly and pointed to the sign 'This is a quiet carriage and has therefore been fitted with a null field to fulfil our traveller Chorus profile.'

'Nothing in or out,' said an older man with a slightly mischievous grin. The important woman spluttered, gathered up her assorted electric toys and left the Luddites to their woodcuts and pamphlets. The older man risked an 'oh dear' look with me then tucked into a triangular bacon, lettuce and tomato sandwich. I was filled with delight. I had just returned from a sustained war with heaven but here people were still defending those tiny little privileges like somewhere peaceful to read a newspaper. I laughed inwardly until Luton Parkway. There the older man got off, still looking pleased with himself. I was sorry to lose his silent companionship. A new assortment joined the null-protected carriage, though for most of them only briefly. I played with my silver anvil, my touchstone throughout all of this – so I knew I hadn't gone completely mad. After about five minutes of watching vanishing points, I walked through to the First-Class section.

The important woman was camped out on a foldout tray, queen of PAN, doing important things with her personal area network, but despite all the real estate and connectivity looking no happier. At the four-seat table opposite sat a man who had clearly spent a lot of money on looking casual. Older, hair a lush white cloud around his head with well-cared-for but crumpled features. Clean-shaven in a world of beards. Cool and calm and, well, Apple-y. It was probably the black polo neck. A travel pack of shortbread sat empty by a cup of tea. Ken Austin. This was why I was here, although it still seemed hard to think about it. An end. A bodyguard appeared, saw my ears and hesitated. How many times had that saved my life in the war? He had a set of augmented-reality visions that Bose and some of the other guys had used. Bose, face down in the street with an arrow in each limb and a hole where his stomach should have been.

'I'm sorry, Mr Austin isn't doing autographs at the moment.' A transdimensional doorkeeper – not often you meet one of them.

'What gave you the idea I was after his autograph? I'm just looking for a seat. The rest of the train is pretty full.'

'This is First Class. You have to have a first-class ticket to be in First Class.' The man looked quite pleased with his logic. As if by magic a train guard appeared and asked the same question. He didn't ask anyone else, just me. As with other life lessons, the Wizard had taught us what not to do. I produced an old-fashioned paper anytime first-class ticket. You could buy a car with an MOT for less. Luckily, Viviana had been quite generous with heaven's gold as reparations.

'She will be armed. She's part of the army of St Albans,' said Mr Austin without looking up from his tablet.

'If we could look in the pack, miss?' I slid my rucksack off my shoulder and handed it over. T-shirts, underwear, a pop-up umbrella, which he popped and then struggled to put away again, sleeping bag and washbag were quickly disgorged onto the table.

'Frisk her.' Ken sounded exasperated. I held my arms out wide and the bodyguard expertly ran his hands down my front, under my boobs, not over them, back and ankles. He exchanged a look with the guard and shrugged.

'Is it normally this hard to get a seat in First Class?' Just to keep up appearances I felt I should be outraged, but it had been a tough week already and I had seen enough guards die.

'I have a train to run, Mr Austin. Miss, sorry for the trouble. Anything off the buffet free of charge by way of apology,' said the guard.

'I'll live. I guess. A can of coke, pork pie and a packet of Quavers, thank you.'

The guard walked off down the aisle. 'Any more tokens, tickets and passes from Wellingborough please.'

I sat down opposite Mr Austin and waited. It was difficult to know where to start. The war was all still jumbled up in my head and seemed more real than this world of tickets and sandwiches. Ken made the mistake of looking up and making eye contact. His eyes narrowed slightly, skin creasing more than he would have liked. His pupils were almost invisible. You could moisturise as much as you liked, but your age still found a way of giving the game away.

'I thought you were that woman on the train.'

I looked around. 'I am.'

'The one with the mirror. You look younger.'

I resisted the urge to be flattered. 'Ah. The one that there was that article about. All about *Under Avalon* and if it's a real place or not?'

'Yes. You look like her. But you also look like I'm not the first person to say that.' He sighed and sat back in his seat, putting the tablet down on the desk. 'Look, the army has tried to get money out of me before.'

'Have they?'

'Someone called Dione Greene, I think.'

'June!' Kneeling in the great hall weighed down by blood loss, angelic fire crackling through her hair, decapitation. Crap way to go and she had come so close.

'I'm pretty sure her name was Dione. Anyway, I made it quite clear to her that while I appreciate your plight, I am not responsible for it.'

'Aren't you?'

'*Under Avalon* is just a game. Sadly it seems to have attracted some extremists and as a result of their activities there have been some unfortunate incidents.'

My meal deal turned up and I opened the can and the Quavers. The pork pie could wait. 'A lot of people have died.'

'As I have said, it is very unfortunate.'

'I tried to stop you before most of those people died but you weren't interested. I was in your office. With Ellie and a cat. And a mouse?' I tried.

There may have been a flicker of recognition over the rodent, but Ken was sticking to the party line and shook his head. 'Look, I don't want to seem unreasonable. But it is just a game. I know, I helped with the treatment, the concept behind it all. A full team wrote the code. I take it as a compliment that people think it so good they confuse it with real life, but it really isn't.'

'Have you not watched the Last Battle on Chorus?'

'I don't have a Chorus account.'

'I discovered that blood contact gave us a way in. So that gave me the means to deliver the ghost army of St Albans to the palace and kill the Queen of Heaven. You appear to have broken your iPad.'

'You were there – and you're here now! Victory!'

'Actually I would say that the angels gave us a pretty good run for our money.'

'The queen must be dead.'

'I shot her.'

'But no missile will pierce the petal armour.'

'No, it won't. And you have no idea how many people told me that, but it misses the point.'

'Which is?'

'Everybody was playing *Under Avalon*. Turning up in chain mail, waving swords, doing the wizardy wish-fulfilment thing. It was very cinematic. But this isn't a game. That's the whole thing. That's why the angels kept winning just enough. Do you mind if I take a picture? Might as well since I'm here. So I thought I would bring a KSG Bullpup shotgun. I wanted an SLR, but it's just impossible to get one. The gun laws are so tight now I had to settle for pump action, and even that's a bit of a grey area. More sort of definitely black area really. Still, fourteen rounds and it's great for corners, and you want me to get to the bit where I kill the queen. And everybody said that no missile will pierce the petal armour and that I was stupid and I should have brought an axe. And you know what?'

'What?'

'It's true. Doesn't matter how hard you strike that petal armour it doesn't let anything through. You look disappointed.'

'You have no idea.'

'But if you hit somebody with a twelve-bore soft-lead slug at very close distance that's a lot of kinetic energy. It doesn't penetrate their bloody magical armour, but it does break whatever bone happens to be behind the impact point. And I shot her skinny arse plenty of times.'

'So the queen is dead?' His face fell. 'She lives.'

'You are not seeing the big picture here. The palace was on fire, the ghost army fought to a standstill. My good friends dying on the marble floor of the great hall in front of the celestial throne. But I've got the queen and I've got the barrel right here.' I pressed my finger against Ken's forehead since he was leaning fully across the table. His skin was hot and dry. 'And then ...'

'And then?'

'Well, you see, Alva thinks you created the game to train humans to kill angels,' I said.

'And you believed her?'

'Well, I mostly sort of didn't. But I had to be sure, and I really didn't like the idea of fighting and probably dying for anyone. Especially someone that fucked up my life so completely and was happy to send thousands of people to their deaths, including me.'

'I didn't pick you.'

'But you did, Ken.' I turned over the phone. I had posted his picture on Chorus with a tag. 'Hail Kenato Orin, the Prince of Hell, the Lord of Elementals, King of the Kobolds, Seraph Friend, Freer of Dwarves, master of debate. All hail Kenato Orin, whose harnessing of magic has brought joy and hope to all the peoples of the world.' It was getting a lot of likes. The counter couldn't refresh fast enough. The survivors of the ghost army of St Albans were pushing it out right across Chorus.

'I had a good job, and a fiancé, and dreams. Well, that's what I'm telling myself. But you decided that we were all anonymous monsters that you could wind up and point at somebody you wanted dead. And it turned out to be true, shame on us. But you created us, the howling mob that stormed the barricades and brought down heaven. You made me a nameless killer.'

'It wasn't like that. She tried to kill me—'

I didn't let him finish. 'Bose and June spent a lot of time trying to work out what the trigger for the war was. It didn't help them, and I don't care.'

'Are you going to kill me?'

I laughed then. 'I want my life back. If I execute you now I spend the next twenty-five years in a psychiatric ward being that mad woman with the mirror who murdered Ken Austin. Let's face it, after what I've been through that's a realistic prospect whether you live or die.' My hand went protectively to the anvil again.

'Next stop, Leicester. Please make sure you have all your personal items with you before you leave the train.'

'You must have done a deal to walk away from the palace.'

'Actually, it was the other way round. But I just wanted to be sure that you really are Kenato Orin and that part at least of what she said is true. And now I am.' I picked up my rucksack and walked away from Ken and his tea and biscuits. Other passengers were getting their bags together and lining up by the exit. We slowed and went through a tunnel. The LED lights were bright but cold.

'Miss, you've forgotten your phone.' The bodyguard had come after me.

'Keep it. I'm going back to fax.' He looked puzzled but spun the mobile in his hand and turned away. The train stopped and passengers began dragging too much luggage from the racks to the platform. One lady, pink hair, green jeans, was going for the full bag, baby and buggy combo. I helped her. Less supportive people trying to get on muttered and ran to other doors.

The station manager whistled. 'Quickly, please.' The buggy was free at last and the door began to slide back flush with the hull. I pressed the open button and pulled my brolly out. I stretched it into the open frame until it clicked. The door tried to close again, metal digging deeply into rubber, holding it in place. The door quivered and stopped. Ken and the bouncer were looking out of the window, shouting. A lot of commuters and staff joined in. But with the door jammed the train couldn't start moving again. In the distance I could hear angelic hunting horns echoing across the station. The guard was asking me to pull the umbrella out. I didn't think I could if I wanted to. Which I didn't. Behind me the sun shone brightly on the Last Host of Heaven as it crested the end of the platform and swept towards the carriages. Angels with flaming swords leapt from their horses, running towards my umbrella.

The shouts inside the train turned to shrieks. A war hammer opened the side of the carriage like a zip, allowing a full-on Japanese monster to ease himself out, pushing aside the torn metal like tinfoil. He was still recognisable as Ken as he stood among the shattered glass and torn seat cushions, just with more tusks. He stretched to his full height. Viviana would have been proud of my language. Hefting the two-metre hammer in his right hand and a shimmering phone in his left, he began to run towards Alva. She was trying to dismount from her horse, hampered by the splints on her legs and arm. I did feel slightly guilty at that point.

Drawing on the power of the phone in a way I recognised from *UA*, Ken was unstoppable, swiping angels out of the way, determined to get to Alva. At his back, the bodyguard pulled out a square-looking pistol and fired in two-round bursts to protect his new-look boss. I recognised the dull ringing bell sound of bullets bouncing off impenetrable armour. He dropped an empty magazine onto the platform and reloaded. A lot of people, who had been calmly watching the big monster fighting his way across the platform through iridescent swordsfolk, only now screamed and ran from this more understandable threat. Halfway through the second clip the bodyguard switched to head shots, but he was too late. A flaming sword took off his arm at the elbow while another passed untroubled through his chest. He collapsed between two dead angels.

Ken had knocked over Alva's horse and trapped her under it. He put a giant foot on the struggling beast, pinning it and his unwitting lover beneath. Although I'd said I didn't care Grerr had filled me in on the whole Alva, Lorcan, Ken thing. Maybe when you are a god a war seems like a reasonable response. But I hadn't killed anyone when Tim and Sofia had done their thing. Ken was saying something, but I couldn't hear it above crying commuters and the sirens of the approaching armed response vehicles. He raised the flaming mobile and, in its blinding light, saw the shadow above him. Alva had condensed a column of cloud and water from the air creating a vast sky-bound river that reached down from far, far above like an apocalyptic exclamation mark. The angels glowed as they rushed into its shade to save their leader. The storm roiled against its magical binding, then there was a numbing clap of thunder as the heavens opened. The tsunami extinguished the blazing mobile and crushed the old man beneath. The wave crossed the platform faster than thought, taking my legs from under me, washing me towards the back of the train. From the doorway the crouching guard held out his hand as I passed, and I caught it. The water pummelled over me, pulling me into the gap between the train and the platform. For a moment all I could see and hear was the torrent and the blue-shirted arm that I clung to with all my strength. Finally the stream subsided to rivulets from the concrete and the noise to sobs from the passengers.

I found my feet and let go. 'Thank you.' The words seemed inadequate for a life.

The sun returned, shining brightly off the gleaming platform swept clean of angels. A white horse was lying sideways about thirty metres down the track. Washed up against it was a broken bundle of an older Ken. The sodden polo neck and trousers clung tightly to his slight frame, his broken limbs folded too many times around him. His sparse grey hair was plastered to Ken's skull and face while water trickled from his slack mouth. The guard stepped out, massaging life back into his arm, clearly trying to make sense of what he had just witnessed. I noticed the white paint through the glass of the open door as it stood proud of the train. The shadow of the warning showed up darkly in the sunlight.

'Blocking the doors causes delays and can be dangerous.'

HOODED CROW

Also by DJ Gilmour and available on Amazon-

REMNANT KINGS

Arthur, the Undying King, still dominates Europe in 1625. With the death of James VI, Scotland faces an uncertain future as Arthur reasserts his ancient right to rule and Vampires return to the streets of Edinburgh.

Remnant Kings is the story of two Scots from the same village in Argyll caught up in the tragedy and turmoil of a country riven by politics, religion and fear. A place where old certainties are lost and new ideas may have a greater impact than anyone realises.

Some Reviews of Remnant Kings

'Remnant Kings is a colorful and at times graphic representation of a Scotland gone by, fighting off the marauding English with one hand and, in a touch of fantasy/horror, vengeful vampires with the other. It portrays the battles for power between kings, countries, nobility and common people alike and the unwillingness of many to acknowledge the dangers in their midst. A colorful cast of characters all share 1 common trait : a love of Scotland.

Time is needed at the outset to become familiar with the period, setting and people but the plot rapidly gathers pace culminating in fierce battles and a medley of not always favorable outcomes for the entire cast and intrigue as to how this unique and enjoyable representation of Scottish history could evolve in the future. I look forward to any sequels.'

R Cyphus

A spellbinding mix of, presumably, some historical accuracy (I'm not well up on the events in Scotland in 1625), and fantasy/horror. D.J. Gilmour skilfully blends the two in such a way that I was almost inclined to believe in some scenes that the vampires and other dark forces at large across the well-invoked Scottish landscape, were really there at that time. The power struggle between rival factions, both mortal and supernatural aspects, is well captured and builds into a fascinating read as we follow the fortunes of wide-ranging, believable characters.

Much of the action takes place in Edinburgh, depicting the often inhospitable climate and conditions, even in the castle. The graphic description of life in the taverns and on the streets, along with particularly bloodthirsty battles, reveal Gilmour to be a talented writer, and I look forward to reading more of his work.

S Bint

'Not my genre at all but it was recommended to me so I thought I would give it a go. Lots of characters to learn about and to understand their journey but lots of action happening to keep the pages turning. The vampire involvement was an interesting twist but fitted in well with the other characters and kept an edge to the plot. An enjoyable read.'

K Matlock

'A gripping tale of how ordinary people fight for political reform against an autocratic King in league with vampires. Set in Scotland in the 1600's there is both historical context and vivid imagery of Edinburgh. One of the characters Amanda becomes an extraordinary heroine and is pivotal to the story.

Remnant Kings is full of plots, twists, romance, drama and tension. I could not put the book down and it left me hanging right till the end as to whether good or bad would prevail. For the first time ever I found one of the baddies endearing. I very much hope it leads onto another book.'

K Yates

Based in Scotland, but with wild imagination. This is a historical fantasy which includes King Arthur, vampires and battles using muskets and swords. Yet somehow the characters are real, with real emotions.

There are a lot of characters in this novel, and it takes a while to become comfortable with them, but eventually you'll know who you are rooting for. The battles are bloody so avert your eyes if you are squeamish.

R Blake

'Wonderful story and setting! Includes interesting interlude in Sweden, possibly my favourite part. The pace is good but the real strength of this book is its fantastic world building, there's a feeling of a large and lived-in world here. Eagerly awaiting next instalment to see where these characters are heading. Would recommend.'

Alastair Edwards

ROCKET SURGERY

Ben is walking out of Slough. As he does, he thinks about what has led him to this expedition. Of growing up on the west coast of Scotland and working in Slough. Of the human capacity for destruction both self and corporate. The value of friendships. The dangers of company rhetoric and the tricky nature of true love.

Rocket Surgery is being listed as a comedy, which may prove optimistic but it is adult in language and content and should not be read if that is likely to cause offence.

Some Reviews of Rocket Surgery

I really enjoyed this book. Like Iain Banks, Douglas has really captured what it's like to be a teenager in a small Scottish coastal town in the 1980's: and has vividly evoked memories of my experiences in the 70's. The later experiences in the world of work are just amazing: I worked for staid giant corporations and the frantic world of call centres, synthetic management concern, ersatz enthusiasm and sackings was a complete revelation to me. Christmas is Cancelled had me agog - never come across that before!

David Gilmour

Fast moving and entertaining journey into adulthood, work, friendship and love. Being a fellow Scotsman living abroad a lot of references and details ring true. Passionately and cleverly written

Moray Robertson

A great insight in to growing up in a small Scottish town in the eighties, whisks you through the University years and on to office work in the early nineties. It resonated strongly with me having done all three, humorous and engaging has to be recommended. The situations and characters presented were very tangible and rang true, many thanks for a good read, I look forward to the follow up.

Simon Foster

A wry, authentic and witty observation of life and early adulthood. Bringing back memories of growing up in Scotland in the Seventies and Eighties: a well-written, wry, entertaining, and at times laugh-out-loud, account of youth, holidays and surviving teenage foibles and corporate adult life. And for a good cause

Raymond Smears

An emotional rollercoaster of the best and worst of human behaviour. The rollercoaster of life's gains and losses. Of childhood friendships we all valued and then cast aside. No doubt we will all relate to the ill choices we all make re friendships, relationships and work dynamics. An emotional read and I can't wait for the sequel.

Karen Yates

Insightful humour. I loved this book. It lampoons business culture and modern thought trends. There is wry humour and comedic metaphors.

We meet the protagonists when they are young and wild only to follow them into the seeds of career building. There were so many clever bits that I wanted to read out loud. I looked forward to picking it up to read a bit more.

Rosemary Blake

HOODED CROW

Some of you may have wondered what actually happened between Sandi, Eldrun and Aileen in the Pilgrims Rest while Grerr slumbered. As an extra bonus for the first edition here's an account of what occurred-

What happened at the House of Absolution

'An angel has just walked into the bar.' There was a long silence as the bartender looked at the monk. 'I thought that would get a stronger response.'

'I'm waiting for the punchline,' said Sandi as he pulled his hair into a ponytail. 'An angel walks into the bar and the barman says why the long face?'

'That's for horses,' said Eldrun, strolling back towards the door that led to the serving counter. 'Do horses go into bars?'

'Funnily enough I know this – I've just offered a horse a beer and he said he wasn't interested,' said Sandi.

'But anyway, I think we're getting away from the point that an angel has walked into the bar for the first time since I don't know when and that probably covers an age.'

'What does she want?' asked Sandi.

'She claims absolution. But the way that she talks, you get the distinct impression that she has the absolution of others in mind. Possibly alongside a bit of cathartic violence.'

'Sounds like this angel is in the wrong place. Should I go and talk to her?' Sandi offered.

The red-headed bartender shrugged. 'You're the monk. Go give her some fatherly counselling.'

Sandi looked down for confirmation. The giant wooden worry beads lay around his neck and the heavy silks wrapped around an expansive middle. 'Oh yes, so I am.' He got up very slowly. 'You could be a priestess. You know, with a bit of female bonding she might loosen up …' His voice trailed off under Eldrun's withering gaze. 'Just a thought.' The barmaid crossed her arms. 'I'm going. Look, here I am, going.'

Sandi pushed through the orange felt curtain into the bar. He was glad to see the sorcerer, the artificer and the officer had taken his advice and come to the pub first. The rest were all solo travellers who seemed to be lost in their own thoughts and keeping the place quiet. With potential eternal damnation imminent, it usually was. The other tollhouses on the road to hell each tended to be rowdy in their own way. This being the last house on the road, not too many folk felt the need to get this close before they had to. A lot of those people misjudged their timing and skipped it altogether, one way or another.

The angel would have stood out if the bar had been standing room only. She looked so busy being disgusted by her surroundings that she didn't acknowledge his presence. There was clearly no point in waiting for an invitation.

Sandi pulled out a chair and sat beside her. 'Good afternoon, pilgrim.'

She looked up more annoyed than surprised. 'I have come for absolution.'

'So I have heard. And that is a good thing.' Sandi hesitated and the angel looked up at him and fixed him with her bright eyes. 'But a little unusual for one such as yourself.'

'I am a poor traveller looking for absolution.' She repeated the statement without any greater conviction. Sandi risked breaking eye contact and took in the rest of her – a sapphire tiara buried in piles of black hair above a cloud of strategically placed chiffon that pretended to have happened by accident. A broad leather belt carefully worked with some sort of hunting scene pulled the whole thing in to underline that there was a tiny waist in there somewhere. The sword and dagger combo alone must have been worth more than the average peasant saw in a lifetime, probably two, even if the Forest of Souls gave them a good second incarnation. She raised an eyebrow. Somewhere outside the tollhouse some sort of percussion band seemed to have set up.

Sandi took a breath. 'After a long life it is good to have the opportunity and surroundings to reflect on what you have done. Those things might be what you have done that you ought not to have done. Perhaps things that you started doing but left undone.'

'And those things that you have done that you are proud of. You should think about those as well,' said the angel.

'I'm sure that's true. But that's not really part of absolution. Have you attended any of the other tollhouses on the way to your ultimate settling of your journey's account? Like pride for example.' Sandi asked. Eldrun glided by with a bottle of red, two glasses and a fake smile.

'I didn't come by road. I came across the desert.' She pointed to a sun hat that lay on the table beside the wine.

He filled both cups. 'Okay, look … Sorry, what's your name?' Sandi asked.

'Aileen.' That name really rang a bell with Sandi, or would have done if the drummers outside weren't making so much noise.

'Okay, Aileen. See, the way this works is there are twelve tollhouses on the road to hell. The theory is that you visit each one in turn on your way here. You see, each one is themed, gluttony, lust and so on. Until recently my colleague was employed at sloth – you can tell.'

Eldrun gave Sandi an empty grin and a thumbs up from behind the bar. 'It's the best tollhouse of them all. You can never get tired of doing nothing.' She picked up a dubious-looking cloth and dried some glasses with it, whistling in time with the music from outside.

'Anyway. This is the thirteenth house. The idea is that you work your way through each of them, atoning, or, in some cases,' he looked meaningfully at Eldrun, 'catching up on all the ones you missed.'

'Thirteen. But I thought seven sins made up the road to hell,' said Aileen. She seemed to be drumming her fingers in time to the rhythm too. It was getting quite distracting. A pool of water was spreading out from Aileen's chair. She must have got soaked before coming in, which was odd; the Guv always insisted on a few showers a couple of times each week to stop everything drying out, but she usually arranged them at night. The sun hat was dry.

'Thirteen? Yes, well people have got quite inventive over the ages. I guess you being in heaven might have missed out on some of that. Anyway. All that ... creativity pushed the number up to twelve and given that we had almost run out of road at that point, the boss—'

'The boss?'

'Yes, you know, the boss. Depends how you meet him really – the Prince of Hell, the Lord of Elementals, King of the Kobolds, Seraph Friend, Freer of Dwarves, master of debate. All hail Kenato Orin, whose harnessing of magic has brought joy and hope to all the peoples of the world.' Sandi sang the last part, more out of habit than anything.

'Kenato?' asked the angel.

'If you know him personally, which I don't. And I don't think you do either.' Because he doesn't really like angels, thought Sandi. He certainly wouldn't like this one.

'Does he come here?'

'No, he has better things to do than hang around in bars answering stupid questions.' Better things to do. If this angel really wanted absolution, Sandi was worried he was not doing well in his priestly duties.

'You said we are very close to the Gates of Hell. How close are we?'

'Just over the rise. Five miles, maybe six if you're walking, though it's pretty much climbing all of the way these days.'

'So this is the last point of alarm before the gates themselves.'

Sandi looked at Eldrun, trying to remember what the secret signal for summoning the guards was. But she seemed lost, dancing behind the bar. This wasn't right. He had worked with most of the Angels Martial over the millennia in the wars against the small gods, and anyone else who gave Heaven lip. He must know this one. It was just that he had a drum-filled hole where the memory should have been.

'Right, miss, you are really going to have to go.'

'Go?'

'Right back to the start. This road has been running fine for over a thousand years and you can't just skip to the front of the queue because you're an angel.' Sandi stood up and pulled the angel's arm; he had planned to make her stand up but she just slid off the chair looking shorter than ever. The movement seemed to allow the water trapped in her clothes to spread even more. 'And I know it's raining but you're going to just have to set off now. Eldrun, can you please go and tell that band to bugger off – I can't hear myself think!'

His colleague stopped dancing and walked out from behind the bar looking puzzled.

Sandi focused back on the angel. 'Look, lady. This isn't the usual service you get when you reach the priest at the end of the road. But your problem is that you started here when you should have finished here.'

'My problem? I don't think it's my problem. You're not even a priest, are you? I think you are a demon!'

'Of course I am,' said Sandi, 'that's why I work here.'

Eldrun opened the door. 'I hope you lot aren't even thinking of begging round here,' she shouted as she wrenched the handle open.

Sandi could see the bright sun shining down from a clear blue sky. The harsh-edged mountains that surrounded the Gates of Hell were sharp in the clear dry air. There was no sign of a band although the drumming was now loud enough to seem as if it originated inside the bar. Sandi turned slowly to look back at Aileen. The pool of water had spread out from her in a distinct pattern across the floor. Each of the patrons had slumped at their tables looking like they had just been pulled back over the side of a trawler. A churning stream had followed Eldrun to the door and his own feet splashed in a puddle.

'Bollocks,' said Sandi. He tried to jump in his mind to the duty sentinel at the gates, but he could not get a message out over the noise. He was never very good at messaging that way, but he couldn't reach Eldrun as close as she was. The penny dropped; the drums were in everyone's mind to make sure that no one could get a warning out. That no one could think. He unwrapped the heavy beads from around his neck and kept them going in a swinging arc towards Aileen's head. He went to step closer to make certain of the connection, but his feet were held as surely as though in deep mud.

'Eldrun! Alert the gate!' Sandi felt his calves dissolving below the knee. He released the wooden necklace but the angel ducked and they smashed into the shelves of glasses behind the bar.

The barmaid looked back at her shrinking partner. 'Sandi!'

Sandi was already looking up at her as his legs dissolved into gravel. 'The gate!' he shouted.

Eldrun wrapped herself in flame and shot vertically up and out of sight. Sandi watched a waterfall rise up through the door after her. The elemental dropped the priest disguise, and his skin became the red sandstone of his birth. Aileen laughed at her victim as he struggled to escape, contemptuously turning away from him and looking up to where Eldrun had gone. Sandi was down to his waist now and the churning water was keeping him from reforming. He reached out for the table, first with just one finger to drag it closer, then the whole leg was in his fist. The stone elemental threw the heavy furniture at the angel just as there was a loud pop from the sky. Enough of the table made it through the doorway to carry the angel thirty feet across the square.

Sandi stopped struggling for a moment, straining to hear the roar of Eldrun's fire restarting. Instead there was a soft thud of a heavy black cinder, wet in the sunlight, close to where Aileen lay. Sandi cried out. The drums restarted as the broken angel struggled awkwardly to sit up. Large fragments of wood had pierced her through from back to front and she coughed up blood as she looked from the still ember of Eldrun to the head and shoulders of Sandi. Behind her the sun shone brightly on the great Host of Heaven as it crested the top of the hill and swept down towards the House of Absolution.

Printed in Poland
by Amazon Fulfillment
Poland Sp. z o.o., Wrocław
18 September 2023

a6cc15a8-847b-4dc4-96ae-9ddfa9a9e622R01